The Lost Welsh Kingdom

The Lost Welsh Kingdom

JOHN·HUGHES

y Lolfa

First impression: 2015
© John Hughes & Y Lolfa Cyf., 2015

Cover photo: SugarVengeance.com

ISBN: 978 1 78461 169 9

Published and printed in Wales
on paper from well-maintained forests by
Y Lolfa Cyf., Talybont, Ceredigion SY24 5HE
e-mail ylolfa@ylolfa.com
website www.ylolfa.com
tel 01970 832 304
fax 832 782

CHAPTER 1

Early June 1041

As the poet Berddig approached the main hall on his first visit to the Caerfyrddin court he could hear all the familiar sounds of feasting: the laughing, the giggling and the shouting.

The sun was setting after a clear warm day in early June and the surrounding hilltops were turning orange. Soon the hills, trees, houses and hall would fade into the darkness of the coming night before the torches would light up the court to allow the festivities to continue. The final rays would reflect on the smooth surface of the river, before that also would succumb to the night, leaving owls to hunt for shrews, mice and voles as they scuttled about in search of meagre sustenance. But there was no shortage of food and drink in the great hall full of people – some drunk, some getting drunk – all in celebratory mood as he entered.

In his late twenties, but having spent most of his life on the road, he was already slightly weather-beaten. Though he ate and drank his fair share – like all the other poets and entertainers – his walking from court to court kept him in good shape. His square face under a thick thatch of ginger hair was mostly covered by a reddish beard, but his pair of blue, lively, mischievous eyes shone like two well-cut sapphires.

A busy, energetic and bright person, he looked innocuous enough, but was talented and missed nothing with those sharp ears and clear vision.

Always well informed, never absent from important events

any where, be they funerals, celebrations of all kinds – births, successes or anniversaries. They were his daily diet. He helped to console the bereaved and where there was merriment he was at the heart of it. He had charisma, didn't stand on ceremony but joined the crowd, invited or not, and before they knew it he would be leading the singing or telling them his stories.

Having entered through the narrow doorway, his presence immediately turned heads and drew shouts, the most prominent of which were, "Who's this?" and "The dogs have found something."

The poet smiled and confidently greeted those near him, with his northern accent drawing gales of laughter which spread rapidly around the hall, eventually penetrating its darkest crevasses. There were shouts of "What type of Welsh is that?" followed by women's high-pitched laughter.

The men joined in the teasing, joking and laughing and adding to the cacophony. One remarked, "Speak French will you – we'll have a better chance of understanding you."

A woman, perched on a man's lap produced uproar when she shouted, "Go back North young man and come back when you've learnt Welsh."

Berddig simply smiled, experienced enough to ignore the banter.

Looking around he could see there were men, women and children dressed in colourful clothes sitting on the benches around the sides, some sat on stools at tables, some sat on the floor and others stood hugging their jugs of mead and ale. There were also a few dogs sniffing around; they had probably been kicked out more than once, but had wandered back looking for scraps.

It was a chaotic, confused, closely-packed collection of revellers which surrounded the smouldering central fire. A large pot hanging over the fire emitted smoke which swirled up slowly and lazily towards the hole in the roof through which most of it escaped. The grey puffs diverted into the rafters, circulated in the roof space until, disturbed by the drafts there, descended and settled on the occupants leaving them in a smoky haze.

There was a constant movement of people and of their shadows thrown by the fire, some disappearing with those shadows into the dark corners while others were emerging from those gloomy spaces.

A woman appeared before Berddig and presented him with a jug of ale and asked, "Are you a poet?"

He nodded and laughing she challenged him, "Try to tell them a story."

He swallowed a few gulps of ale and walking amongst his potential audience, started telling them jokes to get their attention and give them time to accept his perceived strange accent.

Once he was sure they had tuned their ears to his way of speaking and style of delivery he launched into his story, his entertainment, and his propaganda.

"Let me tell you a story, a true story," he said. "On an evening just like this, with the sun beginning to set and its rays reflecting on a ford crossing a river just like yours, there were archers dressed in black crouched in the bushes, foot soldiers clothed in black nearby, mounted troops robed in black on specially selected black horses hidden in the trees."

He checked they were listening and continued quietly as if telling them a secret, "Two years ago Gruffudd ap Llywelyn and his men were waiting in their soot-covered helmets, watched by the crows in the branches above them. Both men and birds sensed danger, yet were excited at the prospect of what was to come. The crows had not departed for their roosts that night, somehow anticipating the slaughter and feasting ahead. They croaked as they jumped and flew from one perch to the next, high in the trees, viewing the gathering by the river with intense interest."

The hall was quiet as he related to his audience: "There was silence, total and absolute silence. Gruffudd's iron discipline prevailed – no one dared speak, no one dared cough, no one dared to swallow his own spittle. They were alert, eager and ready – psyched up by Gruffudd's determination, attention to detail and his power.

"The archers had their arrows at the ready; the spearmen had their weapons held firmly, the cavalry, slightly further from the crossing and well hidden in the woods, were mounted and ready to draw their swords and charge on their leader's orders."

Berddig had captured their attention now and he continued: "Gruffudd, also in black but with a dark purple cloak over his shoulders, was mounted on his large black stallion, halfway between his foot soldiers and his mounted troops and visible to both groups.

"A large, broad-framed and strong man, he stared straight ahead across the ford towards the opposite bank. All was quiet and peaceful, except for the occasional crow croaking and the soft sound of the river gliding over the shallow crossing point."

His eager listeners were hooked by his storytelling skills as he continued, "The horses were nervous and the air in the trees was soured by the smell of their sweat. The Rhyd y Groes rats had sensed the danger and moved from their usual hiding places by the river into the bushes and trees on the eastern bank as if they had advance knowledge of the outcome."

He was giving nothing away – there was nothing to give away perhaps – as his listeners were well aware of the outcome and of the name of the famous ford of Rhyd y Groes on the Severn. They knew the Romans had crossed there and that the great King Arthur had stopped there, but Berddig, quietly divulging more of the story, continued, "The Saxon earl of Mercia, Leofric, and his influential wife, Lady Godiva, were fearful of the new Welsh king, Gruffudd ap Llywelyn, and decided to dispatch an army, commanded by Leofric's brother, Edwin, to subdue him before he became too powerful.

"It was this Saxon army that was now on the march westwards but, in contrast to the Welsh, Edwin's troops were in jovial mood as they approached the ford, a well-established point of invasion. They were well armed, confident that they would outnumber their adversary when they would face them in battle somewhere in the depths of Powys. They were looking forward to the loot, the women, the honours and rewards they would get after their victory.

"The Saxons had made good progress and their high spirits were reflected in their colourful uniforms and banners carried high, flapping in the evening breeze as though they were going to a party rather than on a perilous hunt for the ruler of Gwynedd. They had marched all day but they were still laughing and joking as they approached Rhyd y Groes. With the sun low in the west, the summits of the hills behind them were already acquiring the glow of the approaching dusk as Edwin led his array of troops into the shallow crossing with the intention of setting up camp on the Powys side."

Berddig paused to gulp some ale and there were shouts for more drink but there were stronger calls for him to continue – they wanted to hear the story and he obeyed.

"Gruffudd, with the sun still warm on his back and a slight breeze blowing through his long black hair and thick black beard, was watching and waiting eagle-eyed as the Saxons and their horses splashed their way into the river.

"The Saxons didn't see him sitting still on his horse with nerves of steel, his face motionless, his breathing effortless and his eyes taking on the hungry look of a sparrow hawk's glare at its prey while judging the right moment to strike.

"The invaders were making good progress into the river when Gruffudd lifted his arm high, sword in hand, and brought it down slowly and deliberately in the direction of the enemy, urging his horse forward at the same time. He knew his men would follow, his commanders knew the plan and as his charger was taking its first steps, their arrows were flying towards someone's eye, throat, chest, belly or leg.

"His cavalry was close behind him as the second round of arrows took flight and he engaged the front of the Saxon column. His beautiful black horse stepped miraculously over the corpses and bodies writhing in agony and confusion under its hooves. His sword swinging at the end of his powerful arm took off a head here and a hand there as his cavalry clattered on the stones behind him and into the already disarrayed Saxon army."

The narrator waved his free arm as though it held a sword, cutting, slicing and piercing bodies to the right and left, simultaneously announcing, "The momentum of the horses charging into their ranks dispersed the enemy even before the foot soldiers moved in on the kill and ruthlessly dispatched Edwin's stunned troops, leaving but their spirits to dwell above the water and banks for a while before evaporating into oblivion."

Holding on tightly to his jar of ale, Berddig moved swiftly amongst his listeners and, putting his free hand to his mouth as if to shout, he added, "Edwin and his commanders were calling their men together to regroup to face the enemy, when the Welsh cavalry, led by their fearless leader now holding a lance he'd removed from the chest of a dying Saxon, charged at them again. He galloped, with the lance stretched out in front, towards the mounted Saxon leader, its blood-covered tip hitting Edwin with such force that it penetrated his body, lifting him out of his saddle and depositing him unceremoniously on the ground some yards away from his shocked and frightened horse."

There were gasps of shock and he knew he had them gripped.

"The strong-armed Gruffudd held on to his lance and plunged it further through the body of the dismounted Saxon, pinning him to the ground on the edge of the river. Then, releasing his hold on the lance, he rode around the already still and dying body of Edwin. Drawing his sword again, he calmly looked around the battle site.

"With his men already in the ascendancy, he called his mounted force together and shouted at them to charge at the tangled mass of wounded and bewildered soldiers on the opposite bank. The charging horses, closely followed by foot soldiers, soon tore into them, with Gruffudd's sword again swinging wildly in the front, and with his strength behind it caused further death and destruction to the demoralised and leaderless mass of Saxons.

"Gruffudd wanted a decisive victory and he got it.

"The crows were not to be disappointed, as the river turned red from the blood oozing out of the bodies, some with their eyes still and staring towards the sky, while others were face down as if searching for something amongst the stones. Some groaned, some asked for mercy, but many begged to be put out of their suffering. Others were in full retreat; some running and some hobbling as fast as they could, chased by Gruffudd's men hell-bent on slaying the stragglers. There was fighting and killing taking place in the river and on both banks, with Saxon soldiers falling everywhere.

"It was a glorious victory for the king and he addressed his soldiers as they returned to the ford. He praised them for their discipline, their bravery and their steadfastness in a battle that would remain in the memory of the Welsh for ever. His soldiers, in turn, cheered him endlessly as he examined the battle area from his horse before dismounting and sitting on a large stone near the river, as he would on his royal chair in his great hall at his capital, Rhuddlan."

Berddig placed his jug on a table as if to stress the importance of the next statement and after a brief pause continued, "Gruffudd's treasurer, the custodians of his crown and royal regalia, in the presence of his chief justice, placed the royal crown on his head and crowned him king of Gwynedd and Powys. Yes, friends, there on the banks of the river Severn, Gruffudd was crowned king of north Wales."

The bard's oration had been received enthusiastically by his Caerfyrddin audience and he was pleased as he picked up his jug of ale. King Gruffudd's personal bard and friend received the cheers and adulation of his audience as though he had himself just been crowned king. He had the ability to relate a story enthusiastically and stir the blood of his listeners.

Having finished and responded to the applause, Berddig sat but his audience shouted that they wanted more, hammering their jugs on the tables as the servants tried to refill them. They wanted to know more about the new king in the north.

They knew the Saxons had been soundly beaten but many worried that the king in the north wouldn't be satisfied by the conquest of Powys and would turn his attention southwards towards Deheubarth, knowing that he had already attacked Llanbadarn immediately after his victory at Rhyd y Groes.

The poet shouted back at them, "Enough. We're here to celebrate a wedding. Let's have no more about war. Let's concentrate on the wedding and the happy event tomorrow."

He was at Caerfyrddin – having invited himself – to participate in the celebrations of the marriage the following day of Hywel, the ruler of Deheubarth, to the beautiful eighteen-year-old Elen at her father's court in Caerfyrddin. Twenty-five-year-old Hywel had inherited the kingdom of

Deheubarth from his father and would arrive at the court early the following morning, but Elen was expected to appear in the hall later that evening to meet her well-wishers.

Berddig's audience however wanted more about Gruffudd ap Llywelyn. This was a golden opportunity for them, for here they had a man who knew the king well. Could he alleviate some of their fears about this powerful king, or would he confirm their anxieties? Inevitably some shouted, "Tell us about Gruffudd ap Llywelyn?"

Then they shouted, "What's he like?"

And inevitably came the question everybody wanted to ask, "What's he planning to do now? Is he satisfied with being king of Gwynedd and Powys?"

"Good question," many muttered.

Berddig's audience was determined, and from various parts of the smoky, bustling hall, including the shadowy corners, came shouts of, "What's he going to do next? Are we safe from him here?"

The poet sensed their determination. These were people content with their lot and he shouted over the incoming questions, "Oh! He is quite happy to stay in the north to rule Gwynedd and Powys."

But they were not satisfied and one called out, "I've heard that he rages at his nobles; all his people have to scrape the floor in his presence – even his dogs have to kneel before him. It's said that if someone says anything that he disagrees with, they are starved to death."

Another added, "I've heard that he is an extremely jealous man – you dare not look at his woman nor show any ambition, as he hangs those who do."

"No, no. He is really loved by his people – he has brought them peace and great wealth. He has given them back land that the Saxons had taken from them generations ago. He has removed the Saxons from fertile lands between the Clwyd mountain range and the western bank of the Dee estuary and absorbed it into his kingdom. His people love him."

Sensing some cynicism Berddig continued, "If he were here with us now, he would be sitting there on the floor with you. He would laugh and joke as you would expect your best friend to behave. He would be asking you if you had enough to eat and drink. He would want to know how your health was and would advise you what remedies to take – he would be like a father to you. He would be most caring for you – advising you not to work too hard and to have good shoes. If your shoes looked a little worn he would get you new ones. That is what he's like – he's a true friend to all his people."

This pacified the gathering but then a red-nosed old man from a side bench articulated their concerns again, "Some here think that he wants to rule the whole of Wales and that he is now looking to Deheubarth here in the south-west as his next target. I'm told he wants all the power he can get."

Berddig reassured them saying, "He won't come here. All he wants is peace along all his borders and for the Saxons to return the land they have taken. He's done that, so he's at peace now that he rules Gwynedd and Powys. I can assure you, he is a charming, friendly, kind and considerate king."

His listeners weren't totally convinced and the same old man demanded, "Can he be trusted to stay in the north?"

Berddig, feeling a little uneasy and realising that some in the audience were not fully satisfied on the subject of the king in the north, decided to avoid the question and changed the subject. "That's enough about Gruffudd. I will sing you a song. Come on, we are here to celebrate the wedding of Elen and Hywel tomorrow. Let's get in the right frame of mind, let's drink to the couple's happiness. We are in the rich land of Deheubarth, the best in Wales and where all the men are handsome and all the women beautiful – never was that truer than for Hywel and Elen."

The jugs were raised, the mouths filled, the smooth mead or ale swallowed and the jugs refilled quickly while the local entertainers took the stage, to Berddig's relief.

A little later Elen made a brief appearance, producing a response of awe at her beauty and elegance.

She was Hywel's equal in every way but status. She wasn't from a royal household but was the daughter of a highly-placed noble family in Caerfyrddin. She was a stunningly beautiful young woman, as was attested by the throng of noblemen who had sought her hand from the time she was a very young child. However, her father was aware of her beauty and held her back from her suitors until one came along of whom he approved. He knew she was fit for a king and when Hywel appeared, showing the appropriate interest, he naturally offered no resistance.

CHAPTER 2

Next day in June 1041

T HE FOLLOWING DAY was also bright and sunny and by mid-morning more seawater had begun its journey up the river. Colourfully decorated boats were beginning to feel the effect of the water seeping under them and lifting them gently to an upright position at their moorings as if to salute Hywel ap Edwin and his entourage's arrival at court in the full regalia of the ruler of Deheubarth.

He was a handsome young man, with fair hair disclosing a Saxon or Viking gene in his makeup. He was tall, broad and strong, with a pleasant yet determined personality. In fact, all the qualities desired of a leader.

Hywel and Elen had first set eyes on each other as adults at a prestigious gathering earlier in the year in Dinefwr, Hywel's main court. Her father knew Hywel would be present and engineered an invitation for Elen, suspecting that if Hywel had any eye for a woman he would notice her and hopefully fall for her beauty. Hywel took to her immediately, as she did to him, and it soon became obvious to all that they had eyes for each other only, and it was not long before Hywel had declared his intention of marrying her. Her parents were delighted and plans for the union had proceeded at a good pace.

Elen had a magnetic personality, with kindness, softness and generosity of spirit oozing from every pore. She was bright and alert, interested in all people, a good conversationalist and knew how to hold herself as she had been trained by her mother to perfection. Yet she appeared relaxed and natural in all company whether noble or royal. Her parents expected much of her, they were proud of her and of their own achievements.

The wedding took place at the ancient church of St Teulyddog, where the two lovers recited their solemn vows to each other, hardly heard by some of the noisy guests still intoxicated from the activities of the previous evening. The priest dutifully recanted verses in Latin, words barely understood even by the sober, but humorously translated quietly at the back by a local poet for everyone's amusement.

Many of the women's thoughts were fixed on the handsome Hywel, while the men were distracted by the beautiful Elen. Others were thinking ahead to the food, drink and entertainment awaiting them and some, at the back of the congregation, drifted out of the small wooden church and made their way to the front of the food queues.

As soon as the young pair had been blessed, the crowd moved rapidly out of the small church and formed a procession behind the newly married couple and followed them towards the west bank of the river Tywi, below the court where the feast was laid out.

The river appeared blue under the cloudless sky; the brown muddy banks below the high-tide mark were obscured by the incoming seawater. The boats were rising on the tide and the slightest of breezes was unfurling the banners of the ruler of Deheubarth and of Elen's family. The tall trees and high flag poles carrying the colourful standards formed an impressive canopy for the event.

The central feature of the feast which produced a wonderfully appetising smell, was the large stag carcass in the middle of the cooking area, turned carefully and expertly above a fire by two bare-chested muscular men with the well-sharpened knives for the carving arranged in stands near to hand.

Between the cooking area and the river bank there was a group of musicians tuning their harps and pipes, ready to entertain the happy couple and their guests, with a space set aside on slightly-raised ground for the poets of both families to stand and amuse their audience.

It was a spectacle, the like of which had not been seen for over a generation or more.

Those who appeared to be least in need of feeding were to be seen at the front of the queue, but of course the poets and singers claimed they had to be fed and oiled first because they would be needed for the entertainment that was to start immediately.

There were speeches galore with, as expected, magnificent tributes paid to Hywel, his ancestors, his wisdom, his bravery and to the beauty of his wife and the obvious love between them. Elen was highly praised, by all the poets, with Berddig's poem to her receiving particular approval and applause; he'd clearly earned his place at the wedding.

With the formalities over, the musicians struck the first notes and, led by the newly-married couple, the guests started dancing and revellers of all ages showed remarkable energy, considerable capacity to devour food and mead while dancing and singing, and a natural ability to enjoy a good party. Things, not surprisingly, got a little out of hand when some of the drunken dancers fell into the river, and other drunks were blamed for pushing them in. Many got very wet but no one drowned and after a few brawls here and there, things settled down with a number of the worst offenders falling asleep.

The merriment was still continuing when the wedded pair, their close family and some special guests, boarded boats with torches blazing, and waved farewell to the remaining guests as they floated downriver on the new tide.

Elen and Hywel standing on the bow of their lantern-lit boat led the small flotilla moving gracefully towards the sea. Barely had they left their moorings than the musicians struck up a tune and the array of boats presented a wonderful sight as it drifted in the fast-approaching darkness down the river and into the wide estuary.

For the young couple it was a gloriously romantic moment and the new happy bride, held tight by her lover in the glow of the lanterns, waved at their supporters gathered on both shores with their own torches to wish them well.

Elen turned her face towards her husband and he instinctively met her look and they shared a moment of exquisite tenderness and affection. He held her tighter, drawing their bodies together and she felt his strength near her and reached for his lips. They kissed long and passionately. She felt elated, as if lifted off her feet, and what started as a slight tingle in the back of her neck travelled down her spine as excitement and reached her lower body. She loved him and wanted him.

Their lips separated and looking up at him she declared, "I love you Hywel."

"I know. I love you too Elen," he said. "You are the most beautiful woman I have ever seen."

"I can't wait until we are alone," she admitted.

"I feel the same and I hope when we get to the lodge everyone will want to go to bed," he said smiling at her.

"Yes, I'm ready too."

A while later they disembarked at the small fishing lodge in Llansteffan. Elen had been prepared well by her mother for the night and was relaxed, confident that her love for Hywel would overcome the few concerns she had.

The day had gone brilliantly without a single hitch; her parents had been there to support her whenever they thought she was faltering or when she herself had sought their advice. Hywel had been a tower of strength to her, always at her side, always there with an encouraging word, always there with a helping hand. She loved him and already could not imagine life without him.

She was ready for her husband in all ways and couldn't wait to be shown to the bedroom and be left alone with him. However, the accompanying throng was ready for yet more drinking, dancing, singing and talking, as were the poets – always keen to hear their own voices.

The party continued until the early hours of the morning, with Elen becoming increasingly concerned that they would be too tired even to go to bed. Eventually the crowd dispersed and the young couple were able to make their way to their own room.

Their bedroom walls were covered in white linen and the bed lifted about a foot above the suspended wooden floor. They knew there would be ears pressed against the doors and the walls listening for any sounds reflecting the success or failure of what was left of the night. The two had spoken about all these possibilities before their wedding. This reflected the closeness of their relationship and they had agreed together to entertain their audience early on, whatever was to happen later.

She was ready for the occasion both physically and mentally. She knew him, she trusted him and was madly in love with him. She had been ready for months, indeed had been yearning for this night to arrive and would have been delighted if he would lift her off her feet, carry her to the bed and lay her on it. However, alone with him in the bedroom, she felt slightly nervous.

Everywhere was still and quiet until they became accustomed to the silence, and then they were aware of the sound of the sea lapping gently against the shoreline and their boats. The sound was faint but easily recognisable. She stood by the bed and looked at him while he ensured the door was closed and that the servants had gone to their other tasks or to their own beds.

He turned to face her – she was beautiful – she was exquisite to look at with her femininity reaching out to him. He stepped towards her to kiss her and the wooden boards creaked causing him to hesitate. She smiled and stepped towards him, taking his hands and resting them either side of her narrow waist. She looked up at him happy, but with her eyes closed as they kissed.

Eventually their lips separated and she whispered, "Let's go to bed." His hands stayed firmly on her waist though she wanted them to have strayed to other places as her mother had warned her they would.

She took his right hand and led him to the edge of the bed. There was a creaking noise again, most probably caused by their own movement on the wooden boards. But their steps had not quite coordinated with the sound so both thought it could perhaps have been caused by someone approaching the door or one of the walls to listen.

Hywel hesitated, but she laughed quietly and fell onto the bed pulling him on after her. She realised that Hywel was not one for throwing her onto the bed. She guessed it would be a slow and loving process – gentleness and patience would be the order of the night. The marriage was consummated and provided some entertainment for those listening at the door and those with their ears pressed against the wooden partitions.

Elen woke happy and pleased. The servants knew by looking at the pair that they were perfectly suited to each other. There could be no doubt that they loved each other and desired each other. Elen could not imagine that she would ever experience a happier time.

They had started on their life together and there were many years ahead of them but their subjects would expect to see her pregnant and deliver a male heir to keep the peace in Deheubarth.

They stayed at the lodge for two nights and then set off, as planned, on a tour of their lands. The guests cheered them as they walked hand in hand from the lodge to their waiting boat and bade farewell to most of the guests, including Berddig, who made sure that he spoke to the couple before they left.

Speaking to Hywel first he said, "What a lovely time it's been. You have a lovely wife who clearly loves you. I wish you the best and hope to see you in a year's time to celebrate the birth of a male heir."

"You are expecting a lot of us. Thank you for the entertainment. I understand your story of the battle at Rhyd y Groes was the highlight of the evening before the wedding. I was very sorry that I missed it. Perhaps I can hear it when you next visit us."

"It did go down well, I have to admit. I will be delighted to tell it again when I'm with you both next."

"Good. Hope to see you soon."

"There's quite a queue waiting to see you. I wish you well." Berddig then moved over to talk to Elen.

He held Elen's hands in his and smiling at her he said, "I wish you well in your married life. Everyone can see that the two of you are made for each other."

"I am so glad you came to our wedding."

"My pleasure."

"It's not often that we see you poets from the north. It's lovely to hear new stories and new poems. I do occasionally get bored with hearing the same ones. Thank you so much."

"I hope you will become pregnant this summer on your tour of your beautiful land."

Elen blushed, though he was only expressing her own wish, "Thank you."

"I will join your subjects in praying for success; it would help to keep the peace in Deheubarth."

"Yes," she said and ventured into the realms of politics.

"I hope you will take the message north that we are a peace-loving people here in Deheubarth and are not looking for strife with anyone. We are content to live at peace with all our neighbours."

"I couldn't agree more and I will say that if ever the opportunity arises. Best wishes Elen. My thoughts will be with you and I will visit again to celebrate the birth of the heir and write a poem for him."

"Yes, please."

"I understand that you are going first to Dinefwr and then on to Pencader – well have a lovely tour of your land – enjoy it. I may call at Pencader on my way to Powys but I will have left before you arrive. Best wishes to you all."

"Have a good journey back," she called to him as he departed.

Hywel and Elen sailed across the estuary and entered the mouth of the river Gwendraeth where they were given a warm welcome by the local people and were joined by Hywel's most trusted commanders and soldiers. They set off in procession, following the course of the river Gwendraeth Fawr for about ten miles before turning north for the royal court at Dinefwr.

Along the Gwendraeth Fawr valley all who met them were taken aback by Elen's beauty and remarked at how happy the two were in each other's company. At Dinefwr the welcome was ecstatic, their subjects saw that they liked each other, were contented, wonderfully happy and fulfilled. They smiled together, they laughed with each other, and their souls radiated that happiness which observers absorbed and which left them with a feeling of wellbeing and success.

It alleviated the drudgery of life for the ordinary people; it brought colour to their grey lives. It bizarrely made them feel better – seeing others happy. Perhaps it gave hope – perhaps it gave something to aim for – somehow, for a while at least, it made them feel life was worth living.

Dinefwr was Hywel's home and the seat of the rulers of Deheubarth. He had spent most of his childhood there. In turn, he visited most of the important courts in Deheubarth during the course of a year – keeping himself informed about his people, their wishes and needs, and ensuring them of his protection in return for their loyalty.

Hywel had decided that he and Elen would embark on a tour of Deheubarth immediately from the royal court, calling first at the court in Pencader then moving on to southern Ceredigion and the west coast, returning to Dinefwr later in the summer. So, as planned, they stayed for two nights at Dinefwr before embarking on the journey to Pencader.

CHAPTER 3

Four days later in June 1041

EVEN AS THEY approached Elen had liked the look of Pencader and when she arrived and entered the court enclosure she was not disappointed, declaring to her husband, "I love this place. I've never been here before. We always tended to go east or west from Caerfyrddin, but never north for some reason."

"It's an excellent court. You always get a warm welcome here. The family has been loyal for decades and they are renowned for their good mead."

The tour was going well with the two welcomed everywhere and Elen thought Pencader was a magical place – a small court, a closely-knit community, surrounded by wonderful countryside and a fast-flowing river nearby. She couldn't help but declare how happy she was with her lot.

As Hywel had predicted, the family had prepared a welcome for them, the entertainment was ready, the food was prepared and the mead was in plentiful supply. The two of them were laughing and joking together happily – deeply in love as the evening progressed.

"The music is excellent. It's lively and it's no wonder so many are dancing," was Elen's observation.

"Pencader is a well-kept secret," laughed Hywel. "I'm so glad you like it here. We can visit often from Dinefwr."

The melodious tunes on the harps, the noises from the shouting, laughing and dancing were carried hundreds of yards by the evening breeze blowing from the south-west, which was making its own music as it pushed its way through the trees and the bushes, rustling the leaves and lifting the sounds over the enclosure's palisade. Also, amongst the cacophony of sounds carried far and wide, there were the screeching sounds of the intoxicated vocalists reaching for the top notes and of the drunks' frantic calls for more mead and ale.

The poets had long since retreated to a slightly quieter corner to compose their poems in praise of their mentors, rulers and paymasters. The sound emanating from the eating area had passed its zenith, though there were still some gluttons foraging around for leftovers.

In the immediate area of the main hall it was these human noises which predominated, the shouting and the laughing drowned out all serious conversation. It was that period in the entertainment where husbands were beginning to think of their wives and wives were beginning to think of their husbands, or of someone better. The unattached were eyeing those whom they might wish to be attached to, having explored the range displayed at the gathering carefully and critically. It was noisy, still very exciting, and minds were being distracted by the most basic of human desires, though some were too bloated to move much.

Elen, Hywel's beautiful wife, was envied by all the women for her beauty, poise and charm. She was equally earnestly desired by all the men regardless of their age. Some were careful not to let their women see them glancing at her, others did not seem to care at being caught, or perhaps they could not help themselves – her magical magnetism was too powerful for many. The old men wished they were younger and the young boys wished they were older.

She was also an enthusiastic and energetic dancer, smiling innocently and sweetly at each dancing partner, during all turns, spins and reels, joyfully lifting her head to meet each pair of eyes. Hywel was with her at the dancing, though worse for wear for his consumption of the local mead, but he was happy and proud of his wife and in love with her as she clearly was with him. Moving occasionally to support him physically, she advised him to rest for a while to regain his breath and composure.

A few of the other local noblewomen, seeing her difficulties, joined her, saying they were encouraging their husbands to take a walk down to the river for fresh air and to sober up a little before they thought of going to bed. Elen saw the wisdom of the suggestion and sent Hywel with the other husbands.

Outside the court's entrance, the track which led south to the ford on the small river of Nant Gwen and the other which led northwards up the hill were both deserted. The view for those men escorted to the court's gates by their womenfolk was that of a peaceful rural scene. On a night not disturbed by a feast, it would have been the sound of birds checking out a place to perch for the night that would have been heard. A blackbird perhaps, disturbed by the thought of a kestrel in the area, or an owl in the distance indicating that it was waking up and strangely alerting the mice to their risky predicament – the normal sounds of a night in the depths of the countryside.

That night, the court's canine residents were howling to the sounds of the festivities and totally distracted from their normal duties. They watched as Hywel and a few of his friends walked out of the court towards the ford. Elen and her friends who had escorted them as far as the gate, laughed as they watched their husbands' unsteady steps downhill towards the river until they were out of sight.

They had barely turned their backs on their menfolk when just above the general din they heard one of the dogs by the gate barking loudly. Elen turned to look at the silly dog, laughing at it, when her gaze was distracted by the sight of a large group of mounted horses galloping towards the court from the north. She could not hear the sound of their hooves because of the noise of the party and the breeze blowing from the south-west.

Initially she was not concerned, assuming they were latecomers to the party, but as they approached she and the others realised that there were too many of them, they were approaching too fast, and finally she could see that their swords were drawn.

She started running and screaming to alert the others, but the attacking soldiers were upon them and she, grabbed by the back of her dress, was lifted off her feet and slung unceremoniously across the shoulders of a horse by one of the mounted attackers.

She screamed at the person who had raised her onto his horse, "Put me down you idiot, I am Hywel's wife." However, with her face smashing against the horse's hard, hairy, leathery, muscular upper front leg, she soon realised that shouting was impractical and it was as much as she could do to breathe because of the lashing her face was receiving.

Surely, she thought, it is someone having fun but that it had already gone too far – she was getting injured and was in fear of her life. She knew Hywel would have to deal with this idiot and she knew he would. This man would be severely punished for this. She was confident that it was a game, after all this was Pencader and nothing much ever happened in Pencader.

She couldn't believe that someone had picked her up so easily and was holding her, the queen, in such an undignified position, her bottom up and her extremities hanging either side of the horse. She was aware of the pressure of a large hand on the small of her back keeping her firmly in her place. She tried to turn her head to see her stupid assailant, but her hair was hanging over her face and she had to strain to look through the strands.

Through her hanging hair she had a fleeting glimpse of her captor's eyes: they were black, angry, threatening and expressed elements of hate and yet pleasure at the same time.

She realised then that this hooligan meant to capture her and kill whoever stood in his way. Was he a Viking raider she thought? No, he had a Welsh look about him and was shouting in Welsh for the other attackers to follow him. He might not have a Deheubarth accent but he was Welsh.

The pressure on her back from the rider's big hand made her feel sick as the horse galloped forward she knew not which way. Suddenly her face and hands were splashed by a warm thick liquid. Some of the wetness entered her gaping mouth and she identified the taste of blood.

Spitting the blood out of her mouth she tried screaming again, "Hywel! Hywel!" Even if her husband were present he could not have heard her appeal above the noise of battle, or more accurately the slaughter. She glimpsed a body being sliced in half with her captor's sword, another time it was a head removed. From the little she could see she knew there was no mercy given and she stopped screaming knowing that she also could be slaughtered within minutes.

Instead, she started praying and spent the last few minutes of the uncompromising and vicious attack on innocent revellers at the court asking her maker for absolution for herself and her dear Hywel. But gradually, the motion of the horse she was slumped over slowed down and she saw, when she opened her eyes, the carnage around her. There were bodies everywhere. People she had been talking to and having fun with minutes earlier were dead and their bodies and parts of their bodies strewn around where her horse had stopped.

She could hear what was said but couldn't see the speakers. "Where's Hywel?" demanded one of the attackers, possibly her captor she thought.

There was a frightened reply, "I don't know. Why don't you ask his wife? She's the one you've got on your horse."

She felt herself lifted by the scruff of her neck and lowered onto her feet by the horse's front hooves. She could not adjust to her vertical position quickly enough to avoid collapsing against the horse's front leg and sliding quickly down past its knee and fetlock which she failed to grasp. The horse reared up on its hind legs and she felt sure he would crush her, but it avoided her when it re-established its front hooves on the ground and was again controlled by its rider with a deep sounding 'whoa'.

She became aware that someone was picking her up again and asking, "Where's Hywel?"

She managed a weak, "I don't know."

Then, from her captor still sitting on his horse, came the instruction, "Wash her face and let me look at her again to see if she is as beautiful as they say she is."

Someone brought a jug full of water and threw it at her face, grabbed her hair behind her head, and turned her to face her captor and told her to, "Speak to your king. Gruffudd wants to know, where's your husband hiding?"

"There is promise there," Gruffudd said, looking at her intently and laughing. He dismounted and, staring at her face, he laughed again and said, "Hywel's run away has he?"

"No. He just isn't here."

"He is here. I know he's here. He surely wouldn't desert his young wife so soon after the wedding," he declared. He laughed in spite and then gave the order, "Search everywhere for him and don't let him get away. I want him dead. Then you can take what you want." But the looting had already started.

CHAPTER 4

Later the same day in June 1041

ONCE THE BULK of his soldiers had dispersed to search for Hywel, Gruffudd turned his attention to Elen again and, gripping her tightly by the hair, marched her towards the main hall. At the entrance his soldiers made way for him and his captive saying, "They're all dead in here except for the women."

Those present in the hall scattered towards the walls when Gruffudd entered with Elen in tow, her head forced downwards.

She tried to push her head upwards so that she could see inside the hall, desperately hoping that someone would miraculously save her from the hands of her savage captor, or that she would find that it was all a bad dream. She could see very little of those present and of those she could see, she recognised none. There were bodies lying slaughtered on the floor in their own pools of blood. She thought they were Hywel's soldiers, who might have tried to resist the attack.

Gruffudd lifted her head and asked, "Is he hiding in here? Is he hiding under your bed? Which is your room?"

Knowing that Hywel was not there, she pointed towards the door separating their room from the main hall. Sword in one hand and a fistful of her hair in the other, he opened the door with his sword and, seeing the room empty, he dragged her behind him into the annexe.

The bed was empty and ready for her and Hywel. Gruffudd looked at her and saw her beauty and her form and, slackening his grip, slowly released her. She instinctively knew what was forming in his mind and attempted to dash for the door but he grabbed her, lifted her off her feet with one arm, threw her onto her own bed and speared his sword into the floorboards, to stand there tall, upright, proud and menacing, within reach of the bed.

She struggled against him, kicked, screamed and tried to bite the hand that held her down. But he was too powerful, too brutish and had his way.

She lay on her own bed, exhausted from her struggle against his will. He held her for a while and occasionally turned to look at her and admire her remarkable beauty in a calmer way. She was exhausted and demoralised by the experience and too shocked to cry.

When it was over he grabbed her by the arm, lifted her off the bed and pulled her into the main hall saying loudly, "He's not here," at which the soldiers present, knowing what had happened, laughed loudly.

The men had already searched the court for Hywel and gathered loot at the same time. Gruffudd, clearly the undisputed leader, addressed the soldiers gathered in the hall, "Take what you want from here and we'll search the surrounding area for Hywel. It will be dark soon."

By now Elen knew that the man who had her in his vice-like grip was Gruffudd ap Llywelyn, the king of north Wales. The ruler of Gwynedd and Powys had ventured south to expand his territory and he wanted Hywel dead so that he could claim the crown of Deheubarth.

He held Elen firmly by her hair but not as tightly as earlier. It was a reflection of her strength of character that she had not fainted. She stood next to him, small in comparison to his large frame, fragile and defenceless, her dress dishevelled, knowing that all present knew exactly what had just happened to her. She felt contaminated and wanted to wash his smell off her. She wanted to run into the river and scrub this man's body out of her own. She wanted to run to Hywel.

"Madog, I'm taking this one with me," Gruffudd called across the hall to one of his commanders. He handed her over to him by the hair. "Keep her safe, I'm beginning to like her." There was more laughter and whispers.

Elen was passed on to Madog who had a broad smile on his face as he took charge of her. His grip was not as tight as that of his leader and she managed, even in her weakened state, a glower of hatred towards him.

She was beginning to absorb her surroundings when Madog said to her, "Go on your knees and pay homage to your new king, Gruffudd ap Llywelyn, the king of Gwynedd, Powys and Deheubarth."

He pushed her on her knees in front of Gruffudd saying to her, "This is your new king."

A soldier stepped forward with a well-polished iron crown in his hands and said to Gruffudd, "This must be Hywel's crown, it was kept in the coffer in their room."

"Let's ask his wife?" Gruffudd said turning to Elen.

She didn't answer. It wasn't necessary; he knew it was Hywel's crown.

"Let's crown the new king of Deheubarth," Madog shouted.

Gruffudd sat in the high chair at the long table, the one, which a few hours earlier, had been occupied by Hywel. Madog placed the crown on his head and hailed him as the new king.

There was a resounding cheer in the hall of, "King Gruffudd ap Llywelyn of Deheubarth, Gwynedd and Powys."

Elen was in despair, in shock and fearful of the future, almost certain that the king would kill her after he had finished with her. There was one ray of hope in her heart, stemming from the fact that they had not caught Hywel, and while he was free she could hope.

Sensing her resistance declining, Madog relaxed his hold and she slid slowly onto her knees on the floor with her head bowed, while her enemies toasted the new king with Deheubarth's best mead. She was left emotionally and physically drained.

She thought of Hywel. Would he return with an army of soldiers, kill her captors and release her and return life to what it was only an hour earlier? Could he gather a force that quickly? Could he get the weapons to beat these men? She knew that his soldiers' weapons were kept in the court and that they were now in the possession of the attackers from the north. Gradually, as she recovered from her ordeal, she realised that Hywel could do very little that evening and she became resigned to her fate.

The attack had been a total surprise and if Hywel had not gone to the river with his friends he would have been killed in the initial minutes of the attack. She hoped that he and his friends had noticed that the sound of the music and revelry had stopped and had been replaced by very different sounds. They would have guessed that something was wrong and returned to investigate, seen what was happening, realised that they could do nothing, and escaped into the woodlands to make their way south. She guessed they would be some distance away from the court by now.

She knew that Hywel would be worried about her and would wish to help her escape but believed he was powerless to achieve her release. He might have been told that all at the court had been killed in the initial attack and so there was no point in trying to rescue her. She convinced herself, that this was the reason he hadn't tried.

Also, implanted in her head was the fact that she had been degraded and humiliated publicly by Gruffudd ap Llywelyn. This scar caused her to fear that Hywel would never look at her in the same way again. She couldn't bear the thought of not seeing his beautiful eyes looking at her lovingly.

It was at this low moment, feeling defiled by the brutish Gruffudd, that she contemplated death as a way of ending her suffering and of never having to face Hywel again, but her love for Hywel came surging back to overwhelm these other feelings. The thought of her lover gave her courage, determination and direction.

She gained the strength to stand up, looked around and faced her captors. Realising that she stood a mere five strides from an open doorway, and that Madog and the others were absorbed in toasting the new king, she saw her opportunity.

She waited for Madog to turn his back on her again and immediately darted for the door. She had no plan, other than to get out, away from those horrible men and run and run.

The first four strides went well but suddenly the doorway was darkened, filled by a bulky soldier on his way in. She collided with his midriff and fell in a heap at his feet, injuring her wrist and acquiring a tiny scratch under her chin.

Madog was there in an instant, embarrassed that he had given her the opportunity to even try to escape, however futile the attempt had been. He grabbed her by one shoulder and lifted her on her feet.

"There's some spirit in you, is there?" Then noticing the blood under her chin, said quietly and mockingly to her, "Be careful not to scar that pretty face of yours, your new king is not one for an ugly face. That face can keep you alive for a while at least, so take care of it lady."

She held his gaze and looked at him in disgust as he tied her to a wooden pillar.

The king had not missed her attempt to escape and he and the others had laughed at her ridiculous efforts.

The soldiers continued to search and gather loot, while others were posted as guards on the outer walls of the court. Elen could overhear the discussion in the hall and understood that the men from the north were preparing to stay the night and leave in the morning, unless they had discovered where Hywel was hiding.

Elen was resigned to further abuse from Gruffudd during the night, but she was left tied to the post and he didn't touch her nor even speak to her. But he did come to look at her and study her face and body as he would if he was judging a horse or some other animal. After an intense study he would grunt and walk away again. She eventually fell asleep, slumped on the floor, but woke in the middle of the night to see him looking at her in the light of a torch. She was scared but he said nothing and did nothing to her.

At first light he came to look at her again and this time moved her hair, and it was this movement that woke her from her sleep that morning. She looked back at him through bleary eyes. He touched her face with the back of his hand and for a second she thought he had smiled at her, but realised it must have been her imagination, her state of exhaustion, her anxiety, or the early morning sun playing tricks with his face.

Madog brought her food and told her they would be leaving soon. She would be going with them and was lucky because she wouldn't have to walk as the king had found a horse for her.

She made no reply but ate the bread and some of the remains of the previous day's food. Though resigned to her destiny she still held some hope that Hywel would have gathered an army overnight and would attack as they left the court or would ambush them somewhere on the road to release her from her plight, so that they could live happily together again.

She was disentangled from the post and taken outside, placed on a horse and tied to it. Gruffudd took a rope attached to her horse and tied it to his own saddle.

Slowly the northern army prepared to move out of the court with Gruffudd leading, followed by Elen, and the rest of the soldiers behind with horses and carts laden with items they had plundered. She had heard that the scout sent out earlier had made no contact with the enemy and there had been no signs of Hywel. A few soldiers were left behind at the court, under instructions to burn everything once the army had left, and then follow the main force northwards.

As they moved across the court towards the gate, Elen could see that corpses lay where they had fallen and were already been picked at by crows and magpies. Most she recognised from the clothes they wore, others were so badly dismembered that they were beyond recognition.

She looked towards the rear of the column to see if there were other women taken captive like her, and thought she could see one or two at the back of the procession, but no one she recognised. She couldn't see any of her friends who had been with her the previous evening at the gate. They could have escaped, they could be dead, or they might have endured a worse fate than her own.

CHAPTER 5

Following day in June 1041

E LEN WASN'T RESCUED that morning; her hopes weren't realised. Instead her horse, tied to the king's, followed his exact steps, slower when the track was rough and faster when the country opened out. She felt that she was considered as one other inanimate object taken as loot to the north.

Gruffudd rarely turned around to check that she was still there, and only showed minimal interest in her.

She, however, had many concerns: Hywel and his whereabouts, her parents, and how they would be worried about her, not knowing what had become of her.

She still believed that Hywel was building up his support and would have gone west to the Preseli Mountains, then to the Teifi estuary to raise a powerful army to march north to ambush Gruffudd's soldiers in the foothills of Pumlumon before they left Ceredigion. She was sure that enough people had witnessed her capture to relate the consequences to Hywel, including her departure north.

Indeed, during the day there were two instances when she thought that an ambush was imminent. First, when some of Gruffudd's scouts returned to express concern about the way ahead, but nothing of significance arose. Secondly, when she felt sure that she had seen soldiers hiding in the woods as they came out of the hills opposite Cors Caron, but again nothing materialised. Gruffudd seemed in no haste to leave Deheubarth; he was immune to all sense of danger, and appeared confident that he could cope with all events.

He sat easy on his horse. He was a big man with broad, strong shoulders and powerful arms, as he had demonstrated when he lifted her onto his horse as if she was a toy doll the previous day. He was a very robust man and his soldiers seemed similarly structured – hard men, prepared to fight hard to the bitter end.

She knew that Gruffudd's intention had been to capture and kill Hywel, so that he would be the undisputed king of Deheubarth. So he must have been seriously dismayed to find that Hywel was not in the court when he attacked.

It was while she was deep in these thoughts that it occurred to her that she might be used as a bait to draw Hywel out of his own territory in Deheubarth to engage in a battle on unfamiliar ground, and be soundly beaten and killed. This possibility appeared to be confirmed by the fact that they were not exactly rushing northwards. In her opinion their pace was slow, obviously to give Hywel time to muster an army and catch up with them. This then worried her.

They kept Cors Caron on their left and crossed the Teifi at the point where it turned to flow eastwards into the western edge of the Cambrian Mountains, where its source lay, and they set up their camp for the night on the northern bank of the river.

Madog was given the task of getting Elen off her horse and sitting her down for the evening meal. She expected to have to share Gruffudd's bed that night and she planned not to resist him. Instead she would try to relax him, get hold of his dagger and plunge it into his heart. And so bring her own misery to an end and save Hywel's life.

She kept an eye in the direction of the setting sun. She waited, hoping any second to hear the rush of horses and soldiers bearing down on them, just as Gruffudd had done at Pencader. She was convinced that it was an ideal direction to attack from, with Gruffudd's men blinded by the sun.

The king's soldiers were in good spirits, pleased with their success at Pencader and delighted with their gains. They were singing, reciting rudimentary poetry and recalling past victories, such as at Rhyd y Groes, as they sat relaxed by the fires. They were already forming rhymes in praise of their king and his latest victory at Pencader, and showed no fear of an imminent attack by a southern force led by Hywel.

It was nauseating for Elen to hear them describe joyfully the way they had shocked, frightened and slaughtered her friends and her fellow revellers at Pencader. The soldiers and their commanders constantly bestowed praise on Gruffudd. They knew that there hadn't been such an influential and powerful king as this for generations, and certainly not one who had ruled over such vast areas of their country.

As they were preparing to bed down for the night Elen was secured firmly to a nearby tree with rope and given a separate bed which was close to the king's. She could not sleep because whenever she heard Gruffudd turning on his bed or grunting in his sleep, she feared he would join her. At other times in the night she listened for the noise of Hywel and his men attacking with a rescuing force. These possibilities, one raising fear and disgust, and the other raising hope and joy, did not materialise that night and eventually, through exhaustion, she fell asleep just before dawn.

She was woken by what was probably a slight kick from the king and a command which demanded, "Get up."

She was dazed and was unsure of where she was, but reality soon dawned on her, as did her disappointment – Hywel hadn't attacked in the night. She was handed a piece of bread and was taken, at the end of a rope, by Madog to wash in the nearby river.

On her way back, she asked her escort, "My husband will be out looking for you with a large army. Why doesn't Gruffudd escape as fast as he can to the north?"

Madog laughed, "He wouldn't dare – we would defeat him and kill him easily. Gruffudd would have liked to have killed him at Pencader, so there would be no dispute about his rule in Deheubarth. I can tell you, Gruffudd is a very disappointed man."

"Hywel is bound to come to get me back."

"Your husband has probably escaped to the south west and it will take him a long time to raise an army to beat Gruffudd in battle," he said, laughing at her again and adding, "Get used to it."

She fell silent, with her expectations dashed, but she had no time to dwell on her feelings as they were soon on their way again, she on her horse tied to the king's.

They journeyed towards the mountains and just south of Pumlumon, some of the Powys men turned east for their homes, while the others continued their journey northwards.

The tracks became rougher and steeper and the scenery more grand. But, as impressive as these mountains were, she much preferred the gentle hills of her home. With every step her horse took northwards, the less likely she was of being rescued by her husband. She wondered what would become of her. Would she become a slave? Would she be made use of until she collapsed from ill health? Would she be used to raise a ransom or become part of a deal over the sovereignty of Deheubarth? She decided that she would ask Madog who she was finding to be more amenable than he had at first appeared.

At the next watering stop, a small stream, she asked Madog, "Where are we going?"

"Rhuddlan."

"I've heard of that place. Is it Gruffudd's capital?"

"Yes, it's a wonderful place, you'll like it there."

"I don't expect to be there long – Hywel will either buy me back or rescue me."

He laughed, "Once you're in Rhuddlan you won't want to leave."

She made an expression with her face as if to say, 'Yes, I will.'

Madog gave her a friendly smile but made no reply. While she could never like the man, he was quite affable with her by now and, when he could, replied to her queries honestly.

During these few conversations with Madog, she became aware that Gruffudd was throwing the occasional glance backwards towards her and even as they were riding he would turn back as if to check that she was still there, something he had hardly done at all the previous day.

They came to the River Dyfi and followed it to the small church at Mallwyd dedicated to St Tydecho. Gruffudd was the true king of these parts and was treated royally by all they met. Elen was obliged to stay on her horse while Gruffudd and a few others, including Madog, entered the small wooden structure where they attended mass. Taking their time, as if, in Elen's mind, they were tempting Hywel north, they camped that night in Dinas Mawddwy.

The following day they climbed to Bwlch y Groes and into the thick mist that covered the high ground. It crossed her mind to escape into the grey cloud but she knew she would not get very far and remained on her horse until they descended into the sunshine in the valley of the Dyfrdwy and Lake Tegid. At the northern end of the lake, many of the soldiers departed and followed the river Tryweryn to their homes in the north west. The king and the remaining soldiers travelled towards the north east and at dusk they arrived at a manor house near Corwen where they stayed the night. There were festivities and celebrations again, with Elen now treated more as a guest than as a captive.

Her hands were freed. Madog was obviously given the task

of keeping an eye on her but Gruffudd was never far away, also keeping an eagle eye on her.

That evening Elen said to Madog, "There is something puzzling me. You said that Gruffudd was very disappointed that he didn't catch Hywel at Pencader. How did he know that he would be there?"

Madog hesitated, surprised by the question, but eventually replied, "He guessed that since you were there, then Hywel must have been there too."

"Did he know I was there?"

"No! It was pure luck."

"Luck?"

"Well for Gruffudd, but obviously not for you," and he moved away from her but she followed him, watched by Gruffudd.

"I am not stupid Madog. That isn't an honest answer. Please tell me the truth."

He shrugged his shoulders and, glancing at the king, said quietly, "He knows everything, he watches everything. Be careful."

That night, when Gruffudd retired to bed, he made sure that Elen was with him, and she knew what to expect. However, he was kind towards her and fell asleep quite quickly. He was up before her, and she was unaware of the fact that he had stood above her for quite a while at dawn, looking at her admiringly, possibly lovingly.

She woke shortly after dawn and sat up in her bed, surprised that her sleep had not been disturbed. Gruffudd had left her to wake in her own time but she could hear his voice in the house, vibrating through the thin walls.

She was taken by the kind lady of the house to throw cold water over her face. Then Elen sat at the table with the king, while Madog and the soldiers prepared to depart with the horses by now gathered, fed and saddled, waiting to be mounted.

Bidding farewell to the family of the manor house, they set off on the final stage of their journey, with Elen's horse no longer tied to the king's. It was expected that her horse would follow the master's horse obediently.

Before long they were looking down the wide expanse of the rich Clwyd valley and within a few hours they were approaching Rhuddlan.

CHAPTER 6
Mid-June 1041

T HEY FOLLOWED THE east bank of the meandering River Clwyd coming to its confluence with the Elwy and from where Elen could see the wooden structures of Rhuddlan rising above the trees in the distance.

The army was much reduced as more soldiers had filtered off to their homes during their progress northwards. However, quite a formidable force remained, and made up for the lack of numbers by their noise, particularly as they approached the royal court.

Madog was enthusiastic, "There's Rhuddlan, it's the most fantastic place you've ever seen. Can you see the roof of the main hall? It's built on a hill above the river and from that hill you can see for miles around. The land is so flat."

For her, it wasn't going to be as fantastic a place as Hywel's courts. Clearly, Madog had not seen the best places in Deheubarth and she asked him sarcastically, "Can you see the sea from Rhuddlan?"

"You don't have to see the sea in Rhuddlan, the sea comes to see us twice daily." He was laughing at her and, at last, it forced a smile out of her.

But she wasn't to be deterred and retorted, "Caerfyrddin is like that also."

Madog was equally determined to exhort the virtues of Rhuddlan, "The sea brings boats of all sizes, shapes and colour to your door."

She replied, "What's new in that?"

"You will like Rhuddlan in time," he replied. But he realised that he was not going to win and allowed her to go ahead while she muttered, "Not much chance of that. I don't want to be here and would like to leave before I arrive."

They passed a large lone oak tree, standing on slightly raised ground about a hundred yards away on their right. It had been left untouched Madog said, because it brought luck to the court. The track then climbed upwards, leaving the river at the base of a steep slope below them. From this higher position they had a clear view of the court, its defensive walls, the towers and the thatched roof of the large main hall.

The track went back down to the riverside again and they passed below the royal court and its outer defences on their right and continued towards the harbour, looking upwards at the court entrance which faced the port.

She could see the boats rocking gently on the outgoing tide. Madog had been right; it was a very striking display of fighting ships, trading ships and numerous small boats. Colourful sails were wrapped about the masts, some tall and some short. Elen was reluctantly impressed by the sight facing her.

Gruffudd turned in his saddle and looked at Elen and said aloud for her and others to hear, "This is your new home. You will grow to like this place and eventually to love it and never wish to leave it." He was happy, yet deadly serious, while most of his audience were gaping open-mouthed at Elen.

The statement was directed at Elen, but it was also intended for all the others who heard it. It signalled to everyone that she was there to stay and they had better get used to a new, beautiful woman at the court, a new queen. Elen didn't see it that way though. It gave her hope that she had a future – at least long enough for Hywel to come and release her from her captivity or to bargain for her freedom.

The king turned his horse to the right to ascend the court's main entrance and meet the residents standing on both sides waiting to greet and welcome the returning soldiers and to cheer the king in his success. Many were welcoming back their husbands, sons or lovers, and so it was a time of emotional excitement with kissing, cuddling and cheering everywhere. Children were running to their fathers and being picked up and thrown in the air, to be caught just before they touched the ground. There hadn't been many casualties on the campaign, so only a few children had no one to run to. It was a very happy occasion and one of relief to many of the women.

Elen sat on her horse watching it all.

As the king arrived at the main entrance, a smart-looking woman approached his horse, clearly expecting to be lifted onto his horse to share his glory and accompany him into court. She looked disappointed when it didn't happen, and then she noticed Elen. The look of disappointment was quickly replaced by that of extreme anger. Her eyes sparkled like black pearls as it dawned on her that she was to be the king's second woman from now on.

This woman was furious. She hated the look of her replacement, she was fuming as she glowered at Elen, her eyes full of loathing. The woman had no intention of shrugging her shoulders and accepting 'such is life'. She clearly wanted to scratch and punch her opposition, drag her off the horse and, among other things, kick her senseless.

Elen looked at her and tried to intimate to her that she did not wish to be in Rhuddlan, never mind in the king's quarters and much less in the king's bed. It was indeed the last thing she wanted.

The woman knew the dangers of attracting the king's wrath, but even so, she couldn't restrain her anger and spat at Elen before screaming a torrent of obscenities at her. Elen, having flinched dramatically with shock, proceeded to wipe the spittle off her neck.

Gruffudd glared at the woman but made no comment to her. He directed his horse away from her and Elen's horse followed. The woman spat at Elen again – the spittle, to the woman's great annoyance, landing this time on the lower part of Elen's clothes, making no impact on the dirty threads in those regions. Elen rode quickly past her, but the woman scuttled after her to catch her and, looking up at her said, "Hello slut. I will gouge your eyes out when you're sleeping, you whore. I will give you no peace, you bitch."

"Don't bother with me. You can keep your king. I have a much handsomer and nicer husband to return to."

The woman, taken aback, made no response except to try again to spit at Elen. But she was equally unsuccessful in her third attempt, with the spittle only narrowly missing her own face as it returned to earth.

"Get out of my way. I have no interest in that brute and it reflects badly on you that you clearly do." She encouraged her horse forward and the woman tried to keep pace but lost heart, probably as a result of Elen's statement.

The woman's final comment was, "I will get you. Don't forget I will be there waiting for you one dark night."

Gruffudd and Elen entered the court through the gates to the sound of more cheers. The king rode up to the hall and dismounted, throwing a glance at Elen as he did so.

Madog was also dismounting nearby and Gruffudd, in Elen's hearing, said to him, "Take care of Mair; let her want for nothing and take her home to Anglesey and stay there with her."

Elen could see clear signs of displeasure on Madog's face. She was disappointed herself, because she felt he was one that she could talk to and believed he might help her.

Madog didn't dare to protest, not even with a facial response, and he knew he had to obey without any indication of annoyance.

"Sail with her on this tide."

He dismissed Madog and turned his back on him. He looked up at Elen who was still on her horse and said, "Get down and come with me." His anger seemed to dissipate as she looked down on him.

She felt that though the instruction was abrupt, she had been more kindly addressed than Madog.

She dismounted her horse and tapped the animal gently on its neck, thanking it quietly and adding, "Wish me well."

Gruffudd beckoned her to follow him saying, "You won't escape from here – not alive anyway. And no husband of yours will rescue you. So you need to accept that you are living here now. This is the royal court; there is plenty of food and drink. We will make you happy here."

"No you won't. I want to return to Hywel. Why don't you sell me back to him?"

"He won't want you back. I've spoiled you for him. He will look for another woman in Ireland to replace you."

"No he won't. He loves me and only me. He's told me that many times and I believe him."

Gruffudd laughed heartily at her.

"You are mine now. I have won you in battle."

"It was not a fair battle. You gave no warning."

"I won. He lost. I am the new king of Deheubarth. That is a fact." He was laughing again.

She knew it was pointless to argue with him. She would have to submit to his will and wait for Hywel to rescue her.

Madog waved goodbye to her as he strode out of the court. Mair was held firmly by two soldiers, but turned round to look at Elen and the king. She shouted abuse at them both, but to no avail, as she was marched out of the gates to a waiting boat.

"Madog has had no rest," complained Elen.

"What's it to you? He was too friendly towards you," he said

49

angrily. "He has disappointed me. I need to get him and Mair out of my sight."

Elen was shocked at the man's lack of fellow feeling and was on the point of telling him that he was a brute, when Mair's screaming, as she was taken towards the boat, reached the court and cut across her chain of thought.

Gruffudd wished to be sure that Mair and Madog were on their way. He stood watching them board the boat. From where they stood they could see the boat being released from its mooring and pushed away from the harbour wall. The sailors were rowing slowly, guiding the boat into the middle of the river and unfurling a sail to make its way towards the sea. Elen waved at Madog and received a deadly look from Gruffudd.

She had been impressed by the fleet of war ships anchored in the harbour when she arrived. Looking at them again she wondered how Hywel could possibly conquer the place. Even if he approached the court from the sea by surprise, he would still have difficulty in overcoming the highly-defended fortress of Rhuddlan.

"Come, let's drink to the future," Gruffudd said, smiling knowingly at her.

She meekly followed him into the hall. She was in no mood to drink a toast but was thirsty and the latter need took priority. She drank also to nullify her despair at her separation from Hywel, and to try and forget that she was, in effect, a prisoner.

She scanned her new home. The hall, constructed of oak, was large, the largest she had seen. It could accommodate about fifty people comfortably. She saw a large table on a raised platform, extending the width of the building, on the side furthest from the entrance. This accommodated the king, his family and the court officers. There was no mistaking Gruffudd's chair; large, higher, and covered in ornate carvings.

Numerous trestle tables were arranged in the body of the

hall, laden with food and drink for the returning king and soldiers. The best meat cuts would be reserved for the top table but those at the other tables would do well that evening. The fire was smouldering, but there was very little smoke in the room. As she looked upwards towards the hole through which the smoke escaped, she realised this building was the highest she had ever been in. The little smoke that was not escaping through the roof, she noticed, remained high in the rafters of the royal court.

Viewing her new abode, she noticed at the end, opposite the large table, there were stairs going up to a loft. It was another feature she hadn't seen before in the Deheubarth courts.

The walls were covered in brightly coloured cloths and furs to keep the drafts out and add interest to the room. These were interspaced with shields of various shapes, sizes and colours. Gruffudd had forbidden the hanging of spears in the hall, and only he was allowed to wear a sword indoors.

While she was still absorbing the magnificent hall, Gruffudd directed her to a chair on the right of his grand chair. Jugs were arranged for them and their plates laden. Gruffudd shouted, "This is a special occasion. I need my silver drinking jug."

He was obeyed immediately and his silver jug full of mead supplied.

"Lift your jugs," he invited. "We are celebrating a successful campaign in Deheubarth." Mugs were raised and cheers accompanied the drinking.

Gruffudd, still on his feet, declared, "Tonight, I'm also celebrating my marriage to Elen. The queen of Deheubarth is now also the queen of Gwynedd and Powys."

There was an uproar of congratulations, cheering and shouting. As the melee subsided, Gruffudd called for Chancellor Llywarch Olbwch, the court's priest and chief cleric to come forward and bless the marriage.

Though sober, as was demanded of his office, the chancellor, given the opportunity would have gone through a lengthy ceremony, under Gruffudd's instructions performed the rudimentary marriage. He was wise enough not to even enquire about consent and merely recited the blessing slowly and publicly declared that the marriage had taken place.

Elen, astounded by the course of events, attempted to protest while regarding the whole event as a sick joke, knowing she was already married happily to Hywel. It was only when the man she was later to know as the court justice invited everyone to raise their jugs to wish the happy couple well and that they be blessed by many children that she realised fully how seriously people were taking the event.

It was typical of Gruffudd, he had his own way at all costs. Elen did not regard herself married to this brute nor did she see herself as the queen of anywhere other than Deheubarth.

The evening continued boisterously. Gruffudd kept a close eye on Elen and was clearly pleased that she was imbibing of his mead. He was in a good mood, and at dusk he took her by the arm and led her to see the sunset. He pointed towards the sea in the distance, with the sun just above the horizon and its red colour reflecting on the river that flowed beneath them. He announced, "That is the most beautiful sunset you'll ever see."

"I have seen its equal," she retorted, but she was impressed by the location.

They quietly stood looking at the sunset for a while, each with very different thoughts in their minds. Eventually, after the sun had disappeared he pronounced, "Let me show you to our room."

He led her into the hall and up the stairs she had seen earlier. He opened a door at the top and entered their bedroom, beckoning her in and saying, "This is where you will be tonight – with me."

She stepped in nervously to see a large room, with a window

at the gable end facing the port and the sunset. It was as much as she could absorb before he gripped her arm firmly, as though he was afraid that it would be now that she would try to make her escape.

She struggled against his vice-like grip and thought of hitting him with her small fist, but reconsidered knowing that he could throw her onto the bed or the floor with the minimum of effort.

He bent over her to kiss her but she turned her head away. He was disappointed, and when she looked up at him quickly before turning away again, she thought, in that brief glance she had into his dark eyes, that he had been hurt.

"Better that than being bitten," he laughed.

They went to bed and she didn't resist him, knowing that it would be a gesture only. While the mead she had drunk helped in that respect, he was aware that it was against her will. She felt some relief in just knowing that the morning would come eventually.

CHAPTER 7

The next day in June 1041

D AWN ARRIVED WITH Elen waking next to the person she hated most in the world and wishing that she lay next to Hywel, the person she loved.

To her, Gruffudd was big, brutish, uncouth and uncommunicative, while Hywel had none of these hateful attributes. He was intelligent, humorous and a cultured man, with the ability to sing, dance, recite and write poetry that had made her laugh. As she remembered Hywel, she was reminded of how happy she had been before that fateful day at Pencader. She wondered if Hywel had completed his task of either raising an army to rescue her or collect the money to pay for her release.

She hadn't been sorry to see the back of Mair. While she felt pity for her, the very last thing she wanted to do was to replace her in the king's bed. But she did feel safer with Mair in Anglesey.

Madog's removal from Rhuddlan was a cause of regret to her because she was at least able to talk to him and question him about things. He had been helpful to her and they had arrived at some sort of understanding. She suspected that Gruffudd had sent Madog from Rhuddlan because he was jealous of the few words they had shared together. A friendship had begun to develop between them.

With the dawn well on its way and the sun appearing between the hills on the eastern horizon, Elen lay awake under the fur skin next to the king. She turned over in her mind what could become of her. She knew that at some point or other she would have to talk to the body still snoring beside her. As more light penetrated the room, she became more aware of her surroundings and, among his clothes on the floor, she noticed the shining hilt of his dagger in its scabbard.

She didn't sleep much after dawn. She catnapped a little and only when she felt him stirring did she wake fully. He raised himself to a sitting position, groaning and sniffling, still with the smell of the previous evening's excess alcohol intake on his breath.

She watched him through one slightly open eye and waited until she was sure that he was getting up from the bed and putting on his clothes. Then she raised herself onto an elbow, making sure that her body was covered.

"What's happening to me today?" she asked.

At first she assumed that he had not heard her because he made no effort to answer. But then he turned to her and looked down on her. She feared that she might have spoken too soon, the way he looked at her. However, a tiny rise at the furthest corners of his mouth showed her that he was wearing a slight smile.

"You are a beautiful creature," he said. "It was worth becoming the king of Deheubarth just to get you." He laughed, obviously pleased with himself, while towering over her, his very presence with his muscular body and powerful arms, intimidating her.

Elen didn't reply to his blunt statement and continued her study of his face. His hooked nose gave him an eagle-like image, while his long, thick, black hair gave him a wild and frightening appearance. That morning, his large, dark, penetrating eyes scared her.

"I will get one of the women to bring your breakfast," he stated matter-of-factly as he turned away from her and disappeared down the steps into the hall. In the distance she could already hear the sounds of the court coming to life.

My God, she thought, is he trying to be kind?

She dressed, washed and ate her breakfast before descending to the hall where Gruffudd sat with his advisers and important court nobles. These men had responsibilities for the horses, ships, harbour and everything else at court, from its defence to its food supply. Their conversation was clearly coming to an end and they were dispersing to their various tasks. The king, as it soon became apparent to Elen, was going hunting and he had already given orders to prepare the hounds and horses.

Taking advantage of a moment alone with Gruffudd before he left, she asked him, "How much ransom have you asked for me?"

He laughed at her. "I am not going to ransom you. I decided on that the moment I saw you. Although I had heard a lot about your beauty, I was still surprised when I saw you. I knew then I would never give you back."

Clearly what had been a nightmare for her had been an enjoyment for him. How two people could have gained such a different experience from the same event mystified her. She had always believed that love between two people was essential to a successful and rewarding relationship and to happiness.

"No ransom? But Hywel will pay well for me. Don't you want his money? The south west is rich and Hywel is rich."

"I want you and that's that."

"There will be war. Hywel will come and rescue me. Many will be killed. Let him know that you will accept a ransom for me. Give me back to him and all will be well. Many lives will be saved."

"I have you and I am keeping you. I am the king of Deheubarth."

"So there will be war? He can come by land or sea – you will never be sure – you will have to be on your guard all the time."

"There's nothing new in that! He can't match my navy. He has to go to Ireland for soldiers to attack me. So we will not hear from him for some time, probably years. Get used to being my queen. I will look after you better than Hywel. No one will steal you from me." He was laughing again as he departed through the door to go hunting, shouting as he went, "Jane will look after you. She's of good stock, hardworking and she knows everything about everything and everyone."

She was relieved to think that he would be out of her life for a few hours.

Jane had been instructed to see to Elen's needs. She was young, very young, hardly thirteen years of age. A plain face, but of strong build and energetic, with a ready smile.

That morning, Elen was waited upon hand and foot by Jane. Other servants of the court came to meet her too, to study her, to assess their new queen, some even to admire her. They were talking to her as though she was going to be at the court for a long time; indeed as though she would spend the rest of her life there with them.

Gradually, as the morning passed, some of the more noble ladies arrived at the hall to meet her. They were curious to know what life was like in Deheubarth. What was in fashion there? Of course, Elen was interested in the fabrics and clothes available at Rhuddlan, which was so heavily influenced by trade with Western Europe. They all soon fell into detailed and excited conversations and time passed quickly for her.

After lunch, two women, including Tangwystl, the wife of Llywarch Olbwch, Gruffudd's chancellor, took her for a walk by the river and showed her the port with the ships tied to the poles on the harbour wall. There were six large, sea-going vessels, warships and traders, built to visit ports in England, Scotland, Ireland and France. The other smaller ships were used to carry goods along the shoreline. The numerous small rowing boats were used to ferry people and animals across river and down the estuary to the sea. They all bobbed rhythmically at anchor.

There were many houses and buildings – some small, some large – outside the court's fortifications and only a short distance from the river. The larger ones, she was told, belonged to members of the nobility and the king's officers.

Elen was surprised at how many people lived by the port. The other woman, the wife of the court justice, told her that Rhuddlan had expanded recently as a result of Gruffudd's successes. Not all the new incomers could now be accommodated within the court boundaries, so a small settlement had grown below the court by the port. This settlement provided security for the port and some of the king's trusted naval commanders lived there.

Elen couldn't help but be impressed by the activity there, the mixture of languages spoken and the sight of the vessels swaying gently on the river. It was an area she liked, as it reminded her of her trip on the Tywi after she was married. But, it also gave her hope of escape. She saw herself hiding on a vessel destined for the south and being carried around the headlands of the west and into Hywel's waiting arms.

Her companions seemingly took every opportunity they had to praise Gruffudd and his achievements. The wife of the court justice pointed to the Clwyd Mountains in the east and said, "Those hills used to be the boundary between Wales and England and all the land between them and the Dyfrdwy estuary had been taken from us since Offa's time. But through Gruffudd's military brilliance and skilful political manoeuvring, all that land has been returned to us and we feel much safer here now. The Saxons will not dare attack us while Gruffudd is king."

This was clearly intended to impress Elen but it didn't have the desired effect. So the speaker continued, "Think of what happened at Rhyd y Groes. It was a famous victory that brought us peace and respite from Saxon attacks."

"Rhyd y Groes?" asked Elen.

"Haven't you heard of it? Everyone knows about that battle. I thought Berddig came to your wedding. It's very unlike him not to have told the story of the battle of Rhyd y Groes."

Elen vaguely remembered having heard that Berddig had told a story of a battle the night before her wedding but she had missed it. Even the wedding now seemed an age ago to her.

"I missed it," she said, still showing little interest.

Tangwystl tried another tack and explained, "Do you know Elen, it was Gruffudd who established this royal court at Rhuddlan. He has given us access to materials, not just from England, Scotland and Ireland but from all the European countries. The clothes we wear are better, finer and more hard-wearing than ever because of the trade he has established across the sea. Oh Elen! He has made our lives so much better."

"Hywel's ships are also trading with France and other countries in Europe. We have fine clothes as well," replied Elen, slightly offended.

The court justice's wife was determined to praise her king, "Gruffudd has built a formidable fleet of fighting ships and no one will dare attack us. We feel much safer with him as king."

Elen said nothing, knowing by now that her companions were strong supporters of Gruffudd. She even thought he might have set them up to influence her in his favour.

They were not finished, and the justice's wife continued with her theme, "Everybody here feels much more secure now that Gruffudd has made the Dyfrdwy the boundary in the east and the Saxons have been so soundly beaten. Gruffudd has made Rhuddlan a wonderful place to live in. The peace he has brought means we can enjoy the grain and food the rich land of the Clwyd Valley provides, and we have easy access to the vast hunting lands and forests to the west. You'll love it here,

Elen. We all do. Gruffudd is a bit rough and ready but he is a good man and he will take good care of you."

These facts related to Elen, in praise of the king and his achievements, didn't change her views of her captor. She hated him and couldn't think any good of him.

She didn't wish to hear him being praised and ventured to ask, "What can you tell me about Mair, the one sent away with Madog?"

There was a brief hesitation before the court justice's wife, choosing her words carefully, said, "She was Gruffudd's partner before you came."

It was clear and unambiguous, it was in the past, firmly in the past and they were of the opinion that there would be no turning back. The king had made a decision and it was final.

"Well, he knows I want to go back south to my husband Hywel."

Her two companions looked at her, frowned at each other and one said, "I would not say that too loudly if I were you. The king would not take kindly to it. He can be quite hard."

"I know about it," she said. "He can't steal another man's wife. Hywel is the king of Deheubarth. He has many friends and they will avenge my capture."

"Gruffudd is now the king of Deheubarth. You will have to be more careful what you say."

"I have made it quite clear to him that I want to go back to my husband because I love him."

"Did he slap you?"

"No."

"Consider yourself lucky and don't say it again. No one can attack Gruffudd here in the north. Everyone knows that he is too powerful and is an excellent leader in battles. He has not lost a battle in all his life, even when he is fighting against the odds. It's a shame you didn't hear Berddig telling his stories."

Elen looked at her.

"When he is at court next we'll get him to tell the story again. Everyone loves it. In the meantime, lie back and enjoy your life with us here. You will get old soon enough and lose your good looks."

They had passed the port and houses built near it and had walked along the river bank until they approached a large willow tree. Her companions decided it was time to turn back which they did, but they continued their unhurried conversation.

They had talked openly with each other about everything other than Elen's predicament and her relationship with Gruffudd. When the conversation was directed by Elen to her capture and, as she saw it, her captivity, it was manoeuvred carefully and sensitively to a less controversial topic and away from matters they did not wish to dwell on for too long.

As much as Elen wanted to know her own future, they were not to enlighten her. Perhaps they had been instructed not to talk to her, or perhaps they knew nothing about it.

In the end she believed the two women were trying to be helpful. They were probably giving her good advice but she couldn't see how she could ever stop loving Hywel. She knew he loved her and, however difficult it would be, she wanted to be back with her husband. That's how she felt and that's how she would feel for ever.

She would be civil to these noble ladies of the court but she had no intention of becoming too friendly with them. She wanted to return home where she was happy. She didn't want to listen to these ladies trying to distract her from that mission.

She would have liked to stay there by the river watching the ships being loaded and unloaded. However, her companions insisted that they should return to the hall to oversee the preparations for the return of the hunters.

So, reluctantly she accompanied them back up the slope

from the riverbank, nodding her head at the keepers as she went through the main gates and towards the hall, her spirit declining with every step.

It wouldn't be long before the men would return from the hunt and she would endure another night, sleeping in a bed she had no wish to occupy.

CHAPTER 8

Same day in June 1041
to spring 1042

WHEN SHE RETURNED to the hall she was surprised to see Berddig sitting at the table with a plate heaped with food and a jug in front of him.

Hywel sprang to her mind immediately – it was the shock of seeing Berddig there – the sweet memories of the wedding were overwhelmed by the pang of missing her true husband. Where was Hywel? Why had he not come for her? At that moment, with blood rushing to her head and her heart pounding, hope leapt in her body; hope that Berddig could tell her that Hywel was on his way or that he was there to start the negotiations for her release.

She was hot, red faced and excited as she approached the story teller but Gruffudd, whom she dismissed from her sight whenever she could, was there sitting in his own chair next to Berddig. The king had returned from the hunt early with a couple of his men to meet his favourite poet and, though not all the hunters had returned, the hall was surprisingly full.

"This is my wife," Gruffudd announced to Berddig. There was no mention of the fact that she was his new wife, most recently acquired wife, or this is who I am living with at present. No – Elen was his wife and that was that. Elen knew that no one could dare ask 'since when?' Or 'does she want to be your wife?' He had declared to all that she was tied to him, woe betide anyone who challenged him or would doubt her status as his wife.

Elen didn't feel nor believe she was his wife. Slightly deflated, but still enthusiastic at seeing the poet, she placed her hands firmly on the table and lent across towards him. "I'm so glad to see you. Have you got news for me?"

Berddig raised his jug to Elen and, looking into her lovely watery eyes, said, "So the most powerful king Wales has ever seen has tied himself to this beautiful lady, how wonderful."

Then turning to the king, "You forget, Gruffudd, I have met this lady before you. I can tell you that she is not just a pretty face. She carries a wise head on those shoulders. I congratulate you on your choice."

Berddig knew Gruffudd well. He knew he could get away with more than most others at the court but he also knew to be careful and knew the value of praise.

Elen was devastated. She straightened herself, taking her hands off the table and in so doing distanced herself from the poet. The joy which had filled her seconds earlier had drained and the hope which had lifted her spirits had been replaced by a crushing feeling in her core.

Berddig stood and slid around the table to Elen, as though sensing her disappointment. He took hold of her right hand, saying loudly, "Let's drink to the most beautiful woman in the kingdom."

He grabbed his jug, raising it to his mouth while he released her hand gently but not before she had felt her hand squeezed.

Encouraged, as they were parting, she tried another tack and asked if he had heard anything of her parents and did he think they knew she was alive and at Rhuddlan. He assured her that they knew she was alive and well looked after. This eased her mind a little and Berddig became distracted by the loud calls for him to tell his audience a story. The court justice's wife, who had accompanied Elen earlier, was among the most keen to demand, "Tell us the story of Rhyd y Groes. Elen hasn't heard it."

"Yes! Yes!" resounded from every direction.

"But, you've heard it before and some of you were there at the battle."

"We want to hear it again," some shouted, while others called out, "Elen hasn't heard it."

Turning to Elen, pretending great reluctance, he said, "Elen, I will tell this story in your honour." Then turning towards Gruffudd with his arms open as if praising God he added, "and in praise of your husband, King Gruffudd."

Those in the hall settled to hear the story of the battle of Rhyd y Groes. Some sat on the floor, some on the side benches, and some on the laps of those who sat on the benches. Elen was directed to sit on the chair kept empty for her next to Gruffudd's cushioned chair.

The story was delivered in great style, just enough stress placed on the right words in the right place, at a perfect pace – slowly, gently and gradually increasing the tension while Gruffudd was waiting for the Saxons to enter the river and then robustly and fast when he led the charge. Praise was loaded on the king – glorifying all his actions, his bravery, his military supremacy – all of which was made to convince his audience of his worthiness to be the king of Wales.

Gruffudd enjoyed every minute. He loved the acclaim and basked in it, occasionally glancing at Elen to see if she was suitably impressed by her husband's skills.

For Elen, however, the dedication attached to the story had marred the rendering of it, but such was Berddig's skill as a story teller that it had not completely spoilt it for her. She had first-hand experience of the king's fighting ability. She was not impressed and any hope Gruffudd had that it might influence her was seriously misplaced.

Superbly self-confident, Gruffudd was ignorant of her opinions and kept her by his side. He jealously guarded her, looked at her frequently, admiring her beauty, her poise, even her serenity which hid her inner turmoil.

She still wished desperately to talk to Berddig, to ask him if he had heard anything of Hywel. She waited for an opportunity but by then she was more realistic and more fearful of his answers. Eventually, Berddig sat in the chair next to her, leaving her with Gruffudd on one side and the poet on the other. Elen waited for Gruffudd to be distracted, took a deep breath and asked Berddig, "What can you tell me about Hywel?"

He almost certainly expected the question and was ready with his reply. "Take my advice and forget Hywel, Deheubarth and your past – it's the past. It's obvious to everyone that Gruffudd is besotted with you. Learn to enjoy your life with him."

His reply left Elen devastated. She had not expected good news but not such a retort. It left no room for hope. She stared at him, tears swelling in her eyes and he took some pity on her and said, "I've heard nothing of Hywel or Deheubarth since I left a few days before you did."

She was about to take umbrage at the idea that she had left Deheubarth when she felt the king's hand on her shoulder. She turned towards him, with an inquisitive look on her face.

"I see you're talking to Berddig. He is the best story teller anywhere."

Annoyed, she asked him, "Is that the only story he knows?"

Gruffudd was too merry to take offence and replied, "He tells many stories wonderfully well. We must make the most of his time here. He's leaving in the morning to attend the funeral of a friend in Arfon."

She turned back towards Berddig to take advantage of his presence and ask him more questions. But he'd left his chair and was mingling with the others and her opportunity had passed.

During the entire evening of the celebration which followed the return of the hunting party, Gruffudd was civil and pleasant to her, ensuring that she had enough to drink and that she had the tastier parts of the cooked fowls. He got the court poet to sing to her, to sing about her beauty and to even sing about her style and elegance. In any other situation she would have been pleased and flattered by the attention, but in his court she most definitely wasn't.

When the merriment, the talking and the dancing were over, he indicated to her that they would retire together for the night and led her up the stairs to their bedroom. She was disappointed that he was not too drunk to climb the steps. Instead, she had to allow him to shower her with compliments about her attractive face, her body, her elegance and her strong character. He told her how he admired her virtue in trying to remain loyal to Hywel, but gave her no hope that she would ever return to her husband.

She did not resist in any way but made it clear by her demeanour that she was not participating willingly in the act. Rather, it was clear that she was resigned to her fate.

Before he fell asleep he turned to her and whispered, "You are the most beautiful woman I have ever seen and I want you to remain here with me forever and love me."

If Hywel had said these words to her she would have found them irresistible and would have responded. But, coming from Gruffudd, she believed they could only be false and it neither lessened her love for her true husband nor her hatred for her captor.

The daily life at Rhuddlan continued very much as it had, with Elen sleeping each night with her oppressor who was becoming increasingly obsessed with his new partner. He brought her gifts of gold, jewellery and fine clothes, bought from merchants arriving from England and Europe.

The court members, noble and common, could see that he was besotted with her.

Alone in their bed, he complimented her on the silky nature of her skin, her beautiful eyes, her lovely lips. His admiration of her knew no bounds, but she wasn't moved. She didn't succumb to his charm, convinced it had to be false, and her heart remained firmly attached to Hywel.

The days went by, turning into weeks and months and the winter came. But there was no sign of Hywel and unbeknown to Elen, Gruffudd made sure that she had no messages from Deheubarth.

There was unrest in Deheubarth following the attack on Pencader. Hywel's key administrative staff had been killed, as had his personal bodyguards. Lawlessness ensued and it took time for Hywel to re-establish his authority and reorganise his supporters. Many took advantage of the weakened ruler and tried to expand their own lands at Hywel's expense. Everyone wanted a piece of Deheubarth. There were attacks from the east by, among others, Gruffudd ap Rhydderch of Morgannwg and there were raids from Ireland to be repelled.

It was all Hywel could do at this time to keep Deheubarth free of invaders. In the early spring of 1042 Caerfyrddin and the surrounding area was attacked from Morgannwg numerous times and Elen's parents were killed during one of these incursions from the east.

It was some weeks before she was told the tragic news by Berddig on one of his visits. She suspected that Gruffudd had known for days but had wanted the poet to break the news to her. Elen was devastated by this blow and Gruffudd was sympathetic to her grief and attempted to console her. But she found it easier to lean on Berddig for comfort as she, at least partly, blamed Gruffudd for the disaster in Deheubarth.

The grief for the loss of her parents weighed heavily on her. Although Gruffudd openly declared his love for her, and she listened to his declarations and received all his compliments, she made no favourable responses and his power over her was still far from complete.

All around them knew he loved her deeply but also observed her coolness towards him. Many of the women would have been overjoyed to be in her shoes. But they also secretly admired her for the love that she had for Hywel. Others, many of whom had never experienced true love, thought she was a cold person and incapable of feeling true love and that her so-called feelings for Hywel were simply a cover to get her out of having to show that there was no love in her soul.

On one thing they could all agree, Gruffudd loved her and did not look at any other woman. He was oblivious to the flirtations of many a young wench at the court who was aware of his desire to be loved.

Declaring his love for Elen became a frequent event that winter and in the spring of 1042 Elen became pregnant.

Her state did not detract in any degree from Gruffudd's love of her. He cared for her and loved her more than ever.

CHAPTER 9

July 1042 to April 1043

ELEN WANTED CHILDREN, but with Hywel. So she was not pleased by her pregnancy. She hated the baby's father and worried as to how she could face Hywel when he came to rescue her.

She carried her baby well, endured her pregnancy stoically and in November of 1042 gave birth to a baby boy, who Gruffudd named Maredudd. Elen loved her baby boy and was delighted by his bright eyes and the other women's comments that he looked like his mother. The king, realising that she genuinely loved her child, became jealous of the baby boy whom, he could see, she loved far more than she loved him.

Then, as if to punish her, the baby was removed from her keeping on the pretext that he was a royal baby and required special treatment. The baby was given to a noblewoman at the court to raise. Elen was devastated and had to be content with seeing the boy for only short periods daily, which caused her to hate the baby's father even more than she had before the birth.

In February 1043, Madog, whom she had befriended on the journey from Pencader, returned to the court on the orders of the king after pressure from Madog's influential family. He was related to the old royal family represented by Cynan ap Iago, the son of Iago ap Idwal who had ruled Gwynedd before Gruffudd. That family still had influence through key members who lived in Ireland, and many of the extended family members living in Gwynedd. Some of this once illustrious and powerful family lived in Rhuddlan and were supporters of Gruffudd. Even

Tangwystl, the chancellor's wife, was a member of the old royal family.

Madog was not accompanied by Mair. She'd remained on Anglesey. Elen had heard nothing of her since she was sent away and had assumed that Mair had found another man to entertain her and was now happily married on the island.

She was delighted at Madog's return to favour and, as soon as she heard he was back, searched him out. He confirmed that Mair was indeed married but he warned her that Gruffudd, a naturally jealous man, could still bring Mair back as a ploy to make Elen jealous.

Elen liked Madog's openness and unwisely admitted to him that she did not care for the king, let alone love him. She would even be happy to be replaced in his bed by Mair. She also reaffirmed her desire to return to her true love, Hywel, though she had heard nothing of him since her capture. Madog told her that Hywel was still living in the south west and, for all he knew, he was in good health because he was causing some annoyance to Gruffudd by calling himself the king of Deheubarth. This news delighted Elen.

A friendship developed between Elen and Madog; they were similar beings and neither was a great admirer of the king. Both had suffered under him. Madog's naturally trusting character meant he told her everything. Facts and figures flowed through him as through a sieve. She trusted him and she confided in him, probably more than was wise for her.

Their friendship did not go unnoticed by others at court, including Gruffudd. Many, as always, were delighted to indulge in gossip about the two and some would ensure that malicious talk would reach the king's ears. Also, some were adept at dropping the occasional innuendo, with the result that Gruffudd was not a happy man.

Madog and Elen occasionally met, always accidentally and

never by arrangement. In court that was quite frequently and they always had something to talk about and they enjoyed the chat. Whatever he knew about life in the south he passed on to her.

Gruffudd, overwhelmed by his love for Elen, wanted her to be equally obsessed with him and so have absolute power over her. Towards the majority of his people he was affable, extravagant, supportive and kind but to others, those who threatened his power in any way, be it his political power or personal power, he was pernicious, untrustworthy and cruel.

Madog had no illusions about Gruffudd's jealousy when it came to his woman or his position. He had on numerous occasions alerted Elen to the king's uncompromising attitude to rivals. He could cite the names of men he had suspected of having amorous thoughts towards Mair. Gruffudd had directly or indirectly had these men killed. One had been suffocated with his own hands, another killed with a knife, another had been pushed to his death over a cliff and a lucky one had been castrated. Gruffudd was ruthless and everyone knew it. No one was immune. If they threatened him, even only in his imagination, be they family members or friends, he would destroy them. He wouldn't tolerate rivals.

Anyone showing signs of leadership ability, those up-and-coming men who might challenge his role in the future, were equally at risk. People around him knew this and had to be discreet if they had any ambition for leadership or for his wife.

It was enough for Gruffudd to suspect or imagine the least threat, for that person to be in peril of being killed or seriously maimed. Thus, he would remove the threat as soon as he identified it. Of course, there were many willing to inform him of a rival's desires, sometimes simply in order to further their own careers and ingratiate themselves with him.

Madog knew the risk of being seen talking to Elen too

frequently, smiling at her and being happy with her. Elen, still young, lacked the understanding of Gruffudd's extreme feelings and moods, to be cautious when required, though warned numerous times by Madog and indeed, on more than one occasion, covertly by her maid Jane.

They enjoyed talking together but Madog's basic survival instinct caused him to avoid talking to her when Gruffudd was about. However, the king watched them through the eyes of others.

Madog had been back at court for only a few months when early one morning, while Elen was busy with her own son, there was a great commotion at the main entrance and the noise and excitement moved into the courtyard outside the hall. This happened occasionally and, as usual, Elen and others around went to see what the cause was. Sometimes, it was nothing more than a particular ship returning or a popular personage arriving, like a well-liked poet, musician or comedian. Other times it was only an exceptionally large catch of fish.

That morning the noise was different with more soldiers than usual about. From the direction of the gate there appeared a group of soldiers escorting a prisoner with his hands bound behind his back. The crowd that had gathered in the courtyard separated to give them a clear path to the hall.

As the group came closer to where Elen stood, she was shocked to recognise the prisoner as Madog. Instantly a wave of panic traversed her body. She looked at him transfixed and he caught her eye momentarily but then turned his face away from her. Her mind was blank, she felt sick, her heart was racing as she desperately tried to make sense of what she had seen. She enquired to those around, "What's happened? What's Madog done?"

There was too much noise and excitement for anyone to hear her questions but as Madog disappeared into the hall, she was further surprised and confused when some soldiers approached her and told her respectfully, but firmly, that on the king's orders she was to go to her room for her own safety.

Elen was escorted into the hall where she saw Madog standing in front of the table behind which the king sat wearing his crown. The court justice was on his right and the court's cleric on his left. She looked at Madog's back. He stood in front of the king, erect and defiant. The king, in his full court regalia, looked thunderous, imposing and, what was more frightening, determined to have his own way.

The king raised his gaze to watch her being ushered up to her room, and nodded his approval at the two soldiers in attendance.

The two soldiers entered the room with her and closed the door but she knew that she could still hear what would be said. So did Gruffudd. Although he didn't wish her to be present, he wanted her to hear the accusation against Madog, and she did. She heard Gruffudd's booming, powerful and dictatorial voice. "This court is convened to try you for the crime of having an affair with the queen. The punishment for such crime is castration or death."

There were gasps of shock inside the hall indicating that the king's supporters were disgusted with the outrage against his wife. Seconds later the news had spread to the people outside and their gasps filtered back into the hall.

Elen was mortified and could neither speak nor move. She knew she hadn't made a complaint against Madog. Furthermore, she also knew that he had not had an affair with her nor interfered with her in any way at any time. She also feared that Gruffudd had the power to make up the law to suit his own wishes.

Turning to the soldiers at the door she demanded, "There is no truth in that accusation. Let me go and tell them."

"We have our orders," said one of the soldiers. "We've been told you are allowed to hear the proceedings but not interfere in any way and you are to stay here until the court hearing is finished."

"But there is a misunderstanding and there will be a miscarriage of justice if I'm not allowed to speak and give evidence."

"Our orders are clear," one soldier said as he moved to block the doorway.

The court was proceeding quickly as was the wont of the king. She heard Madog ask, "What is the evidence against me?"

"There are witnesses," replied the king. "Come forward, Einion ap Maredudd."

There was movement among the audience and a pause while the witness made his way to the front and stood before the bench.

Elen knew that Einion was a friend of Madog's and she had seen them talking and laughing together many times. She was puzzled. He couldn't have seen anything, there was nothing to see, but she was anxious, and that knot in her stomach was getting tighter."

"Tell us the truth, Einion. What do you know about this?" demanded Gruffudd.

Einion said that Madog had told him that he had dreamt one night that he was having an affair with the queen.

Gruffudd was furious and declared, "There, he is guilty and must be executed."

Elen was astounded. She couldn't believe what she was hearing. Surely Madog would not be executed for dreaming that he was having an affair with her. On the other hand, Gruffudd might be jealous of Madog, a handsome man and with whom she was admittedly friendly. Also, it was quite possible that Einion had been tortured and forced to say this about his friend, or perhaps he had been bribed by an offer of land somewhere or other.

She could hear that one of the councillors was agreeing with the king.

Then Madog spoke out, "I won't deny that I have said to Einion that I did dream one night of having an affair with the queen. I did not wish to have an affair with the queen, I only dreamt that I had an affair. A man can't control his dreams."

Silence settled quickly in the hall and the court justice, sitting to the king's right, spoke. "While I agree with the king that Madog has committed a serious crime, we must decide according to the law given to us by Hywel Dda, the great-great-grandfather of this excellent king. In this case I don't think Madog has committed a full crime. It's not even a wish to commit a crime. The prisoner dreamt that he was committing a crime and the punishment should be commensurate with that fact."

He spoke with authority and the king's face dropped further and further as he spoke. The murmurings in the hall suggested that they were agreeing with the wise words of the court justice.

"So, can we execute Madog for bringing the queen to disrepute?" asked Gruffudd.

There was some uncomfortable shuffling of feet and then the court justice announced, "The law states that when a man has interfered with another man's wife, in this case the queen, he should be fined. The magnitude of the fine should reflect the nobility of the woman interfered with. In the case of a queen the fine is one thousand head of cattle to be paid to the king."

Elen was pleased and relieved, though she wondered if Madog's family, as noble as they were, could afford to give one thousand cattle to the king. She knew that Gruffudd would be displeased, as he had hoped for an execution.

Now that her extreme anxiety was fading, she could think clearer and wondered if Gruffudd saw Madog as an obstacle to her falling in love with him. He may have thought that she had fallen in love with Madog. She could think of no other reason for Madog's suffering.

"So, he shall only be fined a thousand head of cattle," said the disappointed Gruffudd.

The court justice spoke again saying, "This would seem unfair. The fine of a thousand cattle is appropriate if the queen had been outraged, but the prisoner only dreamt of outraging the queen. He didn't wish to outrage her, so the guilty man should bring a thousand cattle to the edge of the river so that the king can see their reflection in the water. The reflections should belong to the king and the cattle to the prisoner."

Gruffudd was fuming and protested angrily, his wild eyes shining. But Elen knew that he would be obliged to accept the interpretation of the law as pronounced by the court justice. Thwarted, Gruffudd said that he didn't wish to see the reflection of the cattle and that Madog would be removed from Rhuddlan as he was a danger to the queen.

The court justice agreed with him and, at the same time, praised Gruffudd for his wisdom and his ability to provide fair justice and follow the law. Madog was removed from the hall immediately and much praise was bestowed on the king as the law court dispersed.

The soldiers opened the door for her to join her king but she did not go to the hall immediately. She stayed in her room to reflect on the events and the consequences. She believed naively that Gruffudd, knowing that she did not love him, had staged the event to frighten her and Madog, in case they did think of having an affair.

Jane, who joined her in her room soon after the soldiers had left, was sympathetic to her position. However, she tried carefully and sensitively to disillusion her by suggesting that someone would carry out the king's wishes and kill Madog at the earliest opportunity. The king would, of course, have preferred the court to have decided his fate, as Madog's family was still very influential.

CHAPTER 10

July 1043 to June 1044

FOLLOWING THE COURT case, the witness Einion received land in Powys and left Rhuddlan. However, Gruffudd was, surprisingly, just as attentive as ever to Elen. He didn't scold her in any way, believing the fault was entirely that of the person banished. Seeking her favours, granting her all she wished, offering to get her better servants though she was content with Jane, there was nothing he spared to try to make her happy. He contrived by all means to make her love him.

His love for her was overwhelming and his desire to get her to be equally in love with him surpassed all understanding by others at court. But Elen despised him more than ever and still pined for her Hywel.

There were times when his behaviour in her presence was pitiful, despite the fact that he was a great king and ruled his country with a rod of iron. Elen, though she knew she had some power over him, continued to fear him

Many at Rhuddlan, who knew Gruffudd well, also knew that his fits of jealousy knew no bounds. They had witnessed them as he ascended his path to power. However, his display of love for Elen at this time endeared him to many. Many wished their partners would display such loving feelings for them. They contrasted his warmth, his charm, his care for her with her cold, disinterested and detached attitude towards her lovesick husband.

The winter, particularly January 1044, was hard and long, with snow lying on the ground for weeks. Families were forced to live long periods in each other's company, causing frequent family quarrels and disputes. In particular, the extreme conditions restricted men from going to hunt and forage. They were under the feet of their women longer, in turn curtailing their freedom to interact and enjoy the absence of their menfolk, even if it were for only a few hours at a time.

Similarly, Elen and the king were in close proximity to each other for long periods. She found his constant attendance stifling. Advancing along the road towards accepting that it was to be her role to remain linked to Gruffudd, she, nevertheless, during these winter months found herself desperately wishing that the weather would improve and that he would get out of her sight. She fought hard not to dream of Hywel and imagine how happy she would have been with him even in the depths of a hard winter.

Stories had been reaching Rhuddlan for some months that Madog was doing well in Anglesey. He was gaining power there and increasing his wealth. Very few were surprised, as he was an able person. Then, in March 1044, came the shocking news that Madog had been killed in a hunting accident. He had been thrown off his horse and broken his neck. In the dark secluded corners of the court at Rhuddlan, speculation was rife that he had been killed on Gruffudd's orders because he was a threat to the king's power in Gwynedd. Elen suspected that Madog had been murdered by her husband because he saw him as a hindrance to her own heart.

Elen had no romantic feelings towards Madog but considered him a good friend. His death, equal to the loss of a good friend, saddened her deeply, particularly as she believed she might have been the cause.

As the weather improved, the snow cleared, and the sun's rays began to warm the ground. To her delight, in early April, reports were received at court from a Dublin merchant that

Hywel had raised an army of mercenaries in Ireland, mainly Dublin Vikings, and was planning to set sail for Deheubarth in a week or two. The mercenaries were to be augmented by Hywel's own natural supporters, with the aim of openly challenging Gruffudd to the crown of Deheubarth. There were rumours also that the old Gwynedd royal family were supporting the venture. Some speculated that this was going to happen in response to Madog's death, but members of that family strongly denied any involvement.

Elen could not conceal her joy nor wipe the grin off her face for hours. She struggled to avoid being seen to be too happy, particularly by Gruffudd. Her dream of Hywel coming to rescue her, and carrying her south, was more realistic at last.

While Elen was still in this hopeful state, Gruffudd announced to the whole court that he intended to take an army south to sort out Hywel. He declared that the men of the north had been idle for too long and were itching to go on an expedition to the south to deal with the usurper. Turning to Elen, he told her that he would be taking her with him but leaving their son, Maredudd, at Rhuddlan.

She desperately wanted to take her son with her because she was quietly confident that she would not be returning to Rhuddlan. This was the moment she had been praying for. To her, salvation was near, and her release from captivity was at hand. Her dream of being rescued by her true lover and of being carried in his arms into their court was at last coming true.

The preparation started immediately and within a few days they were ready to depart. There was great excitement as the king, Elen, and the bulk of the court officials, passed out through the main gate to meet the army gathered at the port, before marching southwards along the riverbank. Elen was retracing the journey forced on her three years earlier, but this time she was a happier woman.

Warships and heavily-laden supply ships were also embarking from the port to meet the army at prearranged points to replenish their food supplies and attack Hywel and his fleet.

The army grew in strength and numbers as it moved southwards. It was joined by men from Gwynedd and Powys and it was well organised and they were all in good spirits.

They took the same route they had followed when they returned north from Pencader. Elen was familiar with the mountains and the river crossings but this time she was glad to ford each river. Her spirits rose and a weight lifted off her shoulders – she was getting happier by the mile.

While they were still a few miles from Caerfyrddin and to the west of Pencader, Elen noticed that there was tension building in the men in front of her and more scouts were sent on to check the land ahead. Then she saw a lone figure approaching slowly. She, like the others, could see that he was not a scout returning after having sighted the enemy. He was ambling along as though he had all the time in the world.

Other men they had encountered had scattered out of the way of the advancing army but not this one. He was maintaining a steady pace towards them.

Then from the front she heard the cry, "It's Berddig." An immediate cheer went out throughout the marching column as the news passed backwards along the line. The soldiers were happy to see him. Elen liked him and had always enjoyed his poetry and stories but felt that he had not always been a good omen for her.

As the column approached, Berddig stopped and stood slightly off the track. The king and the leaders joined him to confer briefly in a group, with the marching column slowing down slightly to cheer as they passed him. As Elen passed him he waved at her and smiled broadly calling out, "Best wishes."

She waved and smiled back at him, while Gruffudd turned

on his horse and glowered at her suspiciously as though he disapproved of a friendship between her and the poet. "God, can't I even smile at the story teller?" she muttered quietly to herself at Gruffudd's unhappy and disapproving look.

Gruffudd and his commanders returned to the front of the column and Berddig went on his way northwards.

The king and his leading men were discussing their plans as they progressed southwards. Although Elen was not privy to everything said, there were snippets she heard occasionally and knowing the area well, she was able to deduce with a degree of confidence that Hywel's army was positioned somewhere south of Caerfyrddin and on the west banks of the Tywi.

Hywel would be fighting on his home ground while Gruffudd's supply lines were getting longer by the day. Hywel would know every hill and grove in the area. He would have detailed knowledge of the ebb and flow of the tide in the estuary and could use such information to the advantage of his fleet. Elen was anxious, there was a moment of reckoning coming. But she was quietly confident that with his local knowledge and his Dublin mercenaries, Hywel's soldiers would prevail in the battle ahead.

That afternoon she had heard Gruffudd send orders by a rider to his fleet, then sheltering at Aberdaugleddau, to proceed to the mouth of the Tywi and engage and destroy Hywel's ships at sea and in the estuary.

In the meantime, Gruffudd led his men to a position slightly south west of Caerfyrddin and camped for the night. The guards were checked frequently. Elen was restless all night and barely slept. Gruffudd slept well and at dawn he marched his army further south but slowly and far more cautiously than they had the previous day.

She was concerned that Gruffudd seemed to have a plan and hoped that Hywel had an even better one. She was confident that Hywel's people would be watching Gruffudd's progress and informing Hywel who could, she hoped, ambush them at any time. Elen knew they were going towards Llansteffan, near where she had spent her honeymoon night.

Elen hoped so many things at that moment. She hoped the messenger of the previous day had failed in his errand, stumbled, been ambushed, captured or killed. She had never wished so much harm on an individual she didn't know. She hoped the tide would cause Gruffudd's battleships to be stranded on the treacherous sand and mud banks of the estuary or that the westerly breezes would blow them onto the rocks somewhere after they left their anchorage. Above all, she hoped that Hywel and his Dublin Vikings would smash Gruffudd's ships and sink them all. She felt sure the Vikings would be victorious and felt happier again.

Elen followed in the cart, but now behind the marching soldiers and protected by a rearguard of reliable men. The land was undulating and, as they reached the top of a hill, she could see the sea and a few ships but would soon lose sight of the water again as they went down the other side.

The closer to the sea they got the more they could see the estuary from the hilltops. It was clear that a sea battle was taking place in the wide estuary ahead. Some ships were on fire, others had their masts dipping in the water, many had been boarded and fighting was taking place on their decks.

It was impossible for Elen to decide which ships were Gruffudd's and which were Hywel's. All she could see was a chaotic array of fighting ships. She had no idea who was winning as she and other non-combatants were moved to the rear of the army and away from the shore, thus losing sight of the sea battle. There was speculation that Hywel had attempted to move his army across the estuary to the east bank from its trapped position at Llansteffan. The Tywi and Taf estuaries formed the two sides of the triangular peninsula and Gruffudd's forces were bearing down on him from the northern side.

Some, who knew little of warfare, speculated that Hywel had been taken by surprise at the speed of Gruffudd's march south. Elen, however, felt confident that Hywel and his men would not be surprised by Gruffudd the second time. They would have learnt their lesson from what happened at Pencader.

A messenger arrived ordering them to fall back further from the shore, telling them that there was a big battle about to take place. Gruffudd was taking on the might of the mercenaries from Ireland and Hywel's own native soldiers. He told them that the two armies were manoeuvring for a battle but that Hywel had acquired the high ground above the shoreline and was in the process of moving all his troops to that favourable position.

Elen, at the rear of the army, and relying on speculation and the bits of information brought back by messengers, had to guess what was going on. She assumed that Hywel and his men must have brought Gruffudd's force to a standstill and that soon they would be in full retreat. Hence the message to fall back given to the rear guard.

However, minutes later, another messenger arrived. He seemed to suggest that Hywel had been advised to arrive at some compromise with Gruffudd and concede the crown of Deheubarth to him. But, even so, he wanted them to move back further north. A diplomatic envoy, he said, had been sent to Gruffudd's camp to sue for peace but whatever they offered, Gruffudd would have nothing less than an unconditional surrender, which might be unacceptable to Hywel he guessed. That being the case, the battle would start soon.

Elen's hopes and disappointments were more than she could bear. She walked away from the camp on her own to dream of a continued life with Hywel. She found a small grove, brightly coloured by late May flowers and she prayed for the life that she wanted.

Feeling better, but still very anxious, Elen returned to the others, hoping that her true love, Hywel, had by then outmanoeuvred her captor and father of her child and sent him running back north to lick his wounds, in turn liberating her to live with her man in Deheubarth.

She didn't have long to wait, for within minutes, she saw the unmistakeable figure of Gruffudd, followed by his closest men, approaching and driving their horses hard. Her dreams were turning to reality as her captors were escaping northwards. Her only instant regret was that they had come to pick her up on their way. How could she escape his grasp again? Where was there for her to hide? She regretted that she hadn't stayed hidden in the grove.

But she realised that there was something odd as the riders approached. Gruffudd lifted something spherical from the side of his saddle, and threw it at her feet.

She looked in puzzlement at the object. Then, slowly realising it was someone's head with the shocked eyes looking at her, she turned away disgusted. Then she heard Gruffudd's shout, "Look at it. It's Hywel. He can't kiss you again." He was laughing loudly, as were the men with him.

It was Hywel's head, still dripping congealed blood, that lay at her feet.

She didn't turn to look either at Gruffudd or at the head on the ground beside her. Instead she sank on her knees as though in prayer, whispering, "Please let it not be true."

But she knew it was Hywel's head. Her destiny was now tied to Gruffudd for ever. She wept as she had never wept before, her shoulders shaking, her very soul being dragged out of her. Her king left her there to cry and left the head with her.

It was some time before she managed to get up and walk to

her tent. She was alone. Gruffudd had ordered that she be left to her own devices. However, when she was back in her tent she was comforted by Jane and it was clear to all around her that Elen had lost her reason for living.

Orders were given for the head to be taken around Deheubarth to prove that Hywel was dead. The population was now to pay homage to their undisputed king, King Gruffudd.

Out of Elen's sight, Gruffudd had led his forces fiercely but cleverly. He was master of the art of warfare, a good tactician and strategist, and so his enemy's resistance soon crumbled. Gruffudd also led the final charge into the middle of Hywel's army, coming face to face with Hywel himself and killing him with a spear through the chest.

He had dismounted and decapitated Hywel's body and held the head high shouting, "Victory," and again claiming kingship over Deheubarth. He also privately celebrated the death of the man who, he believed, had stood between him and Elen.

He stood there among the dead bodies, covered in blood, sword in one hand, head in the other, and raised his arms high with the blood from the sword and the head running down his arms. His men cheered him wildly, raising their own swords in salute.

Gruffudd attached Hywel's head to the saddle of his horse and, leaving the battleground to the pillaging men of his army, he departed with a small group to where Elen was camped about a mile away to present her with the severed head.

Elen did not sleep that night and the following day she was taken to the battle site on Gruffudd's orders. He wished her to know that he had taken Hywel out of her life for ever. The battlefield was not far from a place that had held such sweet memories for her but would now and forever more bring painful thoughts which would haunt her for the rest of her life.

She, Gruffudd, and the army spent the next few weeks

travelling around Deheubarth. Elen wanted to return to Rhuddlan if that was her destiny and leave the place where her high hopes had been destroyed. But it was the end of June 1044 before they returned to the royal court.

CHAPTER 11

July 1044 to December 1045

S HE LIVED EACH day at a time, low in spirit and with nothing to look forward to. Gruffudd was very attentive to her, ensuring that she was well looked after and had everything she wanted. If he was away hunting or on affairs of the kingdom, then he made certain that there were trusted people around her to keep her safe and sound.

Her son, Maredudd, helped to keep her sane during the weeks and months following the defeat and death of Hywel. The sight of his head, thrown towards her, still troubled her during the day and night. In daylight the grotesque picture would frequently appear in front of her sometimes on the ground by her feet, sometimes in the bushes and brambles, on the riverbank, even in the shapes of clouds. She could not erase that awful memory.

It's of little surprise that she was traumatised by what Gruffudd had done in killing and beheading her Hywel. In that vile act, his intention was not to shock her but to convince her, once and for all, that she wouldn't be rescued by her lover, nor would she ever return to a life with Hywel. The love of her life was dead and so she should now love him.

She had not simply surmised all this. Gruffudd had actually explained his motives to her on their return journey to Rhuddlan, seemingly unaware that the act had caused her to loathe him even more.

At this time with her spirits very low, she even valued helping her servants with their chores. These simple activities helped her to push reality into the back of her mind occasionally, but only for brief periods. She was living through a permanent November, dark, and getting darker, weather bad and getting worse, no hope and no future.

She needed to demean herself, to punish herself. For what exactly she didn't know, but she found it necessary. She needed to occupy herself in hard, strenuous, demanding tasks. For what purpose escaped her. When she went to bed she needed to be not just tired but exhausted.

It was at this time, when there was no hope for her to have a better and happier life, that she began to think of having revenge on Gruffudd. It was only a fleeting thought at first, borne out of extreme despair, hopelessness and anger at his cruelty.

As things were, she was destined to remain the king's wife and serve him at his will, giving him children until she died in childbirth or was cast aside by him as her good looks faded with age and the children from her body drained it of energy and life. This was not what she had imagined her life would be. Even before Hywel came into her life, she had always assumed that she would marry well due to her upbringing. She assumed she would be in love and loved and produce children who would be happy and healthy. Her present state was therefore harder to take, as her ambitions and assumptions had been so high.

The months of hatred for Gruffudd did pass, even if her despair didn't. The process of recovery started as her spirit of self-preservation came to her rescue. She gradually reduced her participation in the servant's tasks and started to walk more, accompanied of course on the king's explicit orders by a servant or two. According to Gruffudd, the servants were with her to keep her safe. But, from Elen's perspective, they were there to keep an eye on her so that she would not stray or betray him in any way.

He did not trust anyone and he didn't trust her, though she had no intention of attracting his wrath. She knew of his brutality too well. He, sensing she did not love him in the way he loved her, was afraid of the hurt she could cause him in one way or another. He'd removed the threat of Hywel but was now jealous of others who he didn't yet know.

She did not wish to carry any more of his children, as much as she loved Maredudd. Through talking to other women, whom she knew had more children than they needed, she became familiar with the use of witch hazel and kept the mixture close at hand, passing it off as hand cream.

By the summer of 1045 Elen was slowly recovering. Gruffudd's expanded kingdom required him to be away from Rhuddlan frequently on missions to Deheubarth, where his kingship was frequently challenged by one usurper or another. During his absence, Elen had somewhat more freedom and the fact that she did not have to share his bed was a great relief to her.

Though he could not bear to be away from her, because of his affection for her, there were times when Gruffudd had to leave her. He always demanded that she accompanied him on his journeys but she was more frequently than not able to convince him that it was her place to be with their son, though as he grew her argument was weakening. She also occasionally feigned illness and, in particular, a fake back problem which, she claimed, would be seriously aggravated by a journey on a horse or in a cart.

And so, in these periods, she acquired more time to herself, which she valued above all else except for her time with her boy.

When Gruffudd was away overnight, he ensured that a trusted woman would sleep with her, to keep her company. But Elen knew it was to keep an eye on her and ensure that no man entered her bed in the night.

Her enjoyment of life was limited to the court's festivities and the entertainment provided by the poets. She particularly enjoyed Berddig's humour, even if she didn't appreciate his stories in praise of Gruffudd.

Life was humdrum for her. She was bored with life at Rhuddlan, and as her so-called husband would not allow her to bring up her own child, there was nothing for her to do. There was no hope of being rescued, no hope of being whisked away on a horse by fair-haired Hywel. She had nothing constructive to do all day, any day.

She got up every morning from a bed she did not wish to be in, one in which she had dreaded going to the night before. Nightly she had to endure his questioning, "Do you love me? Do you love me more than you loved Hywel? Am I better than Hywel to you? He left you – he did not come after you to rescue you – no one would dare take you from me. He did not care what happened to you. I would have rescued you, which shows I love you more than he did. Why don't you love me as much as you loved Hywel? Why do you love a dead man more than you love me?"

These endless questions, night after night, to which she struggled to find some meaningless answers. All she wished for was for him to go away to sort out disputes somewhere in his kingdom, preferably far away.

One of her set replies to his flow of questions was saying that falling in love took time: once you had, you could not change overnight. All this bluff kept him at bay but, in truth, only served to wet his appetite. He was determined that she would love him as much and more than she had loved Hywel.

Of course, she was afraid of telling him exactly what she thought of him, simply because she was afraid of him, physically and mentally. She was fully aware of how difficult he could make her life if she were to seriously cross him. She had on more than one occasion thought of killing him at night while he slept. It wouldn't be difficult; she knew that his dagger was in its scabbard attached to his belt by the side of the bed.

But she didn't have the cruelty of mind for the deed. Neither was she sure she had the physical strength needed. Nor did she wish to face the consequences of a failed attempt.

She had to concede there were many good points about Gruffudd. He was true to his word, you knew exactly where you stood with him. He was punctual and basically honest in his own way, even if he did murder the occasional rival for a woman or for his kingdom. He was feared but he was also admired, appreciated and respected by his people.

By December 1045 he had welded Gwynedd, Powys and Deheubarth into one nation. He had built his capital Rhuddlan into a great fortress, constructed a great harbour from where his powerful naval fleet patrolled the coastline. He had brought peace, prosperity and pride to his country. For these various reasons he was popular and supported by his people. Elen had to concede that he was the greatest king that the Welsh had seen for a long time.

She lived a life of luxury, with all the power that she wanted at her fingertips. Jewellery, wealth, clothes – there was nothing she could have wished for that was not available to her in an instant. Except, of course, happiness and contentment. She was instead unhappy, unfulfilled, unable to give her love to a man in the way she wished. More dangerously, she was bored.

She knew she wasn't devoid of the ability to love. She knew she was a warm, loving and caring person, but she was none of these things with Gruffudd, and could never be.

CHAPTER 12

January 1046 to December 1046

E LEN HAD ACQUAINTANCES at the court; she knew most of the court's nobles by name and reputation, but had no close friends. The only person she was in close contact with was the king and he was the one person she did not wish even to be friendly with.

She believed that her boredom came from this mental isolation, due to her unique situation as the queen of the court. She yearned for a closer relationship with someone. She knew from her experience with Madog that if she were to be seen associating, even faintly, with a man then that man's life would be in danger. She had no wish to cause anyone to lose their life or even be excluded from the court because of her.

Elen knew that she was being watched continuously, even her nights when the king was away from court were not her own. She spent her time month after month wishing for another life.

During festivities at court she was allowed total freedom to circulate among the courtiers and guests. But she was still aware of being watched and never dallied too long talking to any one person, particularly if they were men of about her own age or younger. She took some liberty with older men and remained talking longer with them, even venturing to laugh and enjoy their humour.

At Christmastime in 1046, the court celebrated the occasion as usual, followed by festivities in the hall. Christmas night was cold and frosty, with a sizeable moon in a relatively clear sky. The hall was full with courtiers and guests who had arrived by ship that day from France. Elen was determined to make an effort to enjoy at least some part of the evening, if only to try and lift some of the gloom hanging over her spirit, which was like a heavy weight on her shoulders.

Berddig was there telling his stories about the king, his exploits, his successes, his generous nature ad infinitum. Although Elen liked his humour and his poetry was good and worth listening to, there were times when she wished she could gag him. But, he had to praise the one who paid him, and the more he pleased Gruffudd the more he was paid in drink, food, fine clothes, good horses, and a comfortable bed.

He would always ask about her health and he was sensitive enough to see that she was unhappy. He probably realised she was miserable, but always gave the same advice, "Be content with your lot and learn to like and love him and all will be well." No one else dared give her any advice. No one even dared tell her they knew she was unhappy.

That evening, with the approval of the king, she acted the part of hostess and welcomed guests and greeted poets and singers while ensuring they had drinks.

People were merry; the mead ensured that. It was noisy and crowded in the hall. Elen became aware that a young man of about her age was standing next to her wanting to engage her in discussion. She knew him vaguely, in that she had noticed him around the court in recent weeks.

Eventually, she turned to face him with her full jug pointing towards his empty one as though to ask him, "Do you want more?"

He looked back at her and she asked, "Mead?"

"No. Thank you," he replied, smiling at her. "I'm Rhys."

She started to tell him who she was as she didn't want any misunderstanding but before she had uttered the first two words he said, "I know who you are."

"Most people seem to know me," she said.

"I've been representing the king at our court in Caerfyrddin," he announced naively, thinking that it would please her.

It hurt her and she visibly winced and managed a quiet, "Oh!"

He was disappointed at her response and it showed clearly on his face.

"I knew that court in better times."

He nodded, his face still down as he probably realised that it was a most stupid conversation starter with the queen.

She gave him the slightest of smiles and turned away from him.

Inside she was devastated and disappointed that the young man had been so crass as to tell her that he had been doing Gruffudd's work at Caerfyrddin. The court there had meant so much to her with regard to her parents, her upbringing, her wedding and her Hywel. Did the fool not know as much?

She wondered if he was naive and had been set up by someone to annoy her. She occasionally glanced at the young man across the room and could see that he was quite a handsome man with a pleasant attractive face. He was well dressed and of noble birth obviously, otherwise he would not have been representing Gruffudd in Caerfyrddin.

The evening went well and she did not speak to Rhys during the rest of the evening because she made sure she kept her distance whenever she saw him. She watched him leave the hall as the festivities drew to an end, and in a strange way she was relieved to see the back of him.

Some days later she was walking in the port viewing the just-landed fish catch. She bent down to have a closer look at a large hake. When she rose and lifted her head she could see the same young man standing a few yards away. He smiled at her and gave the slightest of nods in her direction to signal that he had recognised her. She returned the nod but without even a smile.

He walked on and there was no further communication between them.

However, before the day was totally over, with dusk settling over the court and Gruffudd drinking and talking with an ambassador from Scotland at a table at the far end of the hall, Elen went outside to watch the sun set.

She walked a few yards to where she knew she could see the setting sun. She was almost too late – the sky was orangey-red and the sun was all but out of sight and darkness was creeping fast into the courtyard.

She felt alone in the world and as the day was turning into night so was a dark mood settling on her shoulders. Then she heard a voice from the shadows nearby saying, "Isn't it beautiful."

She was startled and turned to her right where the voice had come from. She could just about discern the outline of the young man, Rhys.

She made no reply.

"We seem to meet frequently."

She was shocked, knowing that if Gruffudd had heard that, the young man would be in trouble. Did he have no idea of how jealously she was guarded by her husband?

"Not intentionally," she replied, frightened. She nodded at him and without another word returned to the hall. Gruffudd glanced up at her as she entered, her heart immediately started pounding. She feared him and what he might do to the young man. Desperately, she picked up a jug of mead and went to him asking, "Do you and your guests want more mead?"

She wanted him distracted and his attention diverted from her entry. She astonished herself at how devious she'd been when motivated by fear. To further show that all was well, she should have stayed to talk to them but she was blushing with guilt – guilt from having exchanged a few words with a young man in the dark. Nervous and anxious, she bade them farewell, saying to the king that she intended to go to her room to wait for him.

She ascended the steps fast, entered their room and was relieved that there was no one there. There were no sounds on the stairs and she looked at the closed window; desperate for air she quickly removed the wooden window shutter, putting it down as quietly as she could underneath and stared out of the gaping hole into the darkness.

The sun had gone and the river was a lighter shade of grey than the land. Torches at the main gate were being lit and smaller lights were appearing here and there in the court and the port. Shadows were beginning to form and the shapes of familiar buildings were just about recognisable.

She scanned the horizon and the court and then leaned out further onto the tips of her toes to stare at the area below her. She could just about discern the outside wall of the hall. Suddenly, she dropped backwards onto her heels – no one had pulled her – it was the shock of seeing someone below in the darkness staring back up at her. She was fearful of there being some consequence – it could have been Gruffudd watching her or one of his many spies checking on her.

As soon as she recovered, she replaced the wooden cover in the window space with some difficulty. Her whole body was trembling, but she managed ultimately and sat on the side of the bed placing her head in her hands. It was a mixture of nerves and fear, but slowly as these two foes subsided, a feeling of some wellbeing replaced them and her self-confidence improved as she wondered if the shadow had belonged to Rhys.

On calming down she realised that if it was Rhys, then most likely he was on Gruffudd's instructions, tempting her and testing her loyalty and fidelity. She would have to be careful and not fall into his trap. She retired to her bed hoping to fall asleep before the king joined her; otherwise she would have to pretend to be asleep, as he was normally, if not too drunk, quite considerate of her sleep and was very unlikely to disturb her.

As she was falling asleep she realised that she was in a slightly happier frame of mind than usual.

CHAPTER 13

May 1047 to June 1048

IN THE SPRING of 1047 there was unrest in Deheubarth. Gruffudd dispatched a large section of his trusted soldiers to Ystrad Tywi to quell the rebellion. But they were ambushed and a hundred and forty of his men were killed. It was a devastating blow.

Speculation was rife that the ambush was intended to kill Gruffudd. But no one was sure who was involved and Berddig, though consulted at length, could throw little light on the matter. Some blamed Vikings from Ireland. Others, with no evidence, pointed a finger at the old Gwynedd royal family, simply to cause mischief. They claimed it was revenge for Madog's death. The king, however, was convinced it was limited to the noble families of Deheubarth rebelling, and he was proved correct.

The impact of the ambush and the loss of so many trusted soldiers was significant. It took Gruffudd almost a year to recover his power in that region of his realm and Elen, as the one living nearest to him, had to suffer his rages day after day for months.

By the spring of the following year, some of the rulers of Deheubarth were still refusing to submit to Gruffudd's over-lordship and were frequently rebelling. This meant that armies from Gwynedd and Powys were frequently dispatched south but with little long-term effect. In May 1048, however, Gruffudd himself decided that he would lead an expedition to destroy the rebels once and for all.

He reluctantly decided to leave Elen at Rhuddlan, agreeing to her request to be near their young boy. Whatever else, he knew she loved their boy and would be his strong defender in any trouble. Also, she had reminded him that her bad back would be aggravated by the journey and was likely to slow their progress southwards.

Gruffudd and his soldiers left in late May, with the fleet moving two days later. They were to meet up with reinforcements from Anglesey and Gwynedd at Dolgellau and the men of Powys further south.

Elen was alone at last, or at least Gruffudd was absent from her life. She felt sure he would have someone watching her but she knew the rules and the boundaries. She would have to be very careful, otherwise she would never be trusted again and thus never left alone again.

She had seen Rhys from a distance more than once but had made sure that she never went near him, not even close enough to smile, let alone speak to him. However, two days after the army left, Rhys called at the hall to ask if everything was well. Elen had assumed that he would have gone south with the army but he explained to her that he had been left behind to ensure her safety and that of her child among other duties.

She was shocked, disappointed and dumbfounded, realising that Rhys, by his own confession, was indeed spying on her for the king.

Despising his low craft, she resolved to be courteous to him but distant. He would be keeping an eye on her during the daytime and the usual woman would sleep in her room at night. Gruffudd had her life all tied up.

With the king away fighting in Deheubarth, Elen felt freer, just as others did at court. Gruffudd was always oppressive and his subjects lived in fear of offending him. But they knew and appreciated the fact that he stood for strong leadership, stability and peace. Also, he had brought wealth to the people – they were richer than they had been in their lives. So they accepted his tough rule and sensed that a strong, determined king was a blessing in the long term.

Though realising that there were people watching her every move, Elen did not feel as confined as when the king was at Rhuddlan. She could go to bed when she wanted and get up when she wanted. But there were times when she was out and about when she felt sure there was someone watching her. On more than one occasion she noticed Rhys looking at her but, on being discovered, turned his head away quickly.

About a week after the king and his army had left, Elen had gone for a walk upriver, with her accompanying women servants trailing about a hundred yards behind her as was her wish. She came face to face with Rhys.

"Good morning Elen," he said with far more confidence than she expected.

"Good morning."

"In case you've forgotten, I'm Rhys."

She pretended to have forgotten. "Oh yes, of course."

She thought she detected some signs of disappointment on his face. She also noted once more that he was a handsome man of strong build but not possessing anything like as powerful a body as the king. He was taller than her but not as tall as Gruffudd. She noted again that he had a kind face, his eyes sparkled and his features were well proportioned to his face, unlike the king's which, in her mind, were all over-pronounced.

On looking at him carefully she could see that he would be attractive to women and the ideal man to use as bait for her.

She didn't say anything while she assessed him physically. He was dressed well – better than Gruffudd – with his clothes hanging better on him. He also had an air of a soldier about him, as did all men of noble birth.

These thoughts and judgments passed through her mind in a flash. He was hardly aware that he had been looked over and his appearance assessed so thoroughly.

"Lovely day for a walk."

He was correct if nothing else. So, she simply confirmed his statement with a yes and left it at that. She had no wish to start a conversation with him.

"I haven't seen you this way before. You normally go downriver to the port and towards the sea. You have surprised me."

She noticed that her two servants had stopped and kept a discreet distance from her and Rhys. She was not sure if they were within hearing distance of the exchange of words. The two were talking but she could not hear what they were saying, but they might well have been talking in low voices or even almost whispering for all she knew.

Rhys noticed her glance towards the servants. He was experienced enough to realise that as Gruffudd's wife she had to be cautious what she said within others' hearing.

"They can't hear what you're saying," he volunteered.

She hesitated a second, thinking how to reply and to give her anger a chance to calm.

"There's nothing that I wish to say to you that I would not be quite content for the entire world to hear and most certainly my servants."

He was shocked, disappointed and alarmed by her reply. "I did not mean to imply that you were going to say anything improper."

He'd chosen the wrong word again.

"Improper?" she quizzed, looking him straight in the eyes.

"I didn't mean anything in any way," he stated, fumbling and searching for the appropriate words as though his tongue was stuck to his back teeth.

She did consider asking if he had been watching where she went for her walks but she didn't. Knowing that she had already won the encounter she pronounced, "I'm turning back now. You can go ahead of me. Nice to have met you again."

"Have a pleasant walk," he said, as he made his way back obediently ahead of her.

She then turned and walked back towards her servants, certain that he had been instructed by her husband to keep an eye on her. He was obviously doing his job to the letter. What an odious man, she thought.

She reached the servants who were instantly aware from her demeanour that she had been annoyed by her conversation with Rhys.

"Anything wrong, my lady?" Jane asked.

She could not declare her world to be perfect and said, "Nothing really. It's just that man annoyed me."

"Did he tell us to go back to court?" asked the other servant.

"Certainly not! He would not dare to be so impertinent."

Venturing some wrath from her mistress, Jane commented, "Well I suppose he has some rights now that he is the steward of the port while the king is away."

Elen turned to her in disbelief and instead of keeping quiet blurted out, "I didn't know that."

"Oh yes, he is in charge. He is well respected by the king and everybody. I thought you would have known, my lady."

Elen stormed past them, now more furious with Gruffudd than anyone else, for not telling her. She had just made a fool of herself. And what did Jane's 'I thought you would have known' mean, she wondered. Even more important to Elen, and what really frightened her was that this Rhys could openly watch her every move, now that he had been given the position of a court steward to the port.

As the gap between her and her servants widened again, she thought she could hear some quiet giggling behind her, which further annoyed her.

CHAPTER 14

Late June 1048

ELEN HAD DECIDED to avoid Rhys as much as possible, convinced that he had been given instructions to keep an eye on her safety, wellbeing and obviously her fidelity. For Gruffudd, she assumed, it meant not talking to other men.

In future she would walk down to the port and towards the sea where more people were about. She would be less likely to be accused of looking for secluded places upriver. In any case, she loved looking at the ships in the port despite the occasional remark from a sailor who was unaware of her rank and of the serious risk he was taking.

A few days after the unfortunate meeting with Rhys, she had gone to the port and noticed that a large colourful vessel had docked. She knew that the colourful vessels were often from France; usually from one of the Breton ports bringing wine, olives, different cheeses and fine clothes in return for honey, mead and various metals

There were no sailors about but the captain was sitting on a grand chair in the bow, obviously resting and viewing the land around. He appeared asleep as she ogled his fine vessel and she dallied a little longer, unaware that she was actually being watched closely by the seemingly sleeping captain. She was dreaming of being taken on the ship to sail to some far exotic place – France would be fine – and experiencing warmer weather and more interesting people than she had to endure at Rhuddlan. To be permanently away from the king would be a great relief to her, but she would miss her contact with her son.

She was stirred back into the real world by an exotic-sounding *Bonjour* from the sleeping captain who, leaving his chair, came to the edge of his ship to talk to her.

"You admire my ship?"

"Yes."

"Ah! My ship is like a beautiful woman, like you madam. That is why I love her so much."

She had to laugh. These sea captains were a law to themselves. She was used to them as many of them visited the court from time to time, sometimes to try to sell their merchandise, sometimes to look for a new wife.

"Would you like a tour of my ship madam?"

She would have liked to go onboard ship but was a little uncertain. However, she picked up the courage and turned to the servants behind her and said "I am going to see this ship. If you can remain here on the quayside, I won't be long."

One nodded in response and Jane replied, "Yes, my lady."

The captain helped her aboard, taking a few liberties with where and how he supported her in the task. But if she was to go onboard she could not afford to be too fussy.

Once she was on the ship he oozed more charm on her. "Where would you like to go? I can show you the beautiful Breton coast. Bordeaux might please you more, or are you set for Rouen and Paris. Rome will take us a little longer but it will be well worth it. State your desired destination."

She was laughing, hearing of places she had minutes earlier dreamt of.

"Come madame, state your pleasure. I know who you are you see. I could never forget such a beautiful face and figure. No madame, your elegance has been engraved on my memory and of course in my heart."

"If you know who I am you also know that I am the king's wife, and seriously spoken for. I am not sure if I should be aboard your ship alone, captain."

"Come, come, Elen. Your husband is far away fighting. How could he leave such a beautiful woman behind? I could never do that. I would have given up my life on the sea for such a beauty as you. He should stay at home and let his commanders go to war."

She made no reply and certainly would not have said to him what was on her mind, the relief she felt when her husband went to war. Indeed, she would not have ventured on the captain's ship if Gruffudd was at the royal court.

Arms waving as though he was behind a stall in a market, he pronounced, "This is the front of my ship and that is the back. This is where I stand when we sail, in the front here. Come here, feel the power I have over my ship. I decide on the direction, how much sail we show and where we go and when."

He assisted her carefully up the steps to the front of the ship, holding her hand gently but firmly. She could feel his strength through his hold on her hand.

After a few minutes of enjoying being in command of the stationary ship he said to her, "The most interesting part of the ship is the hold. Let me show the merchandise we have brought to your royal court. It's worth a close examination, I can assure you."

He walked her towards the steps descending to where the merchandise was kept and led the way down the few steps. But she stopped on the second step down, realising that she would be out of the sight of her servants if she went much lower.

"I mustn't go out of the sight of my servants. They may say things about me to the king that would be untrue."

"Come," he said. "You can see it all in seconds. Your husband is away and may never come back. He may be killed."

I wish, she thought. But immediately felt guilt about wishing Gruffudd dead. It amounted to treason she knew and was against God's will.

The captain was insistent, "Come down two steps and you will be able to see it."

He kept hold of her hand as she succumbed and lifted her foot to take the next step down. She slipped or, as she thought long after the event, he might have tugged her hand and she fell forward. But he was there to catch her, to catch her firmly in his arms and, at the same time, to put his lips on hers. He kissed her and she might have kissed him back. She experienced a rush of blood to all parts of her body, the weakness from such excitement and the accompanying thrill, none of which she had ever experienced with Gruffudd. It brought to her mind memories of her life with Hywel.

When he released her, she was unsure what had happened. Things had happened, things which shouldn't have, and she knew it. He had touched her, aroused her even, but that's all.

"Oh my God if the king hears of this he will kill you. He'll kill us both."

"He won't kill me. I will be long gone by the time he is back. And he won't kill you if you don't tell anyone. Don't be frightened. You can go back up, be calm and act normal. Nobody will know you slipped on that step."

She was recovering slowly, and in some ways regretted the recovery and the return to her normal state.

"I will be docked here tonight. We can meet. I can come to your bed chamber or I can…"

"No you can't," she said with alarm. "The king has a woman sleeping there every night."

"Where can I meet you? I beg you madame, I must meet you again," he appealed to her.

"I must go immediately," she said, going up the steps.

Turning around at the top, she whispered, "What's your name?"

"Michel. How shall we meet?" he whispered back.

"I don't know. We can't. Help me off this ship."

He helped her off, smiling softly and spoke charmingly to the servants. "Bonjour. Good afternoon. Would you like to see my ship?"

They laughed, openly flirting with him as he was with them.

Elen kept her cool and her own counsel and the servants followed her home.

CHAPTER 15
Later the same day in June 1048

S HE PONDERED ON the events of the afternoon late into the night. The captain had had his hands all over her body in the few seconds their lips were locked together and she couldn't deny to herself that it had been exciting. However, she was glad that she had managed to disentangle herself from him when she did, otherwise who knows what would have happened.

The captain wanted to see her again. Bearing in mind what could happen if they were caught – for her the consequences were dire, flogging followed by execution – how could they meet safely?

He, of course, could escape in his ship and never return, which was why he must have been one of the very few men who did not fear the consequence of being caught with the king's wife. She feared she would not meet his like again and so this drove her, just for devilment, to think of a way of meeting him. She could not claim that she had not enjoyed the experience. It had brought some fun into her life to replace her infernal boredom.

These thoughts kept her awake for hours and, by the morning, she had decided to meet him again. She went out early to the quay but was disappointed to see that the ship of interest to her was not there. She thought that the captain might have moved it downriver and went searching for it, but she failed to find the vessel. The ship with the French captain had gone.

She tried to make some enquires without drawing attention to herself, but the only information she could glean was that the ship had sailed at dawn with the morning tide. Disappointed, she spent the rest of the day regretting that she had not made some firm arrangement to meet the forward captain.

Later, Jane came to see her to tell her that she had met Rhys in the market. He had asked her to pass on a message to Elen. The captain of the French ship wanted to give her his regards and visit her before he left. But Rhys had told him that he would pass on the message to Elen. He thought this was wiser because the captain's reputation was not the best and he was not a suitable visitor for the king's wife.

Elen's face was crimson through a mixture of embarrassment and fury. What had the stupid captain told Rhys? How cruel of Rhys to pass such a message to her through her servant? Who else would now be involved? Jane would talk. She was fuming and notched another grievance against Rhys, the king's lackey.

To mellow her fury, she took the opportunity of questioning Jane about Rhys.

"I don't understand why I haven't met Rhys more often, if my husband thinks so much of him as to appoint him a steward of the port."

"He hasn't been here long my lady and I don't know much about him." Elen could see that she wanted to talk and so asked, "I know he has been working for Gruffudd at Caerfyrddin, but where is he from?"

"Judging from his accent, I would say he is from the Conwy area."

"I see, Conwy eh? What do you know of his family then?"

"Nothing much, except I hear they are well respected and may be distantly related to the king. That's why he trusts him. They're also saying that the king was looking for someone with little or no past connection with Rhuddlan, because he could trust such a person not to have formed any close association with anyone here."

Elen thought immediately. She means me.

"What else can you tell me about him, Jane?"

"He was doing work for the king in Deheubarth for some time, I think."

"Yes. He told me that. What else do you know?"

"Nothing, my lady. They say that half the women in the court are after him and have been from the day he arrived, but he keeps his distance from them all."

"He's not married then?"

"No."

"That leaves hope for many. Are you interested in him, Jane."

"Goodness me, my lady. No," she said, blushing.

"Really?"

"He wouldn't look at me. He's above my rank."

"Men don't always follow conventions."

Jane's cheeks remained very red and hesitated as she allowed no out of her lips.

Elen was well aware of what she was doing. She was being bitchy, as Jane was very unlikely to be noticed by a nobleman. But she did not appreciate being chastised through her servant and was, against her own nature, taking it out on Jane. Also, she wondered if Rhys was using her servants to keep tabs on her.

"Tell Rhys that I will take heed of what he is saying."

"Yes, of course, my lady," and she turned to leave assuming that she was being dismissed. But Elen hadn't quite finished. "Did he tell you anything about the progress made by Gruffudd in Deheubarth?"

"No. The talk is that they have not caught any of the outlaws yet. The women here are beginning to miss their husbands, so I don't think they will be away long again."

"Thank you, Jane." Then realising that she had been harsh on her servant who was not to blame for Rhys's interference in her life, and knowing there was no point making an enemy of Jane, she added, "I'm sorry that Rhys has involved you. He should have spoken to me directly, not through you."

"That's what I was thinking, my lady."

Elen, annoyed on more than one count, was also disappointed that she had to ask for news about her husband from her servant. This incident convinced her further that Rhys and possibly Jane were working under her husband's orders to keep an eye on her. She was very much a prisoner even in the king's absence.

Having given it some thought, she decided to meet Rhys and explain her visit to the ship to him face to face, so that he would not be passing false information to Gruffudd. She could, at the same time, ask him in future to report on the army's progress directly to her. Thirdly, she could tell him that using a servant as an intermediary with the queen was not acceptable.

However, as furious as she was with the new master of the port, she resolved not to tell him that his errors all stemmed from the fact that he was inexperienced and lacked good breeding.

CHAPTER 16

Evening of the same day in June 1048

WITHIN HALF AN hour Elen was calling Jane back to her room to ask her where Rhys lived. Elen could account for the occupants of all the buildings inside the court's defensive wall and knew he didn't live in that area.

Jane was very knowledgeable and very willing to help. "He lives in the house by the quay. It's where the ships report when they arrive and where those leaving get permission to depart. You can't miss it, my lady. It's the one overlooking the place where the French ship was anchored the other day."

Of course Elen knew the house. How could she miss it?

"How long has he lived there?"

"That's where he moved to when he arrived from Deheubarth."

"So, he checks the ships as they arrive and depart. Is that all he does? Does he have responsibility for the running of the court as well, now that the king is away?"

"I don't know exactly, my lady."

"I see. He's got power over us all then?"

"Well, he looks after the port and, I suppose, with most of the men gone with the king it's a much easier job. We are less troublesome than the men, well in some ways," she laughed.

"What do people do when they wish to see him? Do they ask for an audience as though he were the king?"

"I don't think so. They just call and see him."

"Well, I would like to see him."

"Shall I call at his place and ask if he will arrange to meet you here in the hall?"

"Good idea, Jane. Please do that."

"It's how it should be, isn't it my lady."

With Gruffudd away, she was gaining more confidence in dealing with Jane. When she was in Caerfyrddin she had servants of her own, all from her own family. At Rhuddlan, however, she had been given servants she didn't know nor trust, and it had made life very difficult for her. She guessed they reported everything to Gruffudd and that he wanted to know everything.

Jane left to meet Rhys and was back shortly, saying that Rhys would be delighted to call on her and would be there within the hour.

Elen, happy with the arrangement, checked that the hall was clear and, while waiting for Rhys, sat in her usual chair at the main table. She went through in her head the issues she wanted to make clear to him, starting with her visit to the French ship, a matter that was more urgent now that she had found out where he lived. He could well have been watching her going aboard and even falling down the stairs. She was unsure how much of the inside of the ship he could see from his house, but hoped it was very little.

Promptly Rhys appeared at the door and entered as Elen got up to meet him. She could have stayed seated, which would have put him in his place, but she decided not to add to the barriers between them.

He addressed her as Elen as he had before, and she called him Rhys as was the custom.

They sat opposite each other at the long dining table towards the higher end of the hall. As instructed, Jane brought them mead and some pieces of bread.

Jane then asked, "Shall I stay, my lady," while looking to Rhys for guidance.

Elen noticed all this and thanked her, but told her she could leave. Elen was convinced by the interchange between Jane and Rhys that her servant was acting under his instructions. She would have to be careful with them both, to make sure that they didn't poison Gruffudd against her.

"I wish to explain to you, why I went onboard the French ship the other day. I understand you saw me from your house."

He didn't answer her nor give any hint that he had actually seen her. The captain's invitation had been quite loud and Rhys might have heard him and gone to the window to see who he was inviting.

Sitting opposite him she realised that he was very young, probably younger than her by a year or two. Gruffudd, who was no fool, must have had great confidence in him, so he must be good at his job.

In her presence, he was very uneasy and nervous and this gave her confidence

"I would like to make it clear that I accepted the French captain's invitation to see his ship simply from curiosity. I'm interested in ships since I lived near the sea in Caerfyrddin and I've always been fascinated by them. The French ship I saw the other day was a particularly interesting and beautiful one, a type I had not seen before."

He remained passive, not saying a word, just listening in a most off-putting manner. It made her think that he didn't believe a word she was saying and that she was covering her true intentions. She was digging herself into a deeper and deeper hole and he was succeeding in making her feel guilty.

She changed tactic, faced by his stony silence, and asked, "Are you interested in boats and ships, Rhys?"

"Very much so. I had my own ship on the Conwy and

I worked in the harbour there. I had the ship with me in Deheubarth and I've brought it with me to Rhuddlan.

"So, you've been sailing. But being a steward is more challenging and you can't have had much experience because you are so young."

"With respect, you are also young to be the queen."

"I have very few responsibilities though; mainly to bear children and smile at the guests. It's not challenging work. You have to deal with the daily activities of the court and the harbour, quite a task."

"The Conwy estuary is as busy as the Clwyd's. I managed that with my father for years. So you could say I know the problems that can arise. After you've done one year the second and following years are just repeats of the first."

"But surely there are important issues to solve?"

"They mainly solve themselves. I check what's arriving and leaving and keep a note of it all. The captains and the sailors lead their own lives. I don't even try to influence who they choose to take onboard and when they leave."

She moved uneasily in her chair at that remark, but didn't rise to the bait, even if it was his intention. Instead she decided that a change of topic was needed.

"What I wanted to talk to you about was how my husband is progressing in Deheubarth. I would like you to tell me directly and not let me find out through my servant. I wonder if you could let me know every week."

"Yes, of course, I will be pleased to. I can report to you here at the end of each week. I send him a brief report by ship every week, just to inform him about the court and various issues. I get requests and messages back. The communications are mainly oral but I receive written communication from the king weekly and I write to him by return of ship. I can report to you on the same day as the boat leaves for Deheubarth."

"Thank you. How long do you think they will be away?"

"It's impossible to say. The king will wish to finish the matter, so it could be a few more weeks."

"That's all I wanted to ask. I hope it's not been too difficult for you to leave your work."

"Not at all, it's my pleasure."

As he left she thought there was a mixture of feelings in him. Part of him was relieved to finish the conversation but a part of him wanted to stay with her. Why was that? Was it to find out more about her so he would be better informed and consequently better placed to inform the king about her? At least she knew her two main guardians at Rhuddlan were Rhys and Jane.

CHAPTER 17

July 1048

FOLLOWING THEIR MEETING, Elen resolved to make life a little more difficult for Rhys. She started walking upriver, thus avoiding his living quarters and his prying eyes and, at the same time, avoiding any contact with lusty sea captains.

The walks upriver were not as interesting, she knew that. But they served their purpose and she began to take interest in the river birds and the landscape around the court. She talked to Jane about inconsequential things only, avoided mentioning the king in case some of her hatred for him showed, and avoided mentioning Rhys, knowing that the story would go back to him quite quickly.

After a week had elapsed, Rhys came to see her and they met again at the main table in the great hall. He was courteous and still a little nervous, she thought.

He told her that he had nothing new to tell her, as the king was still hunting rebels and there was no indication that he would be back soon.

Having delivered this message she expected him to leave her but he didn't. He remained seated and silent, which became embarrassing as the conversation instigated by her became stagnated and forced.

He clearly didn't wish to leave. She wondered why. Was he looking to find out something about her that he could use against her? Something that he hoped would make the king pleased with him.

She returned to her earlier question: "Can you give me

some idea of how long do you think the king will be before he returns home?" Adding, "I'm missing him," while the truth was very different. She was happier when he was away from the court and the longer he stayed away the better as far as she was concerned.

He answered her solemnly, "It's impossible to say."

And she thought, you've given that answer before. Can't you be a little more creative and suggest a time, hopefully well into the future.

"Have there been any battles?"

"None, which I know of."

"So the army is intact?"

"Yes, as far as I know."

What a bore she thought. He can't even make interesting conversation. She noticed that while he was answering her questions he would look at her. But then his gaze would drift to the floor as though he was looking for something there or was he simply feeling too guilty to keep eye contact with her.

Did he know that she was aware that he was keeping an eye on her on behalf of the king? Had he already sent exaggerated and salacious reports about her and the sea captain? She felt sure that she could see guilt written all over his face and in his manners. What a loathsome man she thought.

Rhys overstayed his welcome and, to give him a clear signal that he should leave, she got to her feet to wish him farewell.

His reaction was still slow. She could see that he wanted to stay.

Eventually he stood and she moved towards the door to indicate that she wished to show him out. He had nothing to say and she was exhausted trying to fill the pregnant silences. After much lingering and hesitation he did leave, promising that he would return the following week. Elen was glad to see the back of him.

No sooner was he gone than her other spy came in. Jane was all sweetness and joy. "Things must have gone well between you and Rhys. I could see that you were deep in conversation. Did he have interesting things to say, my lady?"

Elen, frustrated and annoyed, blurted out, "No, nothing of any interest." She could see the disappointment on Jane's face.

Elen continued with her walks upriver, avoiding the port until it was time for Rhys to visit again. The meeting took exactly the same form as the previous one, with Elen learning nothing new and, she believed, Rhys being equally bereft of new information to pass on about her.

However, he did shock her by asking, "Would you like me to report to you on the king's progress more frequently. I could see you twice a week if you wish."

She most certainly did not wish to sit in silent embarrassment with this man. In many ways she was already beginning to regret having requested a weekly meeting.

"I think once a week will be sufficient. After all there doesn't seem to be much happening in Deheubarth."

He shuffled nervously on his chair and surprised her again by looking disappointed and even dejected. She wondered why on earth he wanted to meet her more frequently. What could he possibly gain from these meetings?

She had a similarly difficult time getting him to leave again and was left puzzling about his intentions.

A few days after this third meeting, intrigued by Rhys's attitude, she decided to take a walk to the port. She went alone, giving no notice to her servants.

It was close to high tide and many of the smaller ships had left and the larger vessels were preparing to leave. She walked slowly, taking notice of everything and, at the same time, looking out for Rhys.

She didn't have to look hard. He had seen her approaching

and came to meet her. He looked happy, was smiling, and had a spring in his step. He looked nothing like the lump of dough she had seen in the hall.

"Welcome to my domain. It's very busy here today, the tide is coming in and there are ships leaving and others are already on their way up the estuary."

He was far more relaxed, which in turn relaxed her. "I can see. Don't let me distract you."

"I've always got time for you. Let me show you around."

They walked along the dockside with Rhys telling her what was in each ship's hold and where it was bound for. Two were taking provisions to the king and his army in Deheubarth and another two were going to Anglesey, returning there with supplies of wood for shipbuilding.

He was interesting, lively and enthusiastic; a very different person.

"Let me get you a drink. Its hot work this and I'm quite thirsty. Are your servants not with you?"

"No. They had plenty to do and it's nice to be alone sometimes."

He nodded knowingly, which alarmed her. She hoped that he wouldn't take her remarks the wrong way. She wasn't there to meet another sea captain.

He led the way into his own house, which stood less than fifty yards from the dockside. She followed him inside and he produced some mead and poured them a small jugful each.

"The king's health," he announced, raising his jug.

She could not agree wholeheartedly but raised her jug saying nothing.

"I have no more news for you," he announced and she feared he would revert to his nervous and unsure self.

"I guessed that," she said smiling at him.

Sensing that the conversation would become stinted again,

she opened up the dialogue, "You have a nice place here with an excellent view of the ships and the river."

He recovered his spirit and led her to the back of the house. "Look, from the back here I have a view of the Clwyd Mountains. You can see Moel Hiraddug there. Impressed?"

"You have almost as good a view as we have from the hall," she admitted. "Is this the reason you haven't moved to live at the main court?"

"That and the fact that it's convenient for me here. Look, I have a clear view of the main hall where you live. I can see you sometimes from this side window."

Elen felt uneasy, so she rested her hand on the table to steady herself and to touch something real and solid. She looked at him, realising it was an ideal place for him to watch her. He was smiling and looked innocently at her, yet she knew he was the king's dark eyes watching her and ensuring that no one was even to take a fancy to her.

He was standing close to her, the smile slowly disappearing as his hand gently and very slowly descended to cover her own.

She looked up at him and crucially made no attempt to remove her hand. Perhaps he was thinking that she was unwell and was helping her to steady herself. But what she saw was not concern for her wellbeing but something different.

The fact that she did not withdraw her hand may have misled him to believe that she was condoning his own covering hers because he whispered quietly to her, "I love you."

She kept her upward gaze on his face which was now very close to her own and he kissed her gently on her cheek.

As they separated, he said again, "I love you and have for a long time."

Perhaps he expected her to tell him that she loved him also, but she didn't. She said nothing and they stood close together for a few seconds before he lifted his hand off hers.

She recovered from the shock slowly as he moved backwards a little.

They both placed their jugs of mead on the table. She turned slowly and hesitantly to leave.

"Shall I see you at our arranged meeting in the hall?"

She turned to look back at him and said yes. Though she could not see his face clearly, she thought he looked pleased.

She left and, once out in the light, she realised that her cheeks were wet. She wondered at the cause before realising that her vision was also blurred by the tears in her eyes.

Tears, why would she be tearful? By the time she was halfway to the court's gates, she knew it was because of the kindness in his voice when he told her he loved her. It was also his apparent sincerity, the way he had touched her, the way he had so gently kissed her on her cheek. She was vulnerable and believed he meant what he had said to her and she had not genuinely felt loved for a long time.

CHAPTER 18
Later the same day in July 1048

ELEN RETURNED TO the hall, dazed, bewildered and distressed. She felt people were looking at her and guessing what had happened. She did not know what to make of Rhys's advances, the symbolic covering of her hand, his delicate but effective kiss on her cheek. He had been very daring and very reckless. She could have slapped him with her jug. She could have screamed. Perhaps she should have done both, but she hadn't.

Rhys must have guessed how vulnerable she was to the slightest offer of affection and that she would succumb easily and readily to his advances. He had read her as he would an open book.

How could he have been so presumptuous? Did he know that those words "I love you" would secure her attention, silence and response. It was a long time since she had heard those words from Hywel's lips – the memory of his bloodied head and lips lying on the ground in front of her made her tremble as she sat in her chair.

Jane entered and was surprised to find her mistress there. Jane was the last person Elen wanted to see but it did deflect her mind from that horrendous sight of the head with shocked dead eyes staring up at her. There was a mixture of guilt and relief as the image faded in her mind and she went upstairs to her own room barely acknowledging Jane's presence.

Those words had meant so much to her years ago and it was a shock to hear them spoken to her once again so gently and lovingly. Her king had also said those words to her but she had barely noticed and certainly not responded even at their most intimate time though she knew perfectly well that he did love her in his own way. To him they meant that he wanted to possess her, occupy her, have total power over her and have her at his beck and call. Yes, those words uttered so kindly had distracted her and given her more self-belief than she had experienced in years. Even the birth of her son had not given her quite the same feeling of a meaningful existence as those words spoken by Rhys.

She thought of the sea captain who had been even more daring than Rhys and simply kissed her passionately with far more vigour and determination. She had experienced more amorous advances in the short time the king had been away than in all the years she had been under his yoke and beady eye.

Time, even an hour, calmed her troubled mind and caused her to have other, perhaps more realistic, thoughts. Surely, Rhys had been told by the king to test her fidelity. Had he found her wanting, she wondered. Yes, he must have otherwise she should have tried immediately to remove her hand and slap him across his face when he kissed her. He would be delighted with the report he could send to the king.

She searched for positives and remembered that at least she had been fairly impassive to his advances – she was good at that – she'd had years of practice with Gruffudd. She could state quite honestly that he had advanced at her and surprised her with the kiss. He could not say anything else without lying extensively. Perhaps he was capable of lying. He most certainly lied when he said he loved her. He barely knew her so how could he love her.

She had agreed to his regular briefings on the king's progress in Deheubarth and so she would meet him again in the main hall. She was apprehensive and indeed anxious but also wanted it to happen sooner rather than later to get it over with and tell him that it would be the last such meeting. In future she would have any news through her servant, Jane.

She also wished to set the record straight between them. So she would tell him that he had shocked her so much that she had failed to act in the way she wished or in the way she was contracted to do as the king's wife. She would make it clear to him that if there was any repeat she would oppose it vigorously and report him to Gruffudd.

During the days leading up to their planned meeting she had kept away from the port and any area he might be expected to frequent. He, presumably, had done the same as they didn't meet or see each other even from a distance during that time.

He was punctual as was his habit and she liked that in him. He didn't keep her waiting. He was seated at the main table when she entered the hall, having been informed by Jane that he had arrived and "dressed very smartly" according to Jane's comment.

He left his chair and went to meet her as she entered. He was all smiles and far more confident than during his previous meetings in the hall. He asked about her health and wellbeing and she replied with a smile as she went to her chair at the opposite side of the table.

She knew that she would have to mention what had happened in order to prevent misunderstanding. She steeled herself to do so at the very start and opened her mouth to deliver her planned and well-thought out speech. She timed it carefully making sure that no one was in hearing distance. After she had heard Jane's clogs on the cobbles outside, looking him straight in his eyes and taking a deep breath, she said, "I…"

But she heard his voice, "I hope you have had time to consider the fact that I love you. And that I love you more than anyone else in the world and more than anyone has ever loved you before."

She managed a weak smile but was flummoxed by his renewed declaration.

"I'm the king's wife. You can't say things like that to me. It's treason. He will kill you. He's killed many for far less."

"Your beauty has captured my heart. I love you Elen and there is nothing I can do to change that. As I have come to know you better, I have grown to love you more."

"Stop, someone might hear you."

"I love you and I don't believe you love the king. You are too good for him."

All she could do was recite some of what she had been told many times, "He is a strong and powerful man. He is the best king Wales has had in many centuries. He has regained the territories lost to the English since the time of King Arthur. He has made Wales strong. He has managed all that by being ruthless in all walks of life. I am his, please remember that. He has captured me. Hold your tongue, I do not wish any harm to come to you on my account. My first husband lost his head because of Gruffudd's jealousy. So if you value your life stop and love someone else instead of me."

Tears were welling up in her eyes.

"Yes. He has captured you but I don't believe he has captured your heart."

She looked up at him through her watery eyes and stared at him.

"I love you," he said again. "Give me your love and I will treasure it for ever."

"You are young and inexperienced in life and in love," she ventured. "You have much to learn about our world, its cruelty, its brutishness and its inhumanity. Be careful it will not destroy you on the anvil of love."

"I am no younger than you are. My love for you will endure all these things anyway."

"No, it won't. You may have hope, like I did, but it will not conquer in the end."

She knew that anyone could come into the hall at anytime and, though they were not talking loudly, anyone seeing her in tears and the manner of their communication would suspect something. He didn't seem to care. He was on one path only – he was determined to win her confidence and her love, however impossible a task that would prove to be.

"Give me your hand," he requested softly. She obeyed lifting her right hand onto the table. He reached for it and held it softly in his much larger hand and stroked the back slowly as though he was stroking the head of his pet cat.

She withdrew her hand slowly and without difficulty as he hardly held it, merely supported it.

"You had better leave now for both our sakes," she said.

This time he obeyed without questioning her and rose from his chair. "I hope we can meet again for me to give you a full report on the king's progress," he said rather louder than necessary but there was no one within hearing range.

She simply nodded affirmation.

He left a happy man, but she was frightened.

Instead of going to her chamber she decided to go and see her son and try to put everything out of her mind till some time had passed.

CHAPTER 19

The next day in July 1048

ELEN THOUGHT A lot about Rhys that night while she lay awake. She suspected in her heart that he was false and was setting a trap for her to fall into so that he could ingratiate himself with the king.

The only way she could check if she could believe him would be for her to set a trap for him. He had said uncomplimentary things about the king in her hearing. There were no witnesses but he had said them. The fact that he had said that he "loved her" and that "she was too good for Gruffudd" were both treasonable statements.

Dwelling as she did on what had happened to her, an idea began to form in her mind. Rhys's attention had flattered her and raised her spirits to a level that she hadn't experienced for years, but she was fully aware of the dangers involved.

She knew that Rhys was sending messages to the king and receiving messages back. He had said that most were verbal but a few were written, presumably under seal. These were secret messages meant for the king only. She was sure that any report on her behaviour would be confidential and in a written statement under seal. Rhys would not rely on an oral message regarding the behaviour of the queen.

The messages were delivered by ship which carried provisions and special supplies to the army. She needed to find out what was he saying about her to the king in his sealed reports. She puzzled on this and gradually developed a plan.

She could write a note to the king to tell him how his son

was progressing. She could seal it and give it to Rhys the day before it was to be taken by ship. Then, shortly before the ship's departure, she could go and claim the letter back as she wanted to add a sentence. This would cause a distraction and she could take the opportunity to extract Rhys's letter somehow without being noticed, open the seal and read it to see what he was saying about her. It was a challenging plan but she was determined and her life depended on it.

There was no time to waste and she set to on her plan immediately. First her letter. She had all the necessary components – a small piece of parchment, ink and a quill. Her privileged upbringing had given her the ability to read and write reasonably well, even better than many, including Gruffudd himself.

That morning in her room she wrote her letter, addressing it to the king of Wales. It was brief and to the point. It started, 'Hope you are well and leading a successful campaign.' She realised that this was about the kindest greeting she had extended to him ever. The letter continued, 'Your son is well and looking forward to your return.' She did not include herself in this sentence for fear he would smell a rat and neither did she wish him well at the end, other than to say, 'Regards, your wife.' To have signed it Elen would have been too personal and intimate for her. She wished she could have written 'Your captive'. As she was writing these final words, she wondered and hoped that he had captured another woman on his campaign.

She rolled the parchment up and, using the central fire in the hall, melted a lump of wax, placed the tags to her parchment in it and stamped her ring into it. Her letter was ready.

The next task was to find out as much as she could about the dispatches to the king, including which ship would take them and when. To do that she would have to meet and question Rhys.

The letter finished, she went towards the port, hoping to see him as she walked slowly along the quayside. She admired each ship, looked at a catch of fish being landed, caskets of wine being offloaded from another ship, and took her time to smile appropriately at the port workers. There were a few small rowing boats arriving and departing, with individuals bringing their goods to be traded and others leaving after having made a profitable bargain. The port, as always when the tide came in, was a busy, entertaining and colourful place.

Then, inevitably, her quarry appeared. He was all charm, but she only saw the serpent that had tempted Eve long ago. Life at Rhuddlan had taught her to mistrust people.

"Come with me," he said. "You can view the port from my house – I won't ask you inside this time."

She went with him willingly, of course.

They sat outside his house facing the river in the July sunshine. After the initial pleasantries, she asked him, "When will your next dispatch to my husband be sent?"

"It will leave on that ship you just passed, that one there," he said, pointing. It will leave about this time tomorrow just as the tide comes in, with the hope of going through the Menai Straits before the tide has retreated. It's a tall order but some make it, depending on the wind. Otherwise they sail around Anglesey which takes half a day longer. Only a very few risk the Straits at night. Are you a good sailor?"

"I used to sail quite frequently in the Tywi estuary."

"I have a small ship, some would call it a boat. Let's say I have a large boat that I could use to take you for a trip along the coast."

She was careful not to commit herself and simply smiled at him.

It was enough encouragement in his mind to say, "I find I need to tell you again that I am in love with you and constantly desire your company. You are in my mind throughout the day. Can you imagine the pleasure it gave me to see you walking along the quay."

"Please stop."

"It was sheer joy for me to see your face with the sun reflecting from the water on it. You're a beautiful woman, Elen."

She did not want him to stop but knew that she had to insist that he did. He was too effervescent with words to mean what he said. "I insist you stop. I am the king's wife. If any of your words were to come into his hearing, he would kill you and in the most unpleasant manner he could imagine."

It silenced him.

"I have come to ask you a favour. I would like to send a note to the king to tell him how his son is changing while he is away. Can I send it with your dispatch to him, tomorrow if possible?"

"Yes, of course," he said without hesitation.

"When will you be placing your report on the ship?"

"I will be taking the dispatches in a bag to the ship in the morning. Bring your letter here this evening or tomorrow morning or wait till next week if you wish. I have written my report and it's ready to go. But I have not sealed it in case there is something I need to add tonight."

"Thank you."

"Will it be a long letter?" he enquired.

"No, it will be very brief, and will take very little space on the ship."

She thanked him again and, to avoid having to admonish him for more indiscreet comments and pretending that she had to write her letter for the morning, she bade him farewell and walked back to the court.

Chapter 20
Later the same day in July 1048

WHILE ON HER way back she planned her next move. She would take her genuine letter to him later that evening and attempt a swap in the morning.

About two hours later she was at his door again. She surprised him as he was eating but he offered to share his meal with her. She declined. She was very nervous and was losing confidence in her plan, knowing that a great deal of luck was needed for it to work.

She held her missive in her hand, and said, "Can you put this in with yours please?"

She was aware that she was trembling as she handed him the rolled up parchment. Did he notice her state she wondered? But he did not show it as he said, "Here we are. This is my dispatch, nothing very big." He held up a rolled parchment just like hers – it looked as if his parchment was a little wider but otherwise there was little difference between them. She was delighted and struggled not to show it.

He took her letter and placed it next to his.

"Oh!" she exclaimed. "Have I addressed it properly? I have not sent him a note before. How do you address yours?"

"I simply address it to the king of Wales," and he brought it to her to show her. She studied every aspect of the rolled parchment, noting its size, shape, the seal and the writing.

He was more interested in her note to her husband. "You have very clear and beautiful handwriting," he remarked. "Just like everything else about you."

She was nervous and blushed but she was also flattered and thinking, if only this man was genuine.

"It's the result of a privileged upbringing. I must leave now. It would not do for the queen to be compromised by staying for long in a stranger's house."

"But I'm not a stranger any more," he complained.

She turned and left, knowing that the most difficult part of the plan was ahead of her. But she was pleased with the progress she had made.

At home she set to addressing another parchment to Gruffudd. This time she left the parchment blank on the inside, addressed it to the king of Wales in a handwriting that from memory she thought resembled Rhys's. She placed a wax blob on the tag which she flattened on both sides, while it was still hot, roughly to the dimensions of Rhys's seal. She hoped that the fact that there were no identification marks on the seal would pass unnoticed.

She could not sleep that night knowing what was ahead of her and knowing the risks she would have to take even if fate was on her side.

Avoiding Jane early the following morning and while the tide was still at bay, she walked down to the port guessing that Rhys would be up and about, as indeed he was. He was standing in the doorway viewing the surrounding landscape when he saw her.

She had the small, rolled-up, blank parchment wedged and well hidden below her breasts.

He was delighted to see her, though she was too anxious to notice it as she walked towards him. "I'm sorry, but I should have said on my letter who it was from. Can I borrow your quill to write, 'from the queen' on the outside please."

"Yes, of course, if you think it's necessary." She followed him into the house and he got her a quill and some ink and she sat by his table to add the extra words. He brought the bag containing her genuine letter and his report to the table. She could not believe her luck but had no idea what guile she would have to use to access his report.

Placing his hand in the bag he brought both letters out and placed them on the table. "There, that's yours."

He stood above her as she took hold of her letter, dipped her quill into the ink carefully and while her quill hovered over the parchment, she looked up at him appealingly and said that she was nervous writing under someone's gaze. She was trembling from anxiety but he didn't know it as he turned his back on her and moved away towards the door facing the port.

Instantly she took the new blank parchment from its secure place under her breasts, sliding it out quickly and silently through a slit that she had made in her dress. Then she took his report and pushed it through the purposely-made concealed tear. There was resistance; his rolled up parchment refused to slide in. She could hear his steps behind her as he approached the table. She picked the quill up again and slowly and deliberately finished the word queen.

By now he was standing above her again. The writing was finished but she said, "I'll wait for it to dry."

She was sweating and knew that his parchment roll had not gone into its desired place. She stayed seated and lent forward at the table to conceal as much as she could of what protruded from under her breasts.

The ink dried and she had to place both rolls in the bag, which he picked up and said he would take to the ship when she left.

As she rose from the table she did so turning her back to him. Again she surreptitiously tried to push his report into its place but it had somehow become wedged halfway in. She wished she had practised this part of the plan more instead of concentrating on extracting the document from its hiding place. Standing upright, she hoped the document would move easier and, without it appearing strange to Rhys, she pushed at it again and this time it moved with very little effort into what she believed was a more secure position. She was greatly relieved.

"I will take this bag with me now and you can see that it will be placed safely on the ship."

She took a step towards the door and there was a distinct thud followed by a hard click on the floor. She knew instantly that the parchment had fallen on the floor and the sharp click was the seal striking the hard wood at her feet and possibly cracking or breaking.

He looked at the floor with a puzzled look and bent down to pick it up. But she was quicker and had picked it up and dashed to the sunlight in the doorway. With the seal broken, she opened the parchment quickly and started reading it. It was very short. She scanned it for her name or any reference to her in it, but found nothing. It was merely a record of the shipping at the port, the state of the grain and the possibility of a good harvest. Then a list of the three who had died at the court and the two women who had given birth, one of whom had died. It ended by saying all was peaceful and wished the king happy hunting for the traitors in the south.

He made no effort to snatch it from her hands but stood back.

There was no mention of her in the report. She lifted her head to find Rhys standing next to her, looking a bit puzzled but not unduly alarmed.

She cried, the strain had been too much for her. To avoid being seen weeping on his doorstep she returned indoors.

In a release of tension and through her tears and sobbing she said, "I thought you were telling the king that I was not faithful to him. I thought you were spying on me for him. And that you were telling me you loved me to trap me and prove that I would be unfaithful and thus somehow curry favour with the king."

He listened to her raving in silence.

Shocked, she turned slowly to face him. "You have not mentioned me in your letter, there is nothing bad about me in there."

He placed his arm around her shoulders, "I love you. I would not say anything bad about you to anyone, least of all to Gruffudd."

She turned her face towards him and, looking intently into her eyes, he whispered to her, "You are very beautiful and I love you."

Their lips met. He kissed her and this time she kissed him back with a passion that had been pent-up for years. She had not kissed like that since she and Hywel were together and she wasn't sure if even then.

She had no resistance left; she had no wish to resist. Recovering slowly, she knew that she was a new woman. Those last few minutes with this man had been the most strikingly lovely time of her life.

They knew they had to separate. They regretted separating; they wanted to be together longer.

She took charge: "Reseal your report and I will take both mine back with me."

He must have been listening to her but there were more urgent matters on his mind, "When can we meet again?"

Arranging and shaking her dress and her hair she said, "Come to the hall for our usual meeting."

As she was going he said softly, "I love you."

She turned back to look at him from the doorway and whispered to him, "I think I love you too."

He could only see her silhouette in the doorway, but heard her words clearly as she left him.

CHAPTER 21

July to August 1048

S HE COULDN'T THINK of going straight back to the court and
the hall; it would be too confining for her soul. She wanted
space, she wanted fresh air, she wanted to climb a mountain, she
wanted to fly and soar high above Rhuddlan.

She wanted the feeling of being set free from her chains to
last and she somehow wanted the world to know that she had
gained her freedom. She felt human, she felt her body was her
own now, she felt loved – genuinely loved.

She walked upriver along the bank below the court, enjoying
the senses that had been awakened in her. Eventually she stopped
but didn't want to go back. Instead she turned away from the
flowing water on her right and went into the trees and bushes
covering the slight slope rising from the river. She came to the
large oak tree that she had seen in the distance many times before
and lent backwards against its rough, wide trunk wishing that
her newly-found lover was there with her. She rested, canopied
by branches laden with gently flapping leaves and hidden from
the river path by the tall vegetation of high grass, foxglove plants,
thistles and bramble. Above her she heard the soothing sound
of the leaves rustling and looking up she could see the strong,
dark, twisted branches sheltering her from the real world. She
decided that she would think of that space under the oak tree
as her home.

When she opened her eyes and stood on the tips of her toes,
her position there under the majestic old oak tree on the slight
rise gave her a view of the riverside track in both directions. It

was some distance from the court but below the confluence of the Elwy with the Clwyd. The tide did not reach that far inland except on occasions of very high tides during the winter months and when the river was in full flood.

What a day! How wonderful she felt! She had been found by a man who loved her in the way she wanted to be loved. He cared for her, for who she was, what she looked like and how she behaved. She was very happy. How could she have mistrusted him? How was it that she had doubted his open and brave declarations of his love for her? He had already risked his life for her.

Her body and spirit were filled with delight because she was loved by a man she could love back.

Even though her body was satisfied, her mind would not rest. Did she feel guilty? She didn't think she did because the hate that had smouldered within her for years had been released. Strangely she believed she had obtained some revenge for years of suffering. She had been unfaithful to him and was happy about it and wished she could say to Gruffudd "Look what I have done… look what I can do."

But she knew she couldn't and that what she had done had been for love, the love of a man that she, from her own free will, loved. Revenge was an afterthought but it also had its pleasurable aspect.

She knew that she would meet Rhys again and that they would have to be careful not to let the king or anyone suspect anything. The future? No, she wouldn't think of that because only if the king were to be killed or die would they have a future together.

When she was ready she left her secure place under the oak tree and worked her way through the network of brambles towards the river. The thick prickly brambles soon reminded her of Gruffudd's arms entwining around her, stifling her movement, captivating her in his prison. Dark shadows passed over her spirits as she thought of Gruffudd getting to know about what had happened. He would have Rhys brought before the courts and would demand the death penalty and, if the court would fail him, he would have him killed anyway. There were many who would do his bidding; some from fear, others through some form of admiration for the king, some because they believed that the king's will was God's will and so justified everything the king did. Her whole body shuddered at the memory of Hywel's severed head lying there at her feet. She could see Rhys's head similarly thrown at her and the king forcing her publicly to kiss it before her own hanging.

She shook her head as though she had tasted a very bitter fruit. She determined not to have her joy overshadowed by thoughts of Gruffudd. She placed Rhys in the front of her mind and, as she came out of brambles onto the track by the riverbank she was happy, content and ready to go back to the court with a lively step.

As Elen entered the hall she was shaken out of her wonderful reverie by Jane's voice: "We thought you had gone missing, my lady. We were worried about how the king would blame us for not keeping tabs on you."

Elen was furious at these words but, while normally she would have replied firmly, this time she was content to smile and simply nod at her, as good as to say mind your own business.

She went to see her son and then returned to her room. The time passed very slowly and the next meeting with Rhys, in three days' time, seemed an eternity away. But on the morning of the second day, after their intimate time together, he appeared in the hall and asked for her.

Elen was in the hall like a flash – excited but nervous that he might say he did not want to meet her again or that it was too dangerous for them to meet. She was anxious and deliriously happy at the same time.

He met her calmly, smiled and inclined his head. "Good day. Shall I report to you outside today and we can enjoy the summer sun."

She willingly and happily obliged and went out with him. Some yards away from the hall's entrance he turned to her, "I couldn't wait for the meeting tomorrow. I was desperate to see you. I hope we can meet again."

Of course they could meet again, he needn't ask what her feelings were but she was wise enough to say, "Let's walk this way a little, don't smile too much and don't appear too happy. Remember we are discussing the king's progress in the south where, God willing, he may remain."

"Yes."

"I've also been desperate to see you. I've found an old oak tree about a mile upriver – no one goes there. There's a large stone on the riverbank before you come to the tree. Could you go up the river some of the way in a boat or on a horse and I will walk along the river path and we can meet under the oak tree about an hour before dusk tonight. It's a large tree which you can see from the riverside track."

"I know the tree you mean, I'll be there. I've thought of nothing else. I love you so much."

"Be careful, people may be watching us. I'm sure that Gruffudd has asked someone to keep an eye on me and I want you to be safe."

"I know. How will you get away from Jane and the others?"

"Don't worry, leave Jane to me. I'm quite determined and creative when I need to be." She ventured a brief smile at him which he caught and felt reassured.

"We'll meet this evening then."

"Yes, I love you Elen."

They parted formally, he to return through the court gates to his home and she to the hall to sit, steady herself, let her legs recover and control the pleasure swelling inside her.

That evening she set off early on her walk along the riverside. She told Jane that she wasn't feeling well and intended to retire to bed early, and instructed her to go on an errand to the baking house.

As soon as Jane left and was out of sight, Elen left the court and turned south along the track. She wondered if he would take a circular route on his horse or use a small boat. She rather hoped he would ride his horse and in that way wouldn't be seen going in the same direction as her.

When she turned off the path towards the oak tree she thought she heard the noise of a horse. Soon she saw the animal tied to a small tree between the river and her oak tree. She continued past the horse which made a slight snorting noise as if to signal to his master in as discreet a way as possible that there was a stranger about.

Rhys was coming towards her with open arms into which she ran. "I wasn't sure you would come," he said, and she had obviously felt the same, saying, "I was desperately hoping you would be here."

They kissed passionately and he led her under the tree where he had laid a leather cover away from the large exposed roots.

As she had imagined and hoped, he lowered her onto the cover, where they continued their embrace, enjoying the contact with each other and the movement of their bodies and the urgency, as if they had not much time left together. They loved each other and took every second of pleasure from each other's company and bodies.

They lay together staring at the canopy of leaves above them. Now they had all the time in the world, she the queen and he the king's steward. Both had committed treason punishable by death, but were blissfully and wilfully unconscious of the possible consequences. They wanted their time to last and it did. Neither slept, neither spoke. They lay there in each other's company and that was as much as they both wanted and that's what they achieved.

Elen was elated when she eventually rose to her feet to rearrange her hair and clothes. It was all pleasurable, even the adjusting of clothes, as it reminded her of what rapture she had experienced.

Before they parted he asked her if he could take her on his boat down the estuary someday, so they could spend a few hours together afloat and she, of course, jumped at the offer. Doing anything with him was pure pleasure for her.

After much kissing and holding of hands, they were eventually able to prise themselves apart. She left first and followed the path back as the sun was setting. She could have skipped all the way back, but slowed as she approached the court so as not to arouse suspicion.

She had the boat trip to look forward to and didn't sleep that night through excitement. Like a child, she could not accept that such joy and excitement should be dulled or wasted on sleep.

CHAPTER 22

August 1048

ELEN'S LIFE HAD changed. Her son was still important to her but she was experiencing a new zest for life, for enjoying herself, even for simply being happy and being herself again. She was able to think of herself and what she wanted day by day, and it was simple – she wanted Rhys. She wanted to be with him all the time to talk to him, to laugh with him, to lie with him.

She was excited; she couldn't wait to be in his arms again. She was, though, concerned that others would see into her soul and realise that she was someone else now. Her son would not notice of course, he knew she was his mother. Gruffudd and the conventions in Gwynedd, however, had seen to it that her contact with him was not very influential, nothing like that between the lower nobility and their offspring.

The prospect of being alone with Rhys on his boat thrilled her, though she didn't know how he would arrange it. She had confidence in him, a confidence lovers derive from knowing that the feelings between them are mutual.

She continually had to restrain herself from going down to the port to see him and wished she could in some way signal him or wave to him. She thought of waiting at her window until he appeared but, instead, she fetched a white piece of linen and tied it to the bar of the window as if to dry it. Even if it was seen there, she didn't believe that anyone would deduce it was there to show Rhys she loved him.

She left it there for a while, went to the hall for lunch and returned to her window later. She saw Rhys strolling up towards the hall. She was overjoyed at the sight and went out to meet him as calmly as she could, carrying a basket on her arm as if on a mission.

They met casually, smiling appropriately at each other and he asked with some concern, "Is everything alright?"

"Yes," she replied, puzzled, but reacting like a child and feeling the excitement travelling through her body.

"I saw the white cloth in the window and I thought that it might be a signal that you wanted to see me."

"Oh it was. I did want to see you. But that's all, there's no problem."

He was relieved. "Can we meet in three days to go on my boat? We shall have to be careful to get you aboard without anyone seeing you and getting you off again may not be easy. The tide will be going out after midday and returning before dusk. It would give us a good four hours together. How do you fancy that?"

"It will be lovely, can't wait." She was excited, but then anxiety spread over her face and she asked, "But how do I get on your boat?"

"Once you're in the boat the sides are deep enough to hide you and downriver there is no high ground that overlooks the river, so it should be fine. Walk along the harbour and pass my boat which I will have anchored there. I'll wait until it will be too late in the tide for other boats to come up the estuary, and I'll pick you up out of sight at the small landing stage on the far side of the large willow tree. You know the one I mean, it will hide us."

Sensing a little anxiety in her he added, "We'll be fine."

"I'll be there. Why don't you hang a white cloth in your window when it's time for me to start walking."

"I will. If you have a problem then hang a white cloth at your window like you did today."

They agreed to the arrangement and separated. She wanted to kiss him but all that was feasible was for her to shape her mouth into the form of a kiss and he replied likewise.

The day of the boat trip arrived not a moment too soon for Elen. It was a cloudy morning with a fair amount of sea mist, but the sun burnt off most of it as it rose and by midday it was a clear sky. She didn't care what the weather was going to be like. All that mattered to her was that she would be with her lover for the afternoon in his boat, rocked by the sea. The ships that were due to leave had left at high tide and the last of the smaller boats were making the most of the ebbing tide.

The white cloth appeared in his window and she left as the few stragglers were making their way upriver, fighting the tide by now. She walked briskly, knowing that timing was vital. She didn't want them to be marooned on a sand bank at the mouth of the river, though she had confidence in Rhys's knowledge of the tides, river and estuary.

She was soon walking past his boat, giving it a momentary glance only and didn't see Rhys on board. However, about a hundred yards past his boat she looked back and could see him releasing the boat from its anchorage. She quickened her pace, the willow tree appeared in the distance and she was relieved to see that the path ahead was deserted.

As she approached the large willow she instinctively drew her scarf tighter around her head to cover more of her face, so anyone seeing her wouldn't recognise her unless they came close.

She peered into the fine, fully-leaved great willow tree, with its long mournful swinging branches scraping the ground on one side and dipping into the river on the other. She was stunned to see someone standing there. She strained her eyes to see better, and her initial thought that there was a man standing under the willow tree was confirmed.

Though she didn't have a clear view of him because he was well hidden by the low hanging, supple branches touching the muddy ground, she could see that he was a tall, wiry man.

The small landing was just ahead of her on the left, but she was worried that the man had seen her. She pretended not to have seen him and walked past. The landing stage was now immediately on her left and she knew she had to walk past it, which she did. Rhys's boat was now approaching the willow and the man saw it. He seemed to sense some danger and immediately emerged from the cover of the tree, rustling the branches enough for Elen to hear and to turn around and see him leaping onto the path, his long legs and arms outstretched and easily bridging the gap between the riverbank and the raised walkway. He was agile and quick, just like a wolf she had seen leaping a stream, years earlier. Thankfully, he turned away from her, making his way rapidly towards the port, keeping the willow between him and the boat arriving at the landing. Much to her relief, she realised that he was more concerned about the boat than he was about her.

The man didn't turn around but made his way with some haste upriver, making the most of his long legs. Elen took her opportunity, seeing that Rhys's boat was at the landing and using the cover of the willow she stepped onto the wooden staging.

Rhys caught her firmly by her arm and lowered her onto the floor of the boat gently and guided the boat, driven by the tide, away from the small jetty and into the main stream of the tide, smiling down at his delighted catch.

"Did you see that man?"

"Yes. Don't worry he didn't see you coming aboard."

"He wasn't fishing, so what was he doing there?"

"Perhaps he was picking up something thrown there off one of the ships as they pass. Some men do private deals with corrupt captains. The captains throw them some merchandise as they are coming upriver when no one sees them. They sell them for whatever they get and then pay the captains back in kind when they are at the port. There's always someone on the make."

"Is that why he went away so quickly?"

"Yes. He saw my boat and took to his heels. Don't worry, he won't tell anyone. He'll be too frightened of the consequences."

"What would happen to him if he were caught?"

"Depends who he is, but he could be banished or imprisoned. So don't worry, even if he saw anything he won't be talking about it."

"Good. When can I sit up? This is not a very dignified position for a lady." They laughed.

The boat glided gently on the tide down the estuary and into the sea with no effort from its captain. They sat together on cushions he had arranged at the rear of the boat, enjoying the sunshine, the motion of the vessel and the wonderful views of the shoreline for miles along the coast. After taking full advantage of their isolation, they returned up the river with the first signs of the tide turning, exactly as planned by Rhys.

The sun was beginning to set and he assured her there would be no one under the willows when she disembarked. He was right, though she had been a little apprehensive.

She walked back towards the hall, waving at him politely as he secured his boat in the port. She was a happy and contented woman arriving back. It had been one of the best days of her life. She went to bed thinking of how much she loved him and fell asleep happy.

Chapter 23

End of August 1048

She went about the hall, the court and her life with swift feet now. There was a spring in her gait, almost a swagger and she was definitely light-headed, so happy and so in love with Rhys. Nothing was a chore; everything she did reminded her of him and their love for each other. Even the food she ate tasted better.

The weather was perfect with the dry spell continuing to the end of August. The sun was shining on her. True, there were moaners and groaners at the court, complaining about the lack of rain, poor harvest, dust, the drying wells. She sympathised with them but she didn't care; she lived above it all.

As August was drawing to a close, Rhys arrived at the hall to see her at his normal visit to report on the king's progress and, of course, to arrange their next rendezvous. He entered the hall and she could immediately see that there was concern on his face. He didn't keep her waiting.

"I've just received news with the tide this morning that the army and the king are on their way back north and will probably arrive within a day or two."

She sat at the long table with disappointment written all over her face. It was not long before the disappointment turned into fear.

She looked around to see if there was anyone within hearing. She could see no one. "This is unexpected."

"Yes, I'm devastated."

"Do you think he's been told about us?"

Rhys had clearly not thought of that and his face showed almost as much sign of fear as hers. But, after taking a few seconds to absorb the suggestion, he relaxed a little and said, "He surely wouldn't have informed me if he suspected anything. He would have left his army and come back to surprise us. No, I don't think he has been told anything."

"I hope you are right. I was wondering about that man under the willow tree by the river the other day."

"Don't worry about him. If anyone suspects anything it's more likely to be your servant Jane. I don't think we need to be concerned. Gruffudd's probably heard that his enemy in the south has escaped to Ireland or England and he fancies the comfort of home."

She felt better. "What shall we do?"

"For me it is simple, I love you and I want to continue to meet you. Can we meet under our oak tree this evening?"

She stood up next to him and whispered, "I love you too." It was all she could do to restrain herself from kissing him there in the hall. She held back but her eyes welled with tears sensing that his arms wanted to enfold her, caress her and that, he too, wanted to kiss her.

"We'd better separate or I won't be able to stop myself. I love you," she said restraining a tear and turning her back on him.

"Let's meet this evening. Make it an hour earlier than last time, since the nights are beginning to draw in. I love you, Elen."

He left her and the loss was horrific. She was crying now, she couldn't help it. She walked slowly away from the table and then back towards it and sat down again. Her beautiful world had lasted a few weeks only, and it would be destroyed by a husband she didn't and could never love.

Jane entered the hall and asked, "Are you alright?"

"Yes. Yes."

"Only you look as though you've been crying and I thought you'd be happy seeing that the king is returning."

"How did you know?"

"Everybody is talking about it, my lady."

"Have you been crying, my lady?"

She had to think quickly. "They're tears of joy, Jane," she lied.

Elen wondered if Jane was entirely convinced with the answer but made no other comment as she passed her on her way out. Jane was examining her face carefully when she said, "We're all delighted they're on the way home. It's wonderful news isn't it?"

Her mistress managed a weak smile and a yes after she passed her. She breathed the fresh clear air deeply and resolved not to be bothered by Jane, but instead to plan for her evening meeting. They had a day or two left before the king returned. She decided she would make the most of that time by taking two cooked pork chops and a small flagon of the best mead in her basket that evening. She was determined that love like theirs would not be extinguished easily.

When the time came and her basket was prepared, she told Jane that she was going to sit by the river and enjoy a piece of bread and cheese and pray for a safe journey home for the soldiers. Jane asked if she wanted her company but she managed a nonchalant and disinterested no.

Her walk to their oak tree went without hitch and Jane didn't see her leaving with her basket. Others might have, but weren't well enough informed to possibly deduce much from it as it was the beginning of the blackberry season which had ripened early that year because of the fine August they'd experienced.

She and her lover ate and drank under that great old oak tree. They were happy and felt blessed to be in each other's arms, despite a tinge of sadness that the king was returning. They agreed that things would be far more difficult, but they were too much in love not to arrange to meet again and as often as they could.

Neither of them spoke of perhaps what pained them both most. They knew that she would be subjected to the king's lovemaking and dreaded the thought. Of course she also knew that Rhys would know this and dreaded even more what its effect would be on him and on their love. He never mentioned it, but guessed the truth and the reality that faced her.

They parted as much in love as ever, but she was having difficulty in controlling her emotions. She struggled to part from him that night and fought back the tears valiantly.

They agreed that they would signal each other, meet casually when possible and meet as lovers whenever and as often as they could, but their future was uncertain.

At midday, two days later, scouts arrived signalling that the king and his army were less than an hour away. The people of the court went south along the riverbank to greet them. Elen joined them, though welcoming her husband was the last thing on her mind. She felt no guilt about the fact that she had gone to sleep many a night hoping that he would perish in Deheubarth.

The crowds stood not far from her tree. Rhys was there on his horse as part of the main welcoming party. She stood near him admiring his stance, his looks and everything about him, which made her even more desperately unhappy about welcoming the king home.

Soon the dust from the returning army could be seen rising in the distance. There was noise, clatter of hooves, the din of steel hitting steel, the shouting and singing of men.

Then, leading the army, they could see the king, riding high in his saddle, full of the joys of the return. He was smiling and laughing, raising his sword as though he had won a great victory. He was in jubilant mood.

He rode into the middle of the welcoming, noisy crowd. He greeted Rhys and then directed his horse towards Elen, who was trying her best to smile at him. He stopped his horse next to her and all expected him to dismount but he didn't. Instead he leant down and grabbed the back of her dress, lifting her bodily high enough for him to kiss her. The crowd cheered his feat of strength and demonstration of love.

She could have spat at him and was deeply concerned at what Rhys thought of it all. She was greatly relieved when he put her down again. But he had achieved his objective of declaring her his possession.

Elen saw Rhys occasionally that evening, but only to exchange painful glances.

CHAPTER 24

September 1048 – May 1049

L IFE CHANGED AGAIN for Elen on the king's return. Her freedom was severely curtailed, she believed there were more preying eyes on her and gradually things returned to the restrictive drudgery she had faced before Gruffudd had gone south.

She had to share his bed. Excuses of headaches and backaches were of no avail. His possessiveness reflected his love for her, but his strength, power and brutality were never far beneath the surface. It was only when she had managed to fill him with strong mead that she had any peace from him. He was again asking her why couldn't she love him? Why had his absence not made her love him more? She knew he hankered for her love but she knew she could never love him. His absence had further opened the gap between them, as she had experienced true love again with Rhys.

Her life was now spiced by the highly-charged, though infrequent, meetings with her lover. Occasionally they would manage to meet on his boat, sometimes by their oak tree and sometimes in other places. They had found it easier and safer to meet at night when there were fewer people about and when many were drinking their mead prior to going to bed. They would have seconds together in the shadows behind the hall. It was risky but every moment they shared together was precious and rewarding for both.

She used a sheet in her window to indicate to Rhys that she was available to see him. He would respond with his sheet if he could meet her. They developed a detailed signalling pattern: the oak tree would be a white sheet, and a yellow one would mean they would meet at the landing stage downriver. They changed the pattern at the landing with Rhys arriving first in his boat to scatter any unwanted traders from under the willow tree.

They were careful and they knew they had to be. Madog's fate was never far from their minds.

The king visited his other courts around his country, but he normally took his wife with him. Sometimes Rhys would accompany them and sometimes not, and when he was not with her they were both desperately unhappy. But their love endured all the difficulties they encountered.

December 1048 was a tough month, very cold and stormy. By the end of the year, Elen could no longer disguise the fact that she was expecting a baby. This time she was pleased to be pregnant, knowing that the father was Rhys and that it had been conceived on their first boat trip together. Gruffudd was led to believe it had been conceived a few weeks later, immediately on his return from the south. It had worked out well for her.

She knew, from her previous pregnancy, Gruffudd would be intensely jealous and woe betide anyone who looked at her too long even in her enlarged state. After all these years he was still obsessed by her, mesmerised by her beauty and the fruit he could not fully pick. He could not totally possess her spirit, any more than he could get her to love him.

She carried her pregnancy as easily as she had her first. She continued to see Rhys whenever she could. They loved talking together, sharing secrets, and discussing their baby.

Rhys had noticed that she was becoming more concerned than usual about being followed or seen with him. He put it down to her physical state and endeavoured to reassure her that all was well. However, in February, under their oak tree, she confided to him that there was a man she sometimes saw in the port, who she felt gave her a knowing look – as though he was aware that the child growing inside her was not the king's child.

"Oh!" he exclaimed.

"I'm probably imagining it. There is no reason why anyone should suspect anything."

"What exactly have you seen?"

"He looks at me, glances at my tummy and back at my face. I sometimes think he grins as if to say 'I know what you've been up to'."

"Oh."

"Many men leer at me as they do at most women. We don't like it but it's what some men do. It's something we've learnt to endure. This man does not look at my body with any desire and when he looks me in the eyes he keeps staring at me longer than is normal and makes me feel very uneasy."

"Hmm! Does he talk to you?"

"He doesn't say anything, just gives me that look. He grins as I imagine a wolf would grin and salivate at the thought of eating its prey. Also, sometimes, I suspect that he walks slightly out of his way to come closer to me and to meet me face to face."

"If you told the king, he would be dead meat in no time."

"I don't want that," she laughed. "But I would prefer him not to look at me as he does."

"Yes. Tell me what does he look like?"

"He is tall and thin, and he could be the man under the willow tree when we went out to sea in your boat for the first time. Perhaps that is what alarms me the most."

"Tall and thin... I suppose it could be him."

"Yes, I think he's the same man. I've been thinking of asking Jane to find out who he is. But I don't want to raise her suspicion. I fear that he knows something about us and is biding his time before he uses that information."

"Don't be alarmed, but I think I know the one you mean.

His name is Peter and he's probably the man you saw under the willow tree. I have noticed him too and I've also seen that faint knowing smile when he looks at me and I've also wondered what he knows. Probably it's just the way he looks. We feel guilty and are therefore more suspicious of him."

"So I haven't imagined it. Who is this Peter?"

"I've made a point of finding out. He is one of those men who hangs around the port. He has no specific skills but manages to make a living somehow. He makes deals with whomever he can – sea captains, traders and so on. Basically he lives off his wits, collects drift-wood from the river and beaches, snares birds and anything he can catch. Without making it too obvious that I'm interested in him, I have tried to find out more about him, but no one seems to know much. However, in a strange way, he manages to ingratiate himself well with everyone, including the noble families."

"He is the man I saw under the willow, isn't he?"

"I suppose he must be. Remember I didn't have a good view of him then, but I keep thinking, what could he have seen?"

"Perhaps he saw enough to arouse a little suspicion and that he's been watching us ever since. He may suspect even that my baby is yours. I'm frightened Rhys. What if the baby looks exactly like you? I want that, but it frightens me."

He could see that she was alarmed at the thought that someone knew about them. He tried to reassure her again that the man couldn't have seen anything.

"He is a strange man. Sometimes you think he is of even noble birth. But at other times he behaves like a bondman. I'm puzzled by him."

There were tears coming to her eyes and she was holding her tummy. She felt very vulnerable, unsure of herself and her future and that of the child she was carrying.

Rhys did all he could to reassure her and empathised with

her worries. But he was also concerned and said, "I will find out more about this man. He probably looks suspiciously at everyone and we are more sensitive to being watched and are making more of it than we need to. It's probably just his way."

She wasn't totally convinced but returned to the court happier that Rhys was going to find out more about this man, Peter.

A few days later, Rhys was able to reassure her that the man looked suspiciously at everyone and they had come to the wrong conclusion. It was just the way the man was and she would, with the passage of time, get used to ignoring the way he looked at her and would realise that the man was harmless enough.

In May 1049 Elen gave birth to another son. The king was very proud of his new son and so was Rhys. Gruffudd astounded everyone by naming the new baby Idwal, a name associated with Gwynedd's old royal family. In 1039, Gruffudd, from a rival family, had replaced Iago ap Idwal of the old dynasty who had ruled Gwynedd for generations. The talk at court was that it had been done to appease members of the ancient dynasty.

CHAPTER 25

May 1049 to July 1049

E LEN QUICKLY RECOVERED from the birth of her son and she and Rhys continued their clandestine love affair. Idwal was nursed by the same woman who had nursed Maredudd. Preparations were made for him to be brought up like his brother under the supervision of the king and his most trusted family members. While there were no obvious resemblances between Idwal and his father for the courtiers to start gossiping, in Elen's eyes, the baby looked exactly like Rhys, but the king noticed nothing.

As her confidence returned, the tall, thin man's looks at her melted into the background and she learnt to ignore him and, in time, dispel him from her mind.

Shortly after Idwal's birth, Viking mercenaries from Ireland attacked Deheubarth, joining with some of the old noble families of Deheubarth, with the intention of overthrowing Gruffudd ap Llywelyn as king. They were repelled by Gruffudd's own supporters in the area. This victory for Gruffudd, without having to leave his capital at Rhuddlan, confirmed that he was the undisputed ruler of Deheubarth.

The news brought to Rhuddlan by Berddig made it obvious that Gruffudd ruled and commanded the loyalty of the majority of his country. Berddig, an astute reader of military and political events, said to Gruffudd at the dinner table one evening, "You should hold a great feast to celebrate your successes and invite nobles from Gwynedd, Powys and Deheubarth to Rhuddlan and entertain them royally at the court to bind them firmly to your banner."

Elen, listening to the conversation, wondered what effect any new proposals would have on her relationship with Rhys.

The poet continued, "You should display your natural generosity and give your supporters rewards of land and shower the important ones with gifts."

Seeing that he was striking a chord with Gruffudd, and that others at the table were nodding their heads in agreement he continued, "Let those whom you rule see your power in terms of your warships arrayed in the port. Let them see for themselves the splendour of your royal court at Rhuddlan. Let them witness, at first hand, your support for poets, singers and artists."

There was great support for the idea as feasts were always popular. Gruffudd was grinning broadly, clearly hooked by the idea and announced, raising his jug of mead, "Let's hold a feast. We will have the greatest celebration that has ever been seen in Wales."

Berddig added, "We can call it the king's feast." The king agreed.

Elen cringed, while others cheered wildly.

The following morning messengers were dispatched to all parts of Gruffudd's kingdom to invite the powerful families in his land to attend celebrations associated with his official crowning as king of the combined lands of Gwynedd, Powys and Deheubarth.

Ships were dispatched to France to buy the best quality wine, fabrics for gifts, and Arabian herbs for their smells and seasoning of food.

The feast was to last three days. Cattle were chosen to be killed and a large supply of mead acquired from local producers. Carpenters were employed to construct an impressive dais outside the hall for the coronation and a green cloth prepared to drape above it to form a canopy and shelter for the king from the sun or rain, whichever it was to be. Additional tables and benches were constructed to accommodate guests.

Berddig took a key role in producing the programme of events, with himself as the master of ceremonies.

The weeks went by quickly, with the preparations gathering pace as the day of the feast drew closer. Elen and Rhys had difficulty in meeting, but their love for one another remained constant.

The day before the official start of the feast, guests arrived in great numbers. Elen knew that, unless the guests were on their deathbed, they dared not refuse the invitation. Rhiwallon and Bleddyn, Gruffudd's half-brothers from Powys, arrived in splendour to join the good-humoured gathering with the guests clearly looking forward to be royally entertained.

There were nobles and their families from all parts of the king's dominions. All brought gifts of cattle, horses, game, drinks and goods of all kinds. The court and the immediate surrounding areas were packed with tents and other shelters, making the whole area spectacularly colourful and busy.

The harbour was lined with ships. Some had brought guests, others had been arranged to impress the visitors, and they were most certainly achieving their objective.

Elen hated the thought of the celebrations but hoped that it would somehow afford her an opportunity to meet her lover, somewhere or other. Rhys was deeply involved in the preparation and the two of them were hardly able to exchange a knowing glance, let alone meet during the days immediately before the feast.

The king himself, though keeping a close eye on the preparations, was in good humour. Elen did suspect that, after the crowning ceremony, he and the guests would gradually decline into a drunken state which would last for most of the three days. She and Rhys would be moderate in their consumption of alcoholic beverages so as to take advantage of whatever opportunity came their way. They both hoped that the second day, allocated to an all-day hunt in the hills to the west of Rhuddlan, would be favourable to them.

The first day of the feast, the day of the crowning ceremony, was bright and clear with what little mist that had hovered above the river soon burnt off by the sun. People were rushing about getting the sleep from their eyes, dressing in their best clothes, and getting to their allocated places.

At midday, Elen was sitting on the dais on the king's left-hand side with her children, with Gruffudd's court officers arrayed on the right of the platform.

The officers of state, guests and observers had taken their positions long before Berddig led Gruffudd out of the hall and onto the dais, inviting him to sit on a cushioned chair.

Berddig addressed the crowd from the front of the dais, explaining the significance of the occasion and taking every opportunity to shower praise on Gruffudd. He explained that Gruffudd's achievements were the greatest of a Welsh ruler for centuries and didn't miss the opportunity to compare him favourably to the great King Arthur.

The battle of Rhyd y Groes was hailed as one of the greatest Welsh victories. His conquest of Deheubarth was described as the most skilful military campaign in history. The fact that there were so many nobles from that fair land at the ceremony was a testimony to his popularity in that region.

The preliminaries and introductions over, they came to the crowning ceremony. Gruffudd stood and Berddig, with the aid of the chief justice, placed a heavy purple mantle over his shoulders. Gruffudd was then directed to sit in his chair and the highly-polished iron ceremonial crown, claimed by Berddig to have been worn by King Arthur, was placed carefully and solemnly on his head and he was handed the ceremonial iron sceptre. After the cheers subsided, guests representing all parts of the kingdom filed past the king, swearing allegiance to him and receiving his blessing.

The ceremony over, the king rose and, lifting his sword, waved it at the audience to even louder cheers. He then descended from the dais and was surrounded by the enthusiastic crowd. Elen, who had kept her eye on Rhys, took the children to their father to congratulate him before she moved away from the centre stage.

The feasting and merriment started immediately, with people queuing for food while the musicians played. The mead flowed into jugs and the smell of the roasting beef wafted across the court, causing all present to salivate and quell their thirst with more of the excellent mead.

Throughout the afternoon Elen was unable to move from her husband's side. He wanted her near him, to hold, to touch and to kiss. She hated it all but knew that by the evening he, like most of the others, would be totally intoxicated. She knew that the next day the hunt in the upper reaches of the River Clwyd would take him away from the court. Elen was hoping that it would indeed be an all-day hunt, and that she and Rhys would have a day together. It was what kept her going.

The festivities continued late into the night and Elen was concerned that Gruffudd would cancel the hunt the following day. But, he was of a strong constitution and the dogs and horses were ready at dawn. The men left as an army of soldiers, in search and pursuit of their quarry, disappearing into their own dust, having left orders for the preparations of food and drink for their return.

Elen watched them go, waving furiously, knowing that Rhys was not with them. She returned to her room and immediately hung some white linen out of her window and Rhys responded immediately.

She told Jane she was going to view the ships in the port and that Jane, once she had finished her chores, should join the other servants at their own celebrations because they had worked so hard the previous day.

Elen, with a basket on her arm, departed for the port. It was deserted. The ships were arrayed along the side of the harbour with the tide lifting them above the level of the bank and their masts reaching high above her. They were at their best as she walked past towards the willow tree. She could see Rhys's boat leaving its moorings and gently floating away from the bank and she hurried her steps.

She boarded his ship smoothly and sat out of sight of anyone who might be walking on the banks of the estuary. She was happy, relaxed and looking forward to a full day with her lover.

Once out of the narrow estuary, she stood next to Rhys as he guided the ship from the gently flowing waters of the river into the soft swell of the bay.

Elen, truly happy, said, "The first time we had a day on your ship like this you left me with a wonderful present, our boy Idwal is now three months old. He is growing fast and I see you in him and it's a wonderful feeling, Rhys."

"I see him looking like you. I look at him and I want, one day, to put my hand on his shoulder and tell him who I really am."

"Oh! I wish that also. Wouldn't it be lovely if we could live together and have him sharing our lives?"

"Yes, I could teach him how to sail and hunt."

"Life is so frustrating."

He could see that she would soon get overwhelmed by the complexities of their life. He put his arm around her, pulling her closer. "Think of the good things. We love each other and we have wonderful times together. Look at us today. Many in court are living together as man and wife but have little or no feelings for each other. Some hate each other."

"Do you mean me and Gruffudd?"

"Not exactly," he remarked lamely.

"What does that mean? I can tell you honestly I hate him. No, I loathe him. I loathe the sight of him. I hate being near him. I even hate you seeing me near him."

"I know," he said soothingly. "It's difficult."

But she continued her rage with, "He is brutal, he forces his will on all around him. His cruelty knows no bounds and his jealousy is unsurpassed in the whole country. He hates everyone, distrusts everyone, and can turn his friends into enemies in an instant. It's their fear of him that keeps the kingdom together."

"It's the times we live in. He has brought peace and prosperity to our land. You've only to look at the ships in the port."

Having vented her spleen, she began to calm and said reluctantly, "I suppose so."

"Did you see his ship?"

"It was the largest there, wasn't it?"

"Yes. But you don't fully appreciate it when it's in port. Its sails are red and they make a very impressive sight when it's cutting through a blue sea with the wind behind it."

"He would have the best, wouldn't he?"

"The swan figurehead is wonderfully carved and painted. It reflects his wealth and the wealth now at Rhuddlan and in this country."

Abruptly her mood changed. "Wasn't it wonderful that you didn't have to go on the hunt with them today?" Then turning to look up at him she added, "Perhaps you would have preferred to have gone hunting?"

He smiled down at her. "I much prefer to go fishing with you. Goodness knows what you will catch."

"I would love to catch another child with you. I'm ready for another please." She laughed at the shocked look on his face.

She was happy and ready to enjoy herself.

They remained at sea until they had to return in time for the tide. She disembarked at the willow tree without difficulty and made her way slowly back to the hall, walking as if on air.

The hunters returned shortly afterwards and boisterously resumed drinking and eating. Elen could bear it better after such a wonderful day, and was quite willing to help the intoxicated Jane with her task of supplying mead and wine to the guests.

The hunt had been a success. Gruffudd was content and relaxed and slumped, like many of the others, asleep in his chair. The third day was a day for relaxing, with many of the guests taken on a journey down the estuary, while others strolled around admiring the royal court, entertained by the musicians and poets.

The guests departed the following day, declaring the feast to have been a wonderful success. Much praise was genuinely given to the king and his royal court, and there was no doubt that his stature had been further enhanced by the event.

CHAPTER 26

July 1049 to October 1050

Elen and Rhys continued their liaison throughout the autumn and winter following the great feast. The weather favoured them some weeks, while during others it was impossible for them to meet for days.

One pleasant and unusually warm evening in late March 1050, with only a few clouds in the sky and the sun about an hour from setting, Berddig arrived at court. The hunters had returned a short while earlier after a successful day and Gruffudd, in good mood, had instructed the servants to arrange some tables outside the hall for them to eat, drink, chat and enjoy the oncoming sunset.

Most of the court's inhabitants had gathered around tables laden with food and drink. The visitors to the port were also there. Therefore English, French, Breton and Irish was spoken as well as Welsh. The king was outside, like the vast majority, and Elen stayed on the outer fringes of the crowd, as did Rhys, both watching everything and waiting for opportunities to exchange smiles.

As she mingled on the outskirts of the crowd, a gap temporarily appeared giving her a clear view of the top table. She saw the king, in high spirits, putting his jug down on the table and indicating that it needed to be refilled, which Elen saw Jane do while Gruffudd turned away to talk to Berddig. Jane moved on to fill Berddig's jug, which was always empty. Then she saw the hand of another servant adding honey to the mead to sweeten it for the king and accommodate his well-known sweet tooth. Then the jug, servant and the table became obscured by people moving across her line of vision.

She moved a step or two and the jug returned to her view, just as one of the visitors from the port lifted it, presumably mistaking it for his jug, and drank from it. Elen could have laughed but restricted herself to a smile, knowing such mistakes happened in a milling crowd when most were inebriated to some degree or other. She knew that Gruffudd would be furious that his jug had been drunk from and, unless he was in a particularly good and jovial mood, there could well be a rage.

She moved around the fringe of the crowd and, as was her usual practice, she kept out of the way of some, but conducted polite conversation with her acquaintances. She kept an eye out for Rhys.

Then, suddenly, there was a noisy commotion at the centre of the gathering, with people moving away from the area. As the crowd scattered, Elen could see the king in the middle looking downwards, open-mouthed, at the ground where she could see a man lying writhing in agony and frothing at the mouth.

Elen stepped towards the man on the ground, amazed that no one was trying to help him. However, it was not long before the man's movements subsided and it became clear that he had died.

Initially, there was a stunned silence but then every one had questions. "Who is he?" "What's his name?" "Where's he from?" There were few answers, except that he was from one of the ships. Others around were supplying answers to unasked questions. "He's died of a fit," was murmured around. "Seen it before, poor man."

The king, shocked, was in need of more drink and was asking, "Where's my drink?"

"He drank it," someone said.

"Where's my jug?" the king demanded and Berddig pointed it out to him on the table.

As a couple of male servants were about to pick up the body, a man came forward, studied the corpse and said, "That man has died of hemlock poisoning. I've seen it before."

The king stared at him incredulously and the man added quickly, "I mean, I've seen animals die of hemlock poisoning."

The king picked up his jug, peered into it and exclaimed, "It's not empty."

He looked up again, then back into the jug and said, "Someone has tried to poison me."

"Try it on one of the dogs," said the hemlock expert.

The king, followed by some close advisers, took the jug to one of the least popular hunting dogs and gave it to the dog to drink. The animal lapped up the remains of the drink quickly, with a number of people watching it. The dog was fine and the onlookers laughed as the dog wanted more and went sniffing at the empty jug in the king's hand.

The crowd started to disperse in good humor, but Gruffudd, naturally suspicious, stayed and it wasn't long before the dog appeared to be unsteady on its legs and collapsed, frothing at the mouth. Those around the dying dog were silent, shocked and dismayed, knowing the consequences.

Some were announcing loudly, "I wasn't anywhere near the jug."

"Nor I."

"I've only just arrived."

"I was over there."

"I wasn't near the top table."

They were all distancing themselves from the poisoned jug. They all sensed danger and guessed an attempt had been made to poison the king. Elen was sure that she had seen the hand of the assassin but unfortunately not his or her face.

The king immediately took control and called his trusted family guard together. Jane was questioned, but many had seen her filling other jugs and those drinkers had not suffered any adverse effects. Elen didn't reveal what she had seen and it seemed that no one else present had noticed anything either or perhaps they believed it was safer to keep their thoughts to themselves. It was a mystery, but Gruffudd had some of those present arrested that evening, mainly those whom he disliked or distrusted.

During the inquisition Elen found Rhys, who looked apprehensive when she told him quickly and quietly that she had seen a hand pouring what she had thought was extra honey into the jug. That she had not seen the person's face brought a smile to his face and he asked, "Are you sure that it wasn't you?"

Elen wasn't immediately amused but managed a smile before asking him, "Was it you?"

A day later, when they had more time together, they discussed who was behind the attempt on the king's life. Gruffudd had so many enemies: the English king, members of the ancient Welsh royal family or just one of the many individuals who had a personal grievance against him. They agreed that she shouldn't say anything to anyone about what she had seen. He would do the same, it was best for them to show ignorance. It took the court a few weeks to realize that the people involved in trying to poison Gruffudd had been dealt with in a decisive manner and fed to the fish, the eels, the vermin and the birds in the estuary.

Elen felt guilty for wishing that the attempt on the king's life had been successful. Rhys, however, had made it clear to her that he had no guilty feeling for wishing it had succeeded.

In the autumn of 1050, Elen, constantly on the alert, became anxious that the king appeared to be more jealous than usual of her movements and the attention given to her by others. He couldn't take his eyes off her, even if she was talking to another woman. He was watching and would attempt to listen to what was being said, as though he thought the other woman was part of some intrigue.

If she spoke to a man then he would enter the conversation. A prerogative of a king anyway, but she felt sure that he was more suspicious than usual. She spoke to Rhys about it but he hadn't experienced any difference in the king's attitude.

Her female intuition however, strongly suggested to her that there was something different. She felt sure someone had seen something and told Gruffudd.

Then, one day as she walked out of the hall, she came face to face with Peter, the tall, thin man whom she was convinced had been giving her knowing looks. He was talking to Gruffudd, who had his back to her.

The man saw her instantly and smiled at her in a most condescending manner which froze her soul and mind. But it was only for the briefest of instances before he had turned back to face the king. She felt sure that they had been talking about her and the smile was a signal to her husband that she had appeared from the hall.

She could not find it in her heart to smile back at him and struggled to pretend that she was not intimidated by him. She put her head down and turned sharply to the left to avoid the two. She knew it was a mistake because it made her appear guilty.

She didn't look back, she dared not. She feared for herself and Rhys, wondering what they were talking about. Why would a good for nothing from the port be talking to her husband? What on earth would they have to talk about?

Shaken by the experience she wished to talk to Rhys about it as soon as possible, but not immediately as it was too risky. She stood outside the court's gates and looked down over the low roofs towards the sea. As always, when she saw the port, she wished she could sail away with Rhys to Ireland – or anywhere away from Gruffudd – where they would be safe to live together happily.

She thought of her actions minutes earlier, knowing they weren't the wisest. She should have spoken to the two instead of walking past them without saying anything.

She stayed there looking down on the quay for a while and, though tempted to search out Rhys, she decided not to do so in case she was being watched. Eventually, she trekked back to the hall. Peter had gone and there was no sign of the king, so she entered the hall where she found him talking to Jane.

As soon as she appeared Jane turned to her and said, "I've explained to the king that you sometimes air your bedding by putting them in the window. I've said you've always done that."

Jane was clearly distressed about something and Gruffudd was looking suspiciously at them both. Elen went closer and could see that there was a tense atmosphere and, having learnt from her experience half an hour earlier, she asked confidently, "What's the problem? I've always put them out to air. Lots of people do it in the south and I'm told it's very common in France. If the husbands come home smelling of the farmyard then by morning there is a need to aerate the bed clothes."

Jane butted in with, "Yes, many people do it when it's necessary."

Gruffly he said, "I did not know it was done here."

"Frequently," said Elen.

"It was reported to me earlier that sheets are put in the hall windows and the person who reported it was concerned that it was some signal to warships planning to attack the port."

"Are there enemy ships in the estuary?" asked Elen.

"There could be some there and the sheets could let them know when it was safe to attack."

"I won't do it again, but you may have to make do with more smelly bed clothes," Elen replied with growing confidence.

He grunted his consent and Elen led the way out with Jane following her meekly, "Thank you my lady. I was afraid that you would say it was me."

Elen smiled at her, "Don't worry. It's someone wishing to cause you trouble. We'll find out who it is and I won't put them there again."

Jane was grateful and repeated her thanks.

Elen decided to slip out of the court and went directly to the port as fast as it was reasonable to go. She had to warn Rhys as soon as possible. She guessed exactly what had happened. Peter had reported the sheets to the king. But the question in her mind was what else had he told him?

As fate would have it, Rhys was relaxing watching a ship being loaded and prepared for a voyage. He looked contented and happy as she approached him. He was looking towards the river when she surprised him with a hello.

He spun round, recognising her voice instantly, and was delighted to see her. He glanced up at the hall window and saw there was no signal.

"Hello," he said.

"That man, the thin, tall one, you say his name is Peter. He has told Gruffudd that he thinks the bedding I put in the window is a signal to his enemies. Thankfully, he thinks he has enemies everywhere and swallowed the idea, but challenged me and Jane about it. I've told him that I aerate the bedclothes but he does not want me to do it again. I've told him he will have to sleep in his own smells."

Rhys was shocked, yet relieved.

"I saw that Peter talking to him minutes earlier and I'm

sure it was he that reported it. It's going to make it difficult for us to meet isn't it," she said, despairingly, and he could sense her voice breaking.

"Don't worry, we'll arrange the next meeting before we separate each time. Let's meet tomorrow evening by the oak tree."

"I will try my best, but I may not be able to and I won't be able to let you know."

"Don't worry, I'll understand. I love you."

"I'd better go back. I don't want to be seen here now."

"Don't worry about that Peter. He's currying favour with Gruffudd, that's all. We'll be careful," he said as they mimicked a kiss to each other and parted.

They did meet the next day under the oak tree but she had been unsettled and was worried by Peter's involvement and Gruffudd's demands.

"I don't know what to do," she said to Rhys. "I feel that our time together is limited. Gruffudd will catch us and have us executed or murdered, as he did with Madog."

Rhys listened to her quietly.

"I'm desperate to get away from his domineering personality. I find it difficult to breathe without thinking and worrying about what does he know and when will he know everything. What shall we do, Rhys?"

"I feel the same as you do. Short of you killing him in his sleep or me somehow plunging my sword in him when he least expects, I don't know what to do."

Elen looked thoughtfully and then said, "It would be possible for me to wait until he has drunk well and fallen fast asleep, then take his dagger..." her voice tailed off and, shaking her head, she said quietly, "No, I could never plunge a dagger into anyone. First, I'm not made like that and secondly,

I couldn't murder anyone, not even Gruffudd. I can't possibly kill him in his sleep."

He put his arm around her and whispered in her ear, "I know, I know that's why I love you so much. You are such a kind person."

She was weeping and said, "I'm a weak person, you mean."

"If you were to kill him in his sleep, you would be found guilty by the court and executed immediately. I would see much less of you then."

She smiled at him and they kissed.

"We have to bide our time. Murdering him could only make things much worse for us. I can't bear to think about it. We would be caught and the courts wouldn't thank us. He's popular and he has improved people's lives. He is power mad but people benefit from it and they appreciate it. He carries them with him."

"But he has many enemies doesn't he. Surely, someone will want to take revenge on him."

"He has many people who envy him and hate him for what he has done to their fathers, sons and brothers, just because they vaguely threatened his power. But these people also know that he is watching them for any false move and pounces on them when he sees the slightest disloyalty. He disarms his enemies before they become a real threat to him. He's very cunning and powerful."

"There's no easy way for us, is there?"

He shook his head and said no.

It was a life-changing moment for her. There was the threat she felt from Peter and then the realisation she couldn't take matters into her own hands.

CHAPTER 27

October 1050 to March 1051

S HE KNEW THE writing was on the wall for her and Rhys if she took no action but unknown to her, events were moving faster than she expected.

Rhys arranged to meet her under their oak tree not long after the ban on displaying white sheets. Still raw from her recent experience, she walked nervously along the riverside, ambling along as was her way. She knew that Rhys, following their usual pattern, would have ridden eastwards from Rhuddlan and circled back in a south-westerly direction to their oak tree.

The rain had stopped and the sky had cleared, but the river was in full flood and there was an exceptionally high tide expected that afternoon. Before turning off the track towards their oak tree she always ensured that there was no one on the track ahead of her or anyone behind her. She followed the same routine on this occasion.

The track was clear both ways when she turned off it and made her way towards the oak tree. Rhys was there waiting for her and his horse was grazing quietly nearby. She always preferred it when he was there before her.

They embraced and kissed. He had laid down a leather blanket for them to lie on and she was taking food out of her basket when the horse showed some slight signs of agitation.

It was enough to cause them to look at each other. Rhys shrugged his shoulders and said, "It's probably someone passing on the track. Ignore it."

They continued with their preparation and sat next to each

other on the blanket. Rhys poured each a jug of ale. They were happy and relaxed in that peaceful place, but the silence was broken abruptly when the horse neighed loudly and looked agitatedly in the direction of the river. They both stood up instantly, alarmed. Rhys, taller than her, had a better view and whispered, "Someone may have followed you. I think I saw a head above the bushes near the path from the river."

"Who is it?" she whispered with concern.

"I don't know."

"It's him, it's that Peter," she whispered in panic, covering her face with her hands.

"Well, it could be."

"What shall we do?" She was frightened.

Rhys had drawn his sword. "No, don't," she whispered. "Let me face him. Perhaps he doesn't know you are here. I'll walk towards him with my basket on my arm as usual and you come behind me, but don't let him see you. If he attacks me, you'll come and save me, won't you?"

He was unsure since whoever it was had also heard his horse neigh, but he could appreciate the sense in her suggestion and didn't argue, "Of course, but be careful."

Elen casually walked towards the river, uncertain in her mind what she would do. But, with every step she took her natural courage, borne out of years of unhappiness, returned and she became determined to find her stalker, confront him, ask him what he was doing there and threaten that she would tell Gruffudd that he had been following her. Whoever it was would be aware of the consequences and the best thing would be to disappear before being strung up by the king. She was confident that whoever it was would be aware that it was not an empty threat.

She took her time, building up her courage, and when she was about halfway to the riverside track she had a glance of her stalker moving quickly through the low bushes, away from her and towards the river. Even in that brief instant she could see he was a tall, thin man even though he was crouched as low as he could. She saw enough to recognise her stalker as the vile Peter.

She bravely continued towards the riverside track but could not see him anywhere and was disappointed as she had prepared her mind to tackle him.

There was nowhere for him to hide near the track, so he would have to come out into the open and walk on the track. This was the crucial moment, but she couldn't see him.

She reached the track but there was no sign of him. Standing on the track she was about ten yards from the swollen river with its reed covered bank. The usually muddy, steep and slippery riverside was covered by the fast-flowing, dark and cold-looking water.

She was baffled by his disappearance. The track both ways was clear. She was certain that he had not gone into the brush either side of her path to the oak tree. He had to be hiding in the dead sedge and reeds along the banks of the river. He had to be there straight ahead of her somewhere in the thick and faded vegetation. About five yards up river there was a dip in the track where at one time a small stream had crossed it. She realised that he must have slithered in that dip across the track.

Courageously, but aware of the consequence of letting the opportunity pass without confronting Peter, she took a step towards the riverbank, singing gently so as to alert him that she was approaching and giving him a chance to come out and face her.

Taking another step forward, edging towards the river, she could feel her feet sinking into the cold water and soft sedge. She knew she couldn't go much further but, staring into the dead vegetation, she saw a dark form sliding away from her towards the edge of the bank. Suddenly, there was the noise of the sedge separating, and the dark object slid away from her, quickly disappearing over the edge and into the river. She gasped, partly from relief, but the sound she made didn't quite mask another gasp of despair from the river.

She stood there unsure what to do and eventually shouted at the disappeared dark form, "There, serves you right, but I will tell the king you've made passes at me for months."

She waited for an answer but there was no response. All she could hear was the gentle, soothing sound of the river flowing and the slight sound of the water splashing against the withered sedge.

She turned around. The track was clear in both directions and she went back to where Rhys was hiding and told him, "He's gone into the river. I shouted my threat after him. He must have heard but I think he's drowned."

"Good. If he is in that river he'll die of cold soon anyway. You were very brave."

"What shall we do now?"

"Go back quickly, as if nothing has happened. I will cross the river upstream and go down to the port and see if I can see any sign of him from the other side."

"What do I tell Gruffudd?"

"I don't think you need to say anything."

"How will I know if you see him in the river?"

"Come down to the port this evening and we can talk about it. Go now."

"Love you."

"Love you." They parted blowing kisses at each other.

Elen returned to the hall. She was anxious and nervous. Gruffudd was talking to his ship designer and greeted her warmly. It pleased her and gave her confidence to tell him that she had enjoyed a walk by the river and that their children were well.

She busied herself in her room for a while and then left the hall again to go down to the port. Rhys was waiting for her. They met casually near Gruffudd's own royal ship, pretending to admire it.

Rhys, while pointing to the figurehead of the ship, in a low voice told her, "I didn't see Peter, neither in the river nor on the bank anywhere. The bank is so steep and slippery he would have had difficulty climbing out."

"What shall we do?"

"There is no more we can do. Go back to the hall and act normally. If Peter goes there, accuse him of making passes at you. Gruffudd will believe you."

"I hope so."

"I will go a little distance from you. Have a good look at the ships here before you go back. Love you."

She looked at him lovingly as he left. She was anxious, but allowed him to leave her by the ship.

She looked at the river wistfully, wishing as always that she and her lover could be whisked away by the tide to be together somewhere far away from Rhuddlan. The sea was ebbing quickly and the ropes holding the ships to the quay beginning to sag into the water. She didn't wish anyone to think that she had just gone to the port to meet Rhys. So she stayed by the ship for a while and leant over to look casually at the tide flowing through the ropes and between the side of the ship and the quayside. Suddenly she was shocked enough to scream out loud when she realised she was looking down on a white body wedged between the quayside, the ship and the ropes.

She jumped backwards. Rhys came running to her aid. "There's a body in the river there," she shrieked pointing to the spot. "I think it's that Peter."

Rhys stepped to the quayside, looked down and returned to

her saying, "It's the body of a hunting dog; a dog went missing about a fortnight ago."

He shouted for some help and went for a rope ladder. It was not long before they had the dog's body lifted out of the river and placed on the quayside in a pool of water.

Elen left for the hall accompanied by one of the many women who had gathered to see what the commotion was about.

She met Gruffudd as she was approaching the hall and told him that a dog had been found drowned in the port. He could not have been less interested.

Though she was worried about the consequence of Peter's drowning, nothing further happened. She, however, woke many a night seeing the drowned dog wedged there between the quayside and the ship and wondered what had happened to Peter's body.

However, about a fortnight later, a body was seen floating on the outward tide in the estuary. The ship which reported seeing the body had not stopped to retrieve it as the tides were treacherous near the mouth of the river. But it was described as that of a large middle aged man whose body had already begun to decompose and had partly been eaten by rats.

No one had reported Peter missing. His life was one of comings and goings anyway. So the only people to associate the body with Peter were Elen and Rhys. Few questions were asked; no one was interested. It seemed that no husband was lost, no father disappeared, so no one cared. It could well have been the king disposing of someone who had threaten his position, fancied his wife, or simply annoyed him.

Elen suggested to Gruffudd that it was probably a suicide. He repeated it to those in the hall and the suicide story stuck, not least because the king was saying it.

Elen remained deeply worried during the following weeks, knowing that by his very nature her husband distrusted everyone, including her. She wondered what she could do to lessen his suspicions. It was while she sat in her own room by herself that a solution, borne out of extreme anxiety, dawned on her. She would attempt to deceive him by giving herself to him more enthusiastically and get him to believe that, at last, she was falling in love with him. She believed that this would help to save Rhys's life and was therefore a sacrifice worth making.

She was not totally convinced that Peter's death had removed their Sword of Damocles because she believed that Peter might have confided to a friend or a relative what information he had about Rhys and her. So gaining Gruffudd's confidence had to be a priority for her.

Even if fate had been kind to her and her lover in removing Peter she knew the risks they were taking. Gradually, over a period of many months, she worked to convince Gruffudd that first, she had grown to like him and later, over even a longer period of time, worked on making him believe that she was beginning to fall in love with him. So, by appearance, except in Rhys's presence, she was seen to be very kind and considerate towards Gruffudd and, out of desperation, she managed to convince the king that he was conquering her spirit and that she was almost fully his, heart and soul.

This gigantic effort by her did in time gain greater freedom for her and reduced her feeling of being constantly watched by Gruffudd. His jealousy of any admirer of hers declined and he came to accept that some men might look at her wistfully.

Her change of attitude towards the king didn't in any shape or form diminish her love for Rhys. She still desired, indeed hankered for his company, his contact, his hands on her, his kisses, his unstinting love constantly. Her own happiness only he could ensure. Their child she loved most of all – the result of her true love for the father – however guilty deep in her soul it made her feel.

As time passed, observers of the royal family were sure that Elen was now in love with Gruffudd and that there was a greater understanding and even affection between them. They were, of course, unaware that fear of the king's wrath had driven Elen to this position.

The months passed as did the years, with the king and his wife seemingly at ease together, but all that time Elen yearned for Rhys and release from her ties to Gruffudd.

CHAPTER 28

May 1052

IN THE SPRING of 1052, Berddig arrived unexpectedly at the royal court with urgent news for the king; the Vikings and Irish were planning a large raid on Deheubarth again.

Within days, Gruffudd had raised a large army to counter the attack and departed from Rhuddlan hurriedly to resist the impending threat. Such was his haste that much of the supplies were left behind, with orders given that they were to follow them south as soon as they were ready.

Elen was overjoyed at being left behind with Rhys, knowing that they would have greater freedom to be together, to meet, to sail in his boat, and to do the things she dreamt of doing.

Berddig had departed ahead of the main army and things were quiet at the court, which suited her. However, the day after the army left, Rhuddlan was struck by a thunderous storm, great winds rose quickly, lifting the sea into mountainous waves and bending the trees over to touch the land. The powerful wind drove torrential rain horizontally into everything that stood in its way, be it great halls, houses, huts or ships. Gusts of wind uprooted trees in its path around the court at Rhuddlan and sent the sea up the estuary threatening the gates of the court. Ships were violently shaken and the less secure dislodged from their moorings.

They knew the storm must have struck the army as it was crossing the Cambrian Mountains. The rivers would be flooded, the marshland wet and muddy, progress would then be slow, difficult and dangerous. The families at the court were worried and concerned about the wellbeing of their menfolk. No ships sailed, so supplies were stuck in the port.

The storm passed, the sea calmed and a ship arrived from Anglesey. Then, a day later, another arrived from a port on the west coast where it had sheltered from the storm. The captain saw Rhys and told him and all who wished to hear what he had seen.

He described how the storm had risen without warning from the south-west. It had blown all day and night, lifting the sea into enormous heights. He had never witnessed such high waves before and he'd been a sailor for twenty years. None of this was news to those at the royal court, as they had witnessed it themselves out in the estuary. Eventually, he came to the main point; he had heard that the west coast was littered with wrecked ships of a large fleet that had sailed from Ireland into the teeth of the storm. He claimed that experienced sailors and Vikings from Ireland, taken by surprise by the ferocity of the storm, were drowned and their bodies hurled against the coastal rocks.

Elen, Rhys and the others immediately realised the significance of this news. It meant that the threat from Dublin had been wrecked on the rocks and beaches of the west and south-west coastline.

The following day a messenger arrived at court with news direct from the king describing how the storm had caught them crossing the mountains. It had wreaked havoc with the few supply wagons they had taken with them. More significantly, he told them that Gruffudd, who had been expecting news of the invasion in the south-west, was overjoyed to be told that the attacking fleet had floundered and that broken ships and bodies were being washed ashore along the coastline. The news was greeted with jubilation at the court.

People were still in the process of clearing after the storm, but it didn't stop everyone raising their jugs, full of good ale that evening, to the timely storm.

Three days later Berddig walked into court, beaming from ear to ear shouting, "What a success! What an excellent storm! The king is delighted and is conducting a tour of his Deheubarth lands, calling at the important courts on his way."

There were cheers and calls of, "When are they coming back?"

Unusually for him, Berddig was a little elusive in his answer and suggested that the king was disappointed that he hadn't had the opportunity to display his military skills. He hinted that the same sentiments were felt by the men in his army who, after weathering the storm, wanted loot to take home.

Then, putting a finger to his mouth and speaking quietly he whispered, "The truth is Gruffudd has thought long and hard on the disappointment of his men, and with Gwynedd, Powys and Deheubarth now firmly in his grip, he has decide to attack eastwards so as not to disappoint his soldiers."

The questions came thick and fast, "When? Where? How?"

The poet continued, still in a low voice, signifying the secrecy of what he was saying to his attentive audience, "After all, the army was ready, willing and indeed enthusiastic for battle. It is known there are rich pickings in the south-east."

"Can you tell us when he'll attack?"

"Well." He paused and then in very low voice, "They crossed into Morgannwg two days ago," and he laughed.

There were gasps of surprise around the great hall and the questions came again, "Is it a rich area?"

"Very rich indeed," he announced. "I should know, I left there the day before the king crossed the border. Then further east again towards Hereford, there's gold there like you've never seen. I visited a friend in Leominster a short while ago and I can tell you the land is fertile and the people are wealthy beyond your imagination."

"Will we see any of it?" asked a listener.

"It's quite possible. If it depends on the skill of our king, we will in abundance. What you must remember is that much of the land to the east of Morgannwg and Cantref Mawr belonged to us a long time ago and we were able to reap the products of its rich soil. I would think that Gruffudd may wish to reclaim the area and benefit from that fertile land."

That evening he raised interest, expectation and support for an attack on the south-east. In fact, that attack was already in progress.

Berddig departed two days later for Powys, on the very morning Gruffudd was leading his men across Offa's Dyke and through the countryside to the north of Hereford. In the afternoon Gruffudd was met by a large force of English and early Norman settlers in the area. He was not to be stopped, his tail was up and he and his men charged at the enemy.

At the first impact the defending forces buckled in the middle. As Gruffudd's men surged forward, the enemy's troops turned on their heels and bolted the battlefield. The king's men followed them, showing no mercy as they carved their way into the fleeing soldiers, slaughtering and maiming hundreds.

It was a devastating defeat for the defending army, thirteen years to the day since Gruffudd's renowned victory at Rhyd y Groes in Powys.

Local towns and villages were burnt but not before they had yielded their stored crops, cattle, fabrics and precious metals. The pillaging and ravaging of the countryside to the north and west of Hereford and southern Shropshire continued for days.

When Gruffudd's army eventually returned home, they

were laden with plunder. The journey to Rhuddlan had taken longer than usual because of the weight of the booty they carried and the cider they were still drinking.

The victorious soldiers, led by their king, displayed their trophies as they arrived at the royal court. There were carts loaded with implements and goods, followed by fine-looking horses and a large herd of well-fed cattle.

Berddig was with the returning soldiers and in the evening related stories of past battles to the intoxicated gathering. He varied them enough to keep their interest and extended them to include the battle of north Herefordshire and bestow great glory on his king.

Elen could not stomach the story, particularly the part relating to the battle in her own land and left the hall for the duration. Rhys, of course, noticed her absence and wished he could have accompanied her.

CHAPTER 29

January 1053 to December 1055

FOLLOWING THIS SUCCESSFUL invasion of England in the summer of 1052, Gruffudd's ambition to conquer southeast Wales developed and, encouraged by others, he set his mind to plan a campaign to bring the whole of Wales as one kingdom under his rule.

Elen continued her alliance with Rhys and noticed that Gruffudd's obsession with her was declining. He often left her to enjoy her own life without his overbearing presence. As her pretence at loving him took hold, his belief that he had indeed conquered her heart, diminished his possessive desire for her. Some, who noticed the change, speculated that the cause was that her beauty, as she approached her thirtieth birthday, was fading. Though, they also conceded that she was still a startlingly beautiful woman, outshining all others at the court.

Elen still feared her king. She had to be on her guard permanently and she had to be sure that nothing untoward was observed.

One cold, icy day in January 1053, she was in an anxious state. Afraid of slipping on the ice on her way back from visiting Rhys by the oak tree, she held herself tight. In order to avoid being seen returning directly to the court, she strolled towards the port, where she noticed a man leaping off one of the ships, crossing her path about fifty yards ahead of her, and disappearing behind a house opposite.

In itself there was nothing very unusual in what she saw, but it sent a shiver through her body. He was a thin, tall man, with long arms and long strides. He had reminded her of a wolf running for cover and, of course, she had immediately thought of Peter. When she realised the cause of her alarm she calmed and was relieved to remember that he was dead. The man had simply reminded her of Peter's long gait and leap when leaving the willow tree years earlier.

She was so shaken by the memory of Peter that she decided to hang around the port, to enjoy looking at various vessels being loaded and unloaded and the general hustle and bustle of the area. She hoped Rhys would return so she could just mention it to him.

He did indeed return on his horse within a short while and was able, with a smile of reassurance, to say that it was her state of anxiety which had tricked her into thinking that she might have seen Peter. The two of them were close and understood each other well.

Elen's love for Rhys was equally balanced by her loathing of Gruffudd, which was no less than the moment he raised her onto his stallion at Pencader. She would never forgive Gruffudd for throwing Hywel's head at her feet. There were still times in the depth of the night when she wished she had the courage to get out of his bed, take his dagger from his belt, stab him through his heart and calmly go to Rhys to tell him what she had done.

Her overtly servile attitude was purely to ease her own life and to facilitate her continued liaison with Rhys. She despised herself for displaying what she regarded as her sycophantic attitude to him for the sake of achieving some degree of freedom. She found her own compliant mode disgusting and was annoyed when he took her for granted, as if he was now bored with her. And all because she had managed to make him believe she loved him.

Gruffudd, still boosted by his successes in north

Herefordshire in blooding the Saxons and in returning pride to a previously cowed nation, achieved great popularity with his own people.

He was no fool and knew that the Saxons would retaliate sooner or later. He also knew that if he was to establish himself as a king over the whole of Wales, he would have to conquer Morgannwg and Gwent and, at the same time, give the Saxons such a thrashing that they would leave him alone to establish his power over the whole country.

His ambition, often encouraged by Berddig, was clear and simple. He involved the entertainer in his plan, tapping into his extensive knowledge of the country and areas beyond its boundaries.

The year 1054 saw Gruffudd working hard building a powerful mobile army. He was away often at distant courts for long periods, giving Elen and Rhys more time together. Gruffudd knew that beating the Saxons would not be easy and it would be necessary to acquire allies for the battles ahead.

His nearest Saxon neighbour was Leofric, Earl of Mercia, the husband of Lady Godiva, who was powerful but not as ambitious as his son, Ælfgar. He was very outspoken and in 1055 said things he shouldn't have and in so doing committed treason against King Edward of England and was exiled to Ireland in March of that year.

Gruffudd saw an opportunity, knowing that Ælfgar, who was likely to succeed his ageing father as Earl of Mercia, would be disgruntled. Gruffudd sent an envoy to Ireland to arrange a deal with him and, after some skilful negotiations, an alliance was formed between Gruffudd and Ælfgar to attack Herefordshire.

Gruffudd had planned carefully. He knew that he had to gain control of Morgannwg first, an area controlled by one of his old adversaries from Deheubarth, Gruffudd ap Rhydderch, before he could move to Gwent.

By June 1055, Ælfgar had gathered a fleet of eighteen ships in Ireland and Gruffudd had amassed an army of over two thousand men. He'd combined his trusted warriors of Gwynedd, Powys and Deheubarth into a formidable array of soldiers, cavalry and archers for the campaign. He marched this sizeable force towards Brecon.

Elen was with him this time, as if he knew this would be a long campaign and he wanted his woman with him. He now trusted her, knew she was no fool and valued her company, even if he was not quite as besotted with her as he had been. She, in turn, had no wish whatsoever to be on the warpath. She didn't wish to trail behind him into battle, hoping for a miracle that would release her from her long-lasting bondage to him.

She had wasted all her arguments on him to try to convince him to let her stay at Rhuddlan, but it was to no avail. Her desire to stay was made even more desperate when it became clear that Rhys was to remain at Rhuddlan.

Gruffudd was adamant. Having developed her obsequious role with him for her own purpose, she was hoist by her own petard and with him she had to go.

She and Rhys's last meeting was on his boat and, when the time came for him to help her out of it, she wept. He reassured her that she would be back soon and with some luck she might return a free woman.

Understandably, a gloomy mood hung over her as she travelled south with the soldiers. It was June, but for her it was like dreary November, with her spirits low.

With the object of destroying Gruffudd ap Rhydderch's rule in Morgannwg and Gwent, the king and the earl planned a pincer attack. Gruffudd's forces would travel through the rugged terrain of mid-Wales towards the northern boundaries of Morgannwg, while his Saxon ally's ships entered the mouth of the Wye in the Bristol Channel.

In the battle that followed, Gruffudd ap Rhydderch was decisively beaten and killed. Gruffudd ap Llywelyn gained supremacy over the lands of Morgannwg and Gwent, giving him kingship over all Wales as a result.

With the king travelling around his newly-acquired lands imposing his rule, Elen was transported from place to place with nothing to look forward to. There was no Rhys, no oak tree, no boat, not even a glance at her lover, not even a wink from a sparkling eye, nothing to raise her spirits. Whenever a messenger arrived from Rhuddlan, Elen would approach him with some excuse or other to tease out any news of Rhys. But, it was rare that she heard anything about him and was fearful of asking directly.

Eventually, Gruffudd established his base on the south bank of the Wye at Llyswen, giving him easy access to Morgannwg, Gwent and Hereford.

One dusty afternoon in August, while Gruffudd was in Morgannwg with a band of soldiers strengthening his rule in the area, a group of about fifty riders arrived from the north at the Llyswen base. They were expected because Gruffudd had requested fresh cavalry from Gwynedd.

Many went to welcome them with food and drink, and Elen followed. She was rather hoping that one of the riders was Rhys, and examined each horse carefully to see if she recognised his, but didn't. In case he was on a different horse, she then looked carefully into each face and had to move around a little to ensure that she had a good look at each one, but no, he wasn't there.

She turned away disappointed, stepping slowly from the group, when suddenly she could feel anxiety surging into her veins. There was one she had definitely seen at Rhuddlan but as she tried to think who it was, it came to her – it was Peter. She stopped looking. She didn't wish to see him. Then she remembered that he had drowned. She searched again for the one who looked like him, but by then they had been told that the king had gone south and so, to make the most of the daylight left, the riders were encouraged by their leaders to depart immediately.

Elen desperately tried to look at the riders' faces but unfortunately by then many had turned their backs to her, with some already riding away from her. She tried her utmost to see all the faces but barely managed a half. However, the more she thought about it, the more she realised that her imagination had taken over from her rational thoughts in her desperate need to see Rhys.

She was unsettled by it all and wished she had Rhys to talk to.

Shortly after this visitation and the securing of the conquest of Morgannwg and Gwent, and very late in the military campaigning season, Gruffudd moved his army towards Hereford, in support of his ally Ælfgar and the Viking fleet which had sailed up the River Wye.

On 24 October 1055, when Gruffudd and his soldiers were about two miles from the outer defences of Hereford, the city commanders sent out a powerful well-armed force to meet them. Gruffudd arranged his troops into compact fighting blocks, with cavalry on either side. He could depend on the quality and discipline of his own men and he kept the Vikings in reserve on the river.

Elen was at the rear of the advancing column as they approached Hereford. When the city came to sight, the accompanying carts, including hers, were directed to a low hill nearby from where they could view the two armies closing in on each other in the fields outside the city walls.

Gruffudd led the charge at the defenders, hitting them with such force and determination that he dispersed the front ranks and turned the others to face the city walls. Gruffudd had again displayed his military skills and the Saxons were beaten decisively. Accepting the surrender of his foe was never on Gruffudd's mind and the Saxon soldiers were chased into the city by the Welsh soldiers, followed by the Vikings, who were renowned for their brutality.

The city was entered and pillaged, with many of the city's clergy killed. Gruffudd himself was no great respecter of the religious or of their dwellings. Neither were the Vikings from the fleet, and the cathedral was pillaged and burnt.

The defeat was a devastating blow for the Saxons of Herefordshire. King Edward the Confessor sent his wife's brother, Harold Godwinson, to gather an army from the whole of England to recapture the city. When he arrived the victors had left with their trophies and loot of all kinds but he pursued the Welsh army into the hills as far as the Dore valley and he set up his camp at Ewyas in the early winter.

Harold, recognising the strength of the combined power of the Viking fleet and Gruffudd's well-proven military skills and disciplined soldiers, decided not to do battle. In December he signed a peace treaty on the banks of the Wye, south-west of Hereford.

As part of the new treaty, Ælfgar's earldom was returned to him. The Vikings sailed to Chester, where they were paid, and land taken by the Saxons in previous centuries on the Hereford border was returned to the Welsh king.

CHAPTER 30

16 June 1056

FOLLOWING THE PEACE agreement, Gruffudd, realising that the Saxons would wish to regain the ground they had lost, decided to retain essential elements of his army in the Talgarth area between the rivers Wye and Usk. He, his core supporters, and close family spent the winter months moving between the numerous courts in his newly-acquired territory. Sections of his army were billeted in the rich valleys of the rivers Llynfi, Usk and Wye and around the lake at Llangorse.

However, there wasn't an immediate response from the Saxons. Gruffudd knew that his presence in the area deterred an attack. But he also knew that too much land had been gained by the Welsh in the peace accord to be stomached by his enemies for long.

Elen spent a sad Christmas and January away from Rhys. She lived with Gruffudd at the various courts, never moving far from the border and ensuring that the land to the east of Offa's Duke was watched day and night. They stayed at Llyswen, Bronllys, Talgarth, Llangorse and the mountains beyond including the valleys of Morgannwg and Gwent. The king dealt with disputes and crimes, but they never stayed anywhere longer than was necessary.

Elen was bored and pined for her Rhys. She missed him and wished she was with him at Rhuddlan. During the winter months she heard nothing of him but guessed that he was well, otherwise she would probably have heard.

Though she knew her children were well and safe at

Rhuddlan with their minders, she naturally wanted to see them.

In late March 1056, they were at the court in Llyswen, perched above the Wye with its superb view down the wide valley towards Glasbury and the border. Feeling particularly low one day, she asked Gruffudd, "Can I return to Rhuddlan now, so that I can see my children. I know you say they are well but they will want to see their mother and I want to see them. They must be missing me. I have not seen them since we left last year. It's getting on for a year."

"I need you here with me," he replied, becoming agitated.

She knew she would have to be careful not to press her point too hard. "I am of no use to you here. You are busy with your newly-acquired land but I have nothing to do here."

"You have nothing to do in Rhuddlan either. I don't see it makes any difference whether you are here or at Rhuddlan."

"But I miss my children Gruffudd," she looked at him appealingly, utilising all her acquired false charm on him.

"Come on, let me go back," she appealed. "You will be back yourself in a month or two, and it will be nice to make up for the time we have missed. We will be even better together. I will have missed you for two months. I will be waiting for you, my love."

Gruffudd wasn't moved by her words; for him it merely confirmed the fact that she now loved him.

His face was expressionless as she looked into his eyes and reached up with her lips to kiss him, hoping to soften his hard heart to let her go.

He received her kiss with a slight smile. She followed up with, "If I could leave today, I would be in Rhuddlan in three days, stay a week and be back here before you would miss me."

He looked into her eyes and she felt she was winning and said, "I could not be away from you for more than that, I would miss you too much Gruffudd."

But her hold on him had weakened. "Berddig is expected here today. He will want to see you and he may have news for us about what's happening over the border."

Sensing that Berddig would be a distraction to her ambition to return to Rhuddlan, she caused her lips to quiver appealingly, imitating a state she would be at immediately prior to crying. She said in the most affectionate voice she could muster, "But I love you Gruffudd, please let me go back for a few days."

"I need you here with me."

She was totally deflated and could not hold back the tears. He put his arm around her momentarily and rested her head on his large chest. But almost immediately he released her without a word and left her feeling isolated, deserted and guilty. She wept.

Later in the day Berddig could be seen ascending the steep path up to the court, stopping occasionally to appreciate the view. He was happy as usual and it was obvious that, as he was supplied with a jug of ale, he had news for his king.

Berddig had visited them frequently over the winter, bringing information from Rhuddlan, Gwynedd, Powys, Deheubarth and the Hereford countryside. While he was not the only poet and storyteller visiting them at this time, he was always the one given the warmest welcome and the one whose words were listened to most carefully by Gruffudd.

It had been Berddig who had told them in February 1056 that Bishop Æthelstan of Hereford had died and had been replaced by Bishop Leofgar, a far more militant cleric who had immediately started to prepare for war against Gruffudd and the Welsh.

Gruffudd, of course, had prepared for such an event. As the weather improved in April, at the beginning of the fighting season, he again sent orders for those soldiers who had returned home to muster in the area around the lake at Llangorse. This time they were joined by men from Morgannwg and Gwent, where the king had worked hard establishing his power over the winter months. Gruffudd and his entourage remained at Llyswen, determined to hold on to his gains.

At the sight of the approaching poet, Elen's spirits had recovered a little and she welcomed him enthusiastically in Gruffudd's presence. "It's nice to see you. We are very isolated here and I don't know what's going on in the world. Have you travelled far?"

"I was in Rhuddlan a few days ago and I saw your sons. They are both well and changing fast. The little one is changing most of all. You must miss them, Elen."

"I do, but Gruffudd won't let me return, even for a few days to see them. Can't you talk him into changing his mind?"

Berddig laughed. He knew the king too well to tangle himself in any dispute between him and Elen and instead divulged his news. "I was in Hereford yesterday. The new bishop is preparing for war. He is building up a store of weapons of all kinds and choosing commanders for an attack. I think that the bishop himself will be leading the troops."

"Quite a bishop then," remarked someone.

"They won't move until they are fully prepared and think they can overwhelm you."

Gruffudd nodded his head.

"Be sure to be well prepared for them. The attack may be days or weeks away."

"We are gathering our forces and bringing them closer," said Gruffudd.

"I will leave you in a day or two to go north and I'll call at Hereford again on my way back here."

"In the meantime let's enjoy ourselves," said Gruffudd laughing. "It's too dangerous for you to go north now," he said, looking at Elen, who had to struggle to hide her deep-seated hate for him, knowing that she would have to remain with him for the weeks ahead.

True to his word, Berddig joined them in May. He had travelled north on the English side of Offa's Dyke, visiting Rhuddlan. Then he returned south through Powys and Hereford. He spoke at length with Gruffudd in private and later with everyone at the court. Sadly for Elen he never mentioned Rhys, even when she pressed him about the port, saying how much she missed being close to the sea and the ships. He said nothing of interest to her before he left eastwards to stay with some of his friends on the border.

Gruffudd's army gathered in the Llynfi valley. It was a formidable force, well organised, disciplined and above all else, well led.

It was June before Berddig arrived back with news that an attack from Hereford was imminent. Gruffudd organised his men to meet them.

On 16 June the bishop of Hereford led his army along the north bank of the Wye following the old Roman road towards Glasbury. It was assumed by Gruffudd, that they intended to ford the Wye at Glasbury and then advance on the Welsh in the Llynfi valley and Llangorse.

Anticipating the bishop's plan, long before the Saxon army had reached the ford at Glasbury, Gruffudd moved his soldiers across the Wye at points higher up the river, closer to where the River Bachwy joined it.

He led his men by the way of the Bachwy valley to the higher ground above Glasbury and waited in absolute silence and stillness, hidden by trees and bushes. As the Saxons were preparing to ford the Wye he attacked, leading on his heavy black charger, wielding his long sword. Air flowed past his head, pressing his long, jet black hair backwards, with that stern, angry face above his strong jaw showing a determination to win. His eyes focused piercingly on his enemy as he swooped down on them like an eagle with its claws extended before a devastating contact with its target.

His soldiers, to a man, followed his example, some on horses and some running into the enemy's ranks.

The Saxons were falling all around the charging Welsh. Blood and gore splattered onto the faces of the attackers and the dead. Saxons trapped between Gruffudd's soldiers and the wide shallow river, ran into the water as if it would miraculously protect them. The river provided no sanctuary. Gruffudd and his soldiers were at their backs, piercing their leather garments with swords, spears and daggers, bringing them to their deaths in the red river.

The bishop only witnessed the very start of the battle. His eyes were closed very early in the encounter and so he played little part in it. He lay dead on the banks of the Wye, his sword in one hand and his prayer book in the other. Neither had any effect on the bloody encounter. It was not a befitting end for a bishop.

Gruffudd's vastly greater military skill had prevailed.

It was not till the enemy soldiers' had completely deserted the site of the battle that Elen and others were taken in a cart to witness the devastation.

She did not wish to be there. She despised battles. She had boys of her own and was worried about their future. She hoped they would never have to fight any battles and that peace would have descended on her land by the time they were ready to become soldiers.

There were dead men lying about everywhere. She could see blood on the banks of the smooth flowing Wye. Arms and legs were separated from bodies, spears sticking out of bodies, some lying on their backs looking upwards and seeing nothing, faces distorted, faces disfigured and faces hacked into pieces.

The brutality that faced her was overwhelming and she wanted nothing to do with it and walked away from the area.

She found a place by the river, upstream of the battle site. Looking into the clear, clean water she found some peace. It gave her time to recover from what she had seen. She felt nauseous but managed to control her breathing and her racing mind by thinking of Rhys, so far away yet with her every minute of every day.

Gruffudd had more than just survived the battle, he had acquired more power than ever. She would be tied to him till she died. There on her own, by the river, she cried her heart out and it was only the thought of going back to Rhys that kept her sane.

Harold Godwinson was again called to arrange a truce. In the new deal the long-term boundaries of Wales were settled. All west of the Dee estuary and along the eastern boundaries of Powys and Gwent were to belong to Gruffudd. As a result, a new Wales was formed with Gruffudd as king.

Gruffudd led his victorious men back to Rhuddlan, stopping to celebrate at every opportunity. Elen could not reach home quickly enough as she wanted to see Rhys. She wanted to know that he was well and still loved her. She had been away for well over a year. He could have found another woman, another lover; there were plenty of women left behind by their menfolk who would, through sheer need for company, induce him to fall for them.

Another woman could comfort him in her absence, talk to him, encourage him in his life and see to his daily needs. She couldn't bear to think of it. She already loathed the woman, whoever she was, and the closer she came to Rhuddlan the more concerned she became. Anxiety built in her body and she became convinced that Rhys had found another lover.

She was also aware that Gruffudd was losing interest in her, or at least he was not as besotted with her as he used to be. She wondered if he had also found another woman to crave for. Who had he met? She had gone through a list in her mind of women in the camp or living in the vicinity but couldn't think of one whom Gruffudd might have fallen for. Many would have thrown themselves at his feet but she believed she still held enough sway with him to deter them.

However, there was a continuing and very gradual cooling of his feelings towards her which pleased her.

The army plodded homewards slowly, finally following the Clwyd until they arrived at Rhuddlan. The crowds were out waiting for them, cheering, shouting, women running into the arms of their husbands, with some more interested in the loot than their husbands.

Elen was scanning the crowd for her Rhys. He was not there. She was deeply worried. Where was he?

The procession reached the area of the port but still there was no sign of Rhys. She was beside herself with worry.

They entered the court and approached the hall and, with great relief, she saw him there, waiting to welcome the king. He was smiling; yes he was smiling at her. He pursed his lips as to blow her a kiss. She knew their signal and imitated him.

She was happy. They were together again and he still had time for her. All she wanted to know was when could they meet? She was desperate to be with him and in his arms.

CHAPTER 31

July 1056

ONCE BACK AND having seen Rhys and cuddled her sons, Elen concentrated her thoughts on arranging a tryst with Rhys. Her desire to meet him was as powerful as ever. It was urgent – she wanted to know, did he still feel the same towards her? Did he need her as much as she needed him? Were they as madly in love with each other as they were before she was taken south?

That evening Berddig joined the victorious party at Rhuddlan and immediately set about to persuade the king that a grand feast was required to celebrate his new position. The whole of Wales was now under his rule and he was truly the king of Wales. The poet announced to the king's family, his army commanders and all who had returned triumphantly with him, that Gruffudd had achieved a status which had not been achieved by a ruler in Wales since the time of Hywel Dda, the law maker. Of course, any feast arranged as a celebration would have to be grander, bigger and longer-lasting than the feast of July 1049. The king showed no resistance and Berddig's opinion prevailed.

The planning started that very evening and a date was fixed for early August. It would last for four days, reflecting the king's greater power. All invited to the 1049 feast would be invited again but this time the noble families of Gwent and Morgannwg would join them. It was further agreed that the feast was to be called the Feast of the Swans, because of the number of roasted swans planned for the occasion.

On Berddig's advice, Gruffudd decided that evening to depart in two days' time for a tour of western Gwynedd. The long campaign in the south-east had kept him away from his main power base and a visit to the northern courts was long overdue. As soon as she heard of his plan, Elen pleaded to stay at Rhuddlan, and he agreed.

Mixing with the nobles in the hall that night in Rhys's presence was stressful for Elen. She wanted to talk to him, touch him, have him touch her. She wanted to kiss him, she wanted everything with him, then and there, but it was all impossible. They exchanged glances, smiles and even the occasional knowing look. It made her feel better, believing that he still cared for her and loved her.

But how could they meet? She wanted their meeting to be special. It needed to be special. She was nervous, she was anxious – would their kisses be as magical? Would he be excited at being alone with her?

As darkness fell on the court and the sun disappeared below the red sky, she exchanged a glance with him and went out for fresh air. He discreetly followed her and, in that dark moment between the setting of the sun and the torches being fully ignited, they met.

He whispered to her, "How wonderful to have you back."

"Oh! How I've missed you,"

"I heard him telling you that you can stay here while he visits his courts. We can meet by the oak tree early the first day they leave. I've already been told to check on our silver mines in the eastern hills. I will bring a horse for you and we can go towards Dyserth. Will you come?"

"Yes, you fool. You needn't ask. I'm beyond excited at the prospect."

"Excellent, I'll see you by the oak tree early. Wait for the change of guards, then leave."

"Yes, I want to kiss you," she whispered.

"It's too risky. We'll kiss the day after tomorrow. Go back and I'll follow you in a while."

She obediently returned, delighted, but tinged with a slight disappointment because he had not agreed to a kiss. She should have pecked him on the cheek if nothing else. Perhaps he didn't want to kiss her. Perhaps the next day he would tell her it was all over between them and that he had found someone else. But then she remembered the look in his eyes when he saw her. It was a look of joy, she hadn't mistaken that and he'd said, "How wonderful to have you back." All was well.

Gruffudd and his chief courtiers left early for Anglesey on the second day after their return from the south. The preparation for the feast was in full swing. Messengers were dispatched with the invitations and ships sent to European ports to gather supplies. Immediately after the early change of guards at the gates, Elen left and walked slowly, intentionally, seemingly purposelessly upriver towards their oak tree. Rhys was there with a ready-saddled horse for her, but covered in a blanket as though it was carrying a pack.

He gave her one of his own tunics to wear and a flat round cap on top of her plaited hair to disguise her a little. He then helped her into the saddle. They rode towards Dyserth, and turned north passing Moel Hiraddug on their right, where Rhys knew Gruffudd had guards, and climbed to the summit of the Graig hill, where they stopped and dismounted.

They led their horses to a sheltered spot on the hillside where, facing north-east, they could see the northern coastline, the western bank of the Dee estuary and the remains of Offa's Dyke, the old border before Gruffudd's time. They sat together on his blanket surveying the land to the east of the Clwyd mountains regained for the Welsh settlers by Gruffudd.

He began to take food and drink out of a sack. She was

nervous and apprehensive and decided it was best to tell him, "Rhys, I truly love you. I want you to know that now."

And before she could continue further, he responded, "I truly love you too and I've missed you."

"I'm very nervous about us," she ventured. "I'm afraid you won't feel the same way towards me. We've been apart such a long time. My feelings for you have not changed. Have yours for me?"

He was puzzled by her uncertainty and asked, "Can I kiss you?"

The request pleased her greatly and she nodded assent.

He leant over and kissed her gently on her lips. She smiled, "I'm not nervous about myself. I'm nervous about you."

"Don't be. I love you more than ever." He took her in his arms and laid her down gently and within seconds she knew that he loved her as much as before they were apart. Her confidence returned and her fears evaporated.

Resting on the slope, they admired the coastline in the distance, ate their food and drank the mead he had brought. They talked and talked and she remembered to tell him that she had stupidly thought she had seen the drowned Peter at Llyswen. He listened with interest and, after a slight hesitation, said that he had also thought he saw someone resembling him. But, when he had managed a closer look, he realised it wasn't him. Elen wondered if they both had a guilty feeling about his death.

When the time came to return to their real life they left happily, knowing that they were together and would be together in spirit even when apart. Elen arrived back at the court and neither her absence nor her happiness was noticed. It was assumed that she had been on a task related to the feast.

The king returned from his tour, preparations continued apace, and the weeks sped by to the day in August when the guests started to arrive. Elen and Rhys met infrequently in that time as both were involved in the preparations in one way or another.

The king's ship, with its carved swan figurehead painted in gold, was docked in the harbour at the head of a long line of ships of all shapes and sizes. His fleet had almost doubled since the Great Feast of 1049 and the court and its surrounding area had a more affluent look to it. The hall had been renovated and re-roofed and the houses were larger and grander. It all displayed the appearance of wealth and success.

The guests were impressed, some were in awe, others quietly jealous of the inhabitants of the royal court and wished to improve their own lot. Gruffudd's half-brothers, Rhiwallon and Bleddyn from Powys, arrived and were allocated good seats with Elen and her children at the top table. All the nobility, representing the whole of Wales were there, talking, laughing, drinking and eating together.

On the first day, the crowning ceremony commenced about midday. Elen took her position on the left of the dais, with her boys near her and the ceremony followed the same pattern as in July 1049.

The crown, with its ancient history linking Gruffudd to King Arthur according to Berddig, had been beautifully gilded, as had his sceptre. The king's ceremonial purple mantle was new, heavy and made of the finest thick cloth dyed carefully and skilfully, with its fringes brocaded with yellow fabric in the pattern of sea waves and matching the colour of his gold torque.

The gold torque, at Berddig's suggestion, had been borrowed from Merthyr Cynog church near Brecon to where it would be returned after the celebrations at Rhuddlan. It was an ancient, venerable and potent object and no one would dare break a promise in its presence, not even Gruffudd. Berddig had told him that it was the symbol of wealth, power, honour and royal authority to the ancient Celts and that it was befitting for a king of Wales to wear on ceremonial occasions, especially the crowning ceremony.

The sword was his own most trusted friend, sharp and worn with the occasional slight nick on the blade where it had been damaged by the neck bones of his dead enemies. Elen knew too well whose neckbone had caused one of the nicks in the blade. Its hilt was of plain steel, large enough to fit his enormous hand and designed to give him a good grip.

The other object he wouldn't be without was his dagger and he had it in its scabbard attached, like his sword, to his wide belt.

Gruffudd came out of the hall to tumultuous cheering, boosted this time by the families from Morgannwg and Gwent. In response he waved his gold sceptre at his audience. He sat on the purple cushion set on his own beautifully carved chair. The crown was placed on his head and he was declared the king of Wales.

The newly-crowned king led the gathering to the tables laid out ready for the feast. Twenty swans had been roasting above the fires all morning. These were the centrepiece of the meal and were supplemented by geese and a range of other wildfowl.

There followed heavy drinking and feasting on a scale unseen at the royal court. Clerics and poets were present in droves, but the former were kept in their place while the latter were given the freedom to display their entertaining skills to the full. There was music and dancing and the night ended with the guests drunk, fully sated and exhausted.

On the second day, a hunt was organised for three large wild boars, recently captured and released into the woodland a mile away from the court. Each boar had a collar around its neck with a comb stitched to each collar. Gifts of land were to be awarded to the hunters who caught one of these wild boars. This was Berddig's idea, which he got from the ancient story of Culhwch and Olwen he frequently used to entertain his audience with.

The king accompanied the hunt, though it was an opportunity for young men to demonstrate their bravery. Catching and slaying a wild boar was no mean task even with good dogs. If the boar charged at a hunter, it had to be stopped with a spear. That required great skill because if the hunter missed or failed to stop the charging animal, the boar would smash into the hunter's legs and simultaneously lift his head to gore the man's legs with its tusks. In his time Gruffudd had excelled at hunting wild boars.

The men, on horse and foot and with numerous hounds, left early in pursuit of the three wild boars and soon disappeared into the distant hills.

Rhys didn't go with them because he claimed his horse was lame. Instead he and Elen sailed down the estuary in his boat and turned westward along the shore until they rounded a rocky outcrop and came to a long sheltered bay where they went ashore. They had an unobstructed view of the shoreline for about half a mile both ways.

Oblivious of the hunting of the wild boar through the forests further inland, they enjoyed a wonderful day and imagined how they would be together if they were married. There was no Gruffudd there to constantly worry them.

Rhys pointed out to her where St Tudno's church stood on the massive rocky outcrop to the west which obscured their view of Anglesey. He knew the area well from the time he was brought up in Conwy and spoke to her about his childhood and upbringing. She hung on every word. When she asked if he would take her to Deganwy and Conwy one day for her to see his home area, he promised he would.

Reluctantly, they had to leave their heavenly beach and head back for Rhuddlan. Elen arrived back at the court as the hunting party returned, having caught one of the boars. The successful hunter was presented with land in Ceredigion. The feasting and drinking commenced again while the king and his nobles planned to continue the hunt the next day.

On the third day of the festivities, feeling that he couldn't absent himself for another day, Rhys accompanied the hunt, though his heart and soul was with Elen at court.

That afternoon the hunters returned with the other two wild boars, and lands in Powys and Morgannwg were allocated to the successful hunters.

On the final day, entertainment was provided at court. It consisted of feasting on the flesh of all the wild boars caught, sea birds, river birds and more swans too.

In the early afternoon, King Gruffudd gathered everyone together. Standing in his full regalia on the coronation dais, he called Berddig to join him and bestowed on him, his most trusted servant as he put it, a large area of land in Gwent which he had acquired during his fighting in the south-east. Berddig, for the first time ever, was speechless, but accepted the gift graciously to much acclaim from the crowd.

Elen was sad to see the end of the feast, since it had afforded her and Rhys an opportunity to be together and do so many wonderful things as though they were married. They even managed to dance together without drawing any comment from the king.

The guests departed happily on the fifth day, all praising the feast, the royal court, the entertainment, the king and his generosity.

CHAPTER 32

January 1057 to January 1058

B Y THE BEGINNING of 1057, life at the royal court was busier than ever. The king was in possession of additional territory and dealing with more legal issues, making more appointments and ensuring that peace was maintained between his expanded numbers of nobles. He was hardly at Rhuddlan, and no longer needed Elen to accompany him.

She often felt that he was happier without her. She was certainly happier without him. This new arrangement was to her liking. She still made the appropriate noises for him to think that she didn't wish to be left behind. The love between her and Rhys was enduring all the obstacles life was putting in its way.

Since the start of her pretence of loving Gruffudd, she felt that his desire for her had declined significantly and was by now hardly noticeable. She did wonder if he was only interested in women who rejected him and that it was his thirst for their love or power over them which drove him to try to achieve his obsessive control. Whatever, it suited her and she left it at that. Indeed, by the spring of 1057, Gruffudd was showing no interest in her physically, or even as a long-term friend to discuss things with. Their relationship, to all intents and purposes, had ended.

In June Gruffudd left Rhuddlan to meet with his ally Ælfgar with the intention of celebrating their victories which, in the last few years, had brought peace to the borderlands.

Elen didn't accompany him but surprisingly Rhys did. She consoled herself knowing that they were not going on a military campaign and that it was simply a social visit and he would be back in two weeks or less.

About ten days had elapsed when, without any warning, Gruffudd and his band arrived back. Elen could hear the commotion, as awareness of their approach spread through the court. She with others rushed to set out the tables with the best ale and mead and food. The minstrel was called to play his flute as a welcome. She wanted others to think that she was keen and delighted to have Gruffudd return, but it was another man she was waiting for.

The king and his followers rode boldly through the entrance and a cheer went up from the throng waiting for them. Elen was looking forward to have Rhys back again. These days she seemed to miss him more when he was away. Taking a final look at the table with the food and drink arranged on it, the minstrel and the state of the hall, she turned towards the entrance to welcome her husband and her lover.

The king pushed in through the entrance, closely followed by a very young woman, a startlingly pretty young woman. Elen stared at her as Gruffudd announced, "This is my wife, Ealdgyth. She is Earl Ælfgar's daughter. Isn't she the prettiest woman you've ever seen?"

His statement was met by total silence, which lasted too long for the king's comfort. His new wife was bewildered in the gloomy hall and her pretty face dissolved into an inane grin. Elen stood fixed to the floor, unsure as to what was the appropriate thing for her to do. Should she faint? She surely should somehow demonstrate her shock – if she truly loved the king she definitely should. If she couldn't faint then surely she should scream and tear at the newcomer's hair or even make some attempt at taking one of her eyes out. Certainly a deep scratch down her cheek was the least expected of her, she thought. However, she was frozen from tip to toe.

"Let's eat," announced the king, pulling his newly-dearly beloved to the table and ensuring that she sat next to him in Elen's usual chair.

People stared at her. No one dared say anything. Someone started a murmur to the effect that she was very pretty but no one mentioned that she looked very young.

Elen was humiliated, even though she had no feelings for him. Many present felt for her but couldn't show any sympathy for fear of their lives.

Her eyes searched for Rhys, looking for support and guidance. At last he arrived, smiled at her but, reading his eyes, she could see that he was saying 'Such is life'. He confirmed it with a shrug of his shoulders.

She wanted to run to him but knew it would be wrong. She wanted him to take her out of the hellhole she was in, but he couldn't. She wanted to sink into the floor, another impossibility.

Rhys gradually worked his way closer to her and, under the cover of the noisy reception, he said quietly, "Sorry I couldn't warn you. It all happened very quickly. He fell in love with her at a glance and asked her father for her hand. Gruffudd is too powerful an ally to be refused anything. There was hardly any ceremony; he just announced she was his wife and slept with her that night. As for her, she is not enamoured by him, I can tell you. There are a thousand places she'd rather be than next to him."

The final phrase of Rhys's woke her from her shock. "Next to him? Where?" she asked naively.

"Well as you can see at the table," he said. "But be prepared to find yourself in a new bed tonight."

She uttered not a word.

"Don't worry," he assured her. "It's good for us."

This did indeed lift her out of her trance but not out of her confusion and she asked, "Where will I live?"

"I've got room for you with me. But I don't suppose that will do for a while, at least. He may not let you free."

"What shall I do?"

"Bend with the wind. You don't love him and so let it end peacefully."

"But shouldn't I shout and scream? Shouldn't I spit at her? Shouldn't I at least pretend to be offended by this hussy of his?"

"If you say or do too much he will send you away. The best thing now for you and for us is to simply do as he bids. We'll see where it takes us."

"Are you sure? Shouldn't I at least pull out a strand of her hair? Scratch her face perhaps?"

"No. It's Gruffudd. He'll place you in the dungeon at least. He may even accuse you of treason. Then where will you be?"

Her eyes were saying, "I suppose you're right."

They could read each other so well after years of practice. "Look, we've never been able to talk to each other as long as this while he has been around before. He's besotted with her, as he was with you. But you can see this is not where she wants to be."

"But what will people think if I do nothing? They'll put two and two together and link you and me."

"I don't think so, Elen. They know him. They know you don't dare say anything."

It was then that she noticed that Jane was hanging about near her and she turned towards her. She knew she would give her it straight and she did, "We're very impressed by the way you've controlled yourself. I'm sorry this has happened but I will have to call her queen now. I hope you understand."

Elen decided to take it all on the chin and, with Rhys as

support, she was able to say, "I understand Jane." She then added, "I hope you'll be good enough for her. Her father is an earl and her grandmother was Lady Godiva." Instantly she regretted her cutting remarks and added, "I'm sure you will be an excellent servant to the new queen," while thinking to herself thank God I've got Rhys to love me.

The party continued and, between the times she went out for fresh air and spent arranging for more alcohol to be supplied, she miraculously managed to avoid noticing the pitiful glances thrown at her and to stay clear of the top table with the king and his new queen.

Pleased with herself she went out again late in the evening to breathe deeply and rest her soul. This time she was followed by Rhys who, in the gloom, was able to touch her hand without any risk and say to her he loved her.

"I've heard him announce, in front of her, that you are to be housed with Jane and the others till he finds you a more suitable place."

She was angry but knew it was pointless. "I'm one of the servants now am I? Well he needn't expect I'll serve that bitch."

Rhys couldn't help but smile, "Why don't you suggest to him tomorrow that you would like to go out of the court and live down by the port. Say calmly to him that you are deeply offended by the arrival of the new queen and it would be best if you lived out of her way. Say clearly that you do not wish to be sent away somewhere because you have your boys and many friends here at Rhuddlan and you wish to stay near them. Make it clear to him that you will be no trouble to him or his new wife."

She spent that night in the servants' quarters, the most degrading night for her for a long time. But she took the slap with equanimity knowing that it was pointless to resist such a ruthless, unfeeling man.

The following day, when she judged he was sober enough,

she caught him alone and made Rhys's suggestion to him. She also, for good measure and to influence his mind, lied to him and told him she still loved him. He looked slightly embarrassed for a second or two but not too long. But he did agree to find her a place, a good place in the port and saw all the advantages of a suggestion so skilfully put to him.

Within days a place was found for her in the port and Jane allocated to her as her servant.

CHAPTER 33

February 1058 to December 1063

G RUFFUDD WAS BESOTTED with Ealdgyth. Indeed her beauty had a similar effect on most of the men at court but all were wise enough not to show any outer signs of their desire. They were aware that the consequence would be dire if their dreams came to the king's attention.

The new queen behaved impeccably. She didn't complain and kept herself to herself as much as was possible and reasonable. She never looked overjoyed with her role as the wife of King Gruffudd, then in his mid-forties, but bore it all dutifully.

Elen sympathised with her, and often felt sorry for her and wished that she could talk to her openly and share her experience with her. But it was impossible, the risks were too great.

She didn't know what Gruffudd's reaction would be if he were to find out about her relationship with Rhys. Even if he were to be convinced that their relationship had only started after he took to his new wife, she and Rhys took no risks. They continued as they had always done and ensured that no one found out about them.

She was sure that, Gruffudd being Gruffudd, he still regarded her as his wife and that he had the same conjugal rights as he had before the arrival of the new wife. He was not one to stand on ceremony and would not have allowed religion, beliefs and superstition to stand in his way of having two wives.

Her new house suited Elen well. She was much closer to Rhys and they could now talk and see each other on a more equal footing in the sight of others and thus draw less attention from gossips. The vast majority of the court were sympathetic towards Elen and felt that she had been badly treated by her husband. However, no one dared mention it to a neighbour and hardly to their own partner and certainly not in front of their children. They were fully aware of the consequences of such remarks reaching the king.

Elen was happier in her life. The burden of ingratiating herself with the king, of satisfying his needs and, at the same time, loving another man, had been lifted. Now the only thing that disturbed her was the fact that she couldn't, at a time of her own choosing, fall into the arms of the man she loved. Instead she had to search for an opportunity. However, she and Rhys were optimistic that Gruffudd would one day be prepared to release her.

Ealdgyth learned quickly how to take advantage of the king's feelings towards her. She was able to influence him in many ways and she soon acquired skills that were to stand her in good stead in her life at court. She pleased her husband even more when she became pregnant.

So, when in March 1059 the Rhuddlan courtiers set out on their annual hunt in the pleasant valley of the River Dulas to the west of Rhuddlan, the pregnant queen stayed at court. The valley of the Dulas had a narrow entrance from the coast, between high precipitous rock faces but then it opened out to a relatively flat, wide valley which invariably afforded entertaining and successful hunting.

They crossed the Clwyd and followed a track westwards, meeting the seashore less than a mile from Llanddulas. They turned sharply to the left to follow the River Dulas south through the narrow gap.

Gruffudd, as usual, led the noisy band of hunters, family members, guests and dogs. Elen and her sons accompanied the throng, but Rhys was not with them and she had not seen him for a day or two. Elen was near the front of the column while her boys were with the other young people at the very back.

The king was in good spirits and had, like many others, already drunk more mead than was advisable. They were talking, joking, singing and laughing when they came to the narrow gorge at the mouth of the Dulas. Elen, mounted on her horse about thirty yards directly behind the king, became aware of some commotion in front of her. Then, to her utter astonishment, she was narrowly missed by an arrow which struck a foot soldier a few yards behind her squarely in the middle of his chest, lifting him off his feet and hurtling him backwards to lie flat on his back immediately behind Elen.

There was great agitation and shouting at the front of the column. People were shouting "It's an ambush." "They're hiding in the rocks above." "They have fired a volley of arrows at the king." "The king has been hit." Even, "The king is dead," could be heard.

In the next instance Gruffudd on his wild-eyed horse came charging back through the column, scattering horses and walkers to the sides. He was closely followed by other riders and armed men on foot. Clearly the king was not dead but it might have been close.

He was shouting, "Regroup at the rear."

As he passed Elen, he almost threw her off her horse. She struggled to stay on her animal and saw the king urging his horse forward out of the immediate danger. His face showed great anger and blood streamed down the left side of his face, she presumed from an arrow that had glanced off his forehead leaving a bleeding gash. Elen was glad her sons were at the rear and out of danger.

The situation was serious but, like Elen, most were paralyzed for seconds until someone shouted, "Get out of here. Follow the king."

Elen turned her horse to follow Gruffudd and, as she did, glanced up at the rocks above the track where she assumed the arrows had come from. She could see in an instant that there were about half a dozen men there, some reloading their bows, others turning to escape.

"Retreat! Get out of here," someone was shouting but Elen was either mesmerized or too curious. She kept her gaze on the rocks above her where the attackers were escaping upwards over the rocks, scrambling like animals on all fours, their bows now over their shoulders.

One, their leader she assumed, who at first appeared familiar to her, stopped for a brief instant to look down directly at her she thought. For a second or two a wave of extreme anxiety passed through her body as she thought she was to be his target.

She shifted her horse and followed the others as fast as the animal could go until there was about two hundred yards or more between her and the point of ambush.

People were talking around her as she calmed herself and her horse. She could hear, "The king and his men have circled the hillside to cut those thugs off and kill them."

She looked in the direction the king had gone and could see him and a group of soldiers dismounting and leaving their horses to climb the difficult terrain on foot. She watched them disappear over the brow of the hill and out of sight. She waited anxiously while the remaining soldiers formed a defensive line around them.

After about an hour the king and his soldiers returned. Gruffudd explained that the cowards had their own horses on the far side of the hill and had mounted them and ridden westwards into the forest where there was little point following them as they'd had too good a start.

The king decided that the courtiers should return to the royal court while he and some soldiers would track the outlaws.

They would question local villagers to find out what they knew or had seen.

During the return journey there was speculation about all aspects of the attack. Interestingly, no one thought the attackers were outlaws. A group of half a dozen outlaws wouldn't attack what amounted to a small army. It was an ambush and the target was the king and it had been well planned by someone with inside knowledge of the court's activities.

There were many suggestions on that journey back to Rhuddlan as to the culprits' identities. The one which curried most favour was that they were in the payment of the English king. However some were quietly hinting that they could be supporters of Cynan ap Iago, the head of the old Gwynedd royal family. Others, of course, were honest enough to point out that Gruffudd had enemies in many parts of Wales.

Later that evening Elen saw Rhys and told him exactly what had happened. He was also of the opinion that it was an attempt to kill the king. It could have been a group of discontented individuals wishing revenge for some deed.

After days of hunting for the outlaws, no one was found and the questioning of villagers only produced what was already known: there were six of them and they rode off to the west where they had come from. No one had seen them at close quarters or spoken to them.

Time healed the wounds to the flesh, and pride was restored and life returned to normal. However, lessons were learnt.

Gruffudd's new wife enthralled her husband when she gave birth to Nest, a lovely daughter for the king. She was allowed to nurse her own daughter, unlike Elen, who had to leave her boys for others to rear. Boys could not be trusted to her care.

Gruffudd remained the undisputed king of Wales, which he ruled with a rod of iron. No English king dared to attack his territory – a situation that had never existed in living memory.

Even the knowledgeable clerics and historians of the day could not recall such a period of tranquillity. His military skill and the strong alliance with Mercia kept the peace on the borders.

However, the strong and powerful king remained a slave to his young wife and she, understandably, learnt to get her own way by the use of guile. Elen was happier in that she and Rhys met more frequently, but there was always the risk of detection hanging over them.

Life at Rhuddlan became pleasant, comfortable and affluent. The court blossomed and, as always, in a time of plenty the arts, music, storytelling and poetry flourished.

CHAPTER 34

Christmas 1062

THE INHABITANTS OF the royal court at Rhuddlan were in good spirits celebrating Christmas 1062. The king was still head over heels in love with his wife, Ealdgyth, and worshipped the ground that she walked on. Nothing was too much for him to do for her. His only concern, on the domestic front, was the jealousy aroused in him if anyone looked too intensely at her or, worse still, if she took too much interest in another man.

No man was to look at her with a glint in his eye or in any way demonstrate any desire towards this beautiful woman. Everyone knew of his jealously and made certain that they viewed her from a safe distance only. Any desire they had for her had to be kept a very closely guarded secret.

His ambitions achieved on the military and political fronts, the king was now content to enjoy his power, ensure that his realm was ruled firmly and, with the court of justice, deal with disputes promptly even if not always fairly in everyone's opinion.

He had his alliance with Ælfgar, the earl of Mercia, which secured his eastern border and the storms of a decade earlier had pacified the Irish desire to raid across the sea. The country was at peace and his subjects enjoyed it.

His war band was off-duty for the days immediately following Christmas. Many had gone home to their families for the celebrations. On the third night after Christmas, the mist had spread up from the sea towards the estuary to cover all blemishes and faults in the landscape. It was very much like the feeling of wellbeing that had descended gradually over the years on the country to mellow and erase military and political worries.

The royal court woke to a misty, cold and damp morning but, as many proclaimed, it was better than snow. Some were still celebrating Christmas and planned to consume more ale that evening. In the afternoon, Gruffudd had gone down to the port to look at a shipment of silver he was sending to France from his mines in the north east. Rhys was with him, so Elen had remained in her house and was talking to Jane.

She planned to go for a walk later, once the king had returned to the hall, his wife and daughter. She would then visit Rhys and they might well sail on his boat for an hour together. She barely saw the king; she avoided him. It was a great relief to her that she didn't have to submit to his attention. While she didn't envy her replacement, she did experience the unpleasantness associated with being the king's cast-off and of being seen by others as such. She hated their false pity and wished she could tell them about the love of her life.

She was sitting by the fire warming herself ready for her walk later when she heard shouting up by the gate of the court and the noise of a horse galloping towards the port. Then, above the sound of hooves thundering on the stony track, she heard someone shouting, "Look out. We're under attack. Saxon raiders."

Elen went out, as did many others. There were people milling about, confused and bewildered.

"Where's the king?" the rider shouted. Many pointed to his ship.

Gruffudd emerged from the ship and jumped ashore, followed by a number of others, including Rhys.

"Where are they?" Gruffudd shouted at the horseman. "We'll take them on. Back to the court. Get our men into the court."

But the excited, sweaty rider with his horse rearing high on its hind legs, shouted down at the king, "There's not a minute to spare. They are here, half a mile away."

"They came through at Dyserth," he shouted. "There are over a hundred of them on fast, light horses. They may be led by Harold Godwinson. I think it's him. Our beacons were useless because of the mist."

His horse settled with its four hooves on the ground momentarily before being again influenced by the developing chaos and rearing up to its full height.

Gruffudd knew the rider. He knew that he was reliable and had been with him when he met Harold during the peace negotiations near Hereford.

"I was on Moel Hiraddug when I saw them. I only just managed to get ahead of them."

Elen saw that by the time the horse was grounded again, Gruffudd was running, sword in hand, towards the court gates. Others were following him. She could hear his powerful voice booming, "Get my wife and children."

"It's too late. Leave them. Get away," the rider was shouting at him as he followed him towards the gate.

It hit Elen like a bolt that her sons were also in the court and she started running towards the gate. Men, women and children were running in all directions, mostly in panic.

She could hear the messenger on his horse shouting in vain, "You must escape. Leave in the ship. The tide is with you. Turn back."

Gruffudd must have heard him but he didn't even hesitate.

Then, for no apparent reason, people stopped for a few seconds and stood in petrified silence sensing danger and listened. In that silent moment they heard the sound of the pounding hooves of the approaching cavalry – they were close.

Elen reached the gate as Rhys caught up with her. She was fearful for her sons but to her great relief met them at the gate coming out. Maredudd, now aged twenty, took care of Idwal who was only thirteen. She shouted at them, "To the boats."

They were glad to see her and they joined the others running towards the ships. They were hardly halfway when the leading raiders were arriving at the court's open gate.

Elen, still running, turned to glance behind her and saw the first Saxons entering, wielding their swords and axes, easily overpowering the shocked guards. The first three horses disappeared into the court, leaving the guards' bloody bodies prostrated at the entrance.

Then, as the next few riders arrived blocking the entrance, there was an almighty roar, and she and those with her turned to see the middle horse struck by some enormous force and toppled on its side. There appeared, in the space occupied by the tumbled animal, Gruffudd on his powerful charger, a broken lance in his right hand, his sword in the other piercing the chest of the rider on his left. Hanging on to the king's chest was his wife, with her daughter in her arms.

Gruffudd's much larger and heavier horse leapt effortlessly over the fallen horse, avoiding the front part of Gruffudd's lance protruding from its belly and landed firmly on the slope.

Elen could see that Ealdgyth and her daughter were precariously balanced for a few seconds but settled again as the horse continued its gallop to the port with people, including Elen, scattering from its path. The huge animal and its passengers passed with everyone standing in awe at the massive, angry beast and its wild-looking rider.

On arrival at his ship, the king dismounted, lifted his wife and daughter from the animal's saddle-less back and took them onto the royal ship.

"My sons?" he questioned. He then saw them with their

mother and called to them, "Take the horses and ride into the hills. They won't follow you. It's me they want."

The boys followed his instructions, much to Elen's annoyance.

There were horses, including Gruffudd's, running wild, liberated by their owners in an attempt to escape. The boys had no difficulty in grabbing suitable animals, mounting them and dashing towards the ford. The shouting of orders continued, "Take them across the river." "Make for Deganwy and meet the king there."

Elen saw her boys disappearing into the mist, Maredudd on his father's horse. She waved but they were gone.

Gruffudd didn't even glance after them, but did see Elen standing not ten yards away from him. He looked at her, but showed no concern, no emotion. The look told her, 'Well there we are. Find your own way out of this one.'

He didn't care any more. All the love he had for her had gone. He had someone new. He'd had sons from her and that was that. The next instant he was on his own ship, giving firm orders to leave.

Rhys observed the departure and grabbed Elen by the arm and rushed with her towards his own ship. Many others followed him, encouraged as they were by commands of, "Let's get on the ship." and "Make for Deganwy."

Elen heard it all, experienced it all as she boarded the ship, but only as if she were in a dream. The ship was crowded, indeed overcrowded to the point of concern that it was too low in the water to pass over a ford in the estuary.

From her ship, Elen could see a defensive line of soldiers were resisting the advance of the Saxons to the port. The court's treasurer and a few of his men were making their way to another ship about to leave the quayside. They were carrying a large wooden chest, which Elen recognised as the one containing the king's royal garment, cloaks, crown and other valuables.

Then the noise of the attacking cavalry became suddenly louder as they arrived in strength at the gate of the court. The gate keepers were long gone. Men with swords in hand met them at the gate, there was shouting and fighting. The horsemen disappeared in great numbers into the courtyard but other raiders saw the activity by the river and turned their attention in that direction.

In the port many were shouting, "Let's go." "Leave now." "Get on the ships and sail with the tide or cross the river and make for Deganwy."

The brave soldiers blocking the Saxons advance on the port were overwhelmed and the raiders broke through. The ships were full and desperate people were diverted onto other smaller boats or to ford the river upstream. Elen could see the last ship which managed to leave move slowly away from the shore and into the main flow of the tide following the others and the king's royal ship. She could also see that not all the ships were able to leave the quayside in time. Some were boarded by the Saxons.

The small fleet moved slowly downstream with the oars handled clumsily at the beginning. Looking back, Elen could see that the Saxons were in full control of the port, but there was a gap developing between the ships and the quayside.

Spears and lances were thrown from the bank in their direction but to no avail. The ships were separating from the shore, with archers taking their positions on the ships sides facing the attackers. These few archers restored the balance of power, successfully dampening the enthusiasm of the attackers.

The Saxons had obviously overwhelmed the court with speed and ferocity. Their leader was aware that the king had escaped and was getting his men out of the court to search for him, sending more to follow the ships and boats down the estuary.

Looking back from Rhys's side, Elen saw that there was smoke rising from the court. The attackers were setting fire to the great hall. The smoke began to billow upwards in huge large clouds as the roof caught fire. Then, other dwellings were set alight and the flames were spreading. Soon smoke rose from many sources, the dark grey bulging columns of it dissolving into the mist hanging over the Rhuddlan plain.

The horsemen following them along the banks of the widening river were threatening the hapless ships and boats. Then the king took command; he organised the rowing, chastised the weak, and galvanised the able.

They passed the large willow tree and Elen, standing next to Rhys, saw that the riders on the shore were losing ground on them. She became more relaxed but continued to watch them carefully.

The pursuers had to slow down as they entered the marshy ground closer to the sea. Aided by the flowing tide, Gruffudd's flotilla left them behind, but not before they could see that the royal court was fully ablaze, as were the houses, huts and ships in the port.

Suddenly she poked Rhys in the ribs and asked, "Who's the fifth rider from the front?"

"Don't know. They're too far away for me to recognize anyone and I don't know any Saxons anyway."

"Look he's tall and thin. You can see that, even though he is on a horse."

Rhys, smiling at her, reminded her, "There are many tall and thin men, Elen. You can't possibly see his face to recognize him. He's too far from us. He's dead, remember he drowned. Those are Saxons not Welsh soldiers."

She managed a smile and moved closer to him.

He laughed at her and then relieved, shouted, "Look. They're giving up."

"Good." She was also able to breathe easier again as the pursuers disappeared in the distance.

The flotilla moved faster towards the open sea and, to the great relief of all on board the ships and boats, they negotiated the ford successfully.

Gruffudd was raging, but that was all he could do. He raged, but to no avail. Once out of the estuary they headed westward for Deganwy.

CHAPTER 35

Late December 1062
to January 1063

G RUFFUDD'S ROYAL SHIP and its accompanying flotilla
sailed past the long beach where Elen and Rhys had spent
such pleasant times years earlier. It then sailed around the bulky
Gogarth, and arrived at Deganwy in the Conwy estuary before
nightfall.

After suffering one surprise attack they were more prepared
for another, but the Conwy estuary was silent and peaceful.
Darkness was approaching fast. The sun, obscured by the
clouds and the mist rising from the sea, was settling for the
day. They could see torches at the gates of Deganwy being lit
by apprehensive guards watching the small flotilla entering the
estuary.

The ships and boats were guided to anchorage below the
court where they disgorged their passengers. Gruffudd led the
group up the beach slowly and silently, with only the sound of
lapping waves behind them disturbing the peace. The guards
were on high alert above the closed gate and challenged them as
they approached in the gloom, "Who's approaching?"

"Open the gate," boomed the king.

"Who are you?"

"I am the king. Open the gates immediately."

"We thought we recognised your ship, but we had to be sure,"
was the apologetic reply.

The gates were opened and the escapees from Rhuddlan filed in, feeling dejected but relieved that they were safe. The noise and the commotion had alerted all those dwelling in the court and soon everyone was up and about. The fire in the hall was rekindled, food and drink supplied, while the visitors explained their plight to their countrymen.

During the latter part of the evening, those who had escaped from Rhuddlan on horseback arrived, including Elen's boys to her great relief. They brought news of how the court itself and all the ships and boats still left had been burnt. Everything had been destroyed, leaving nothing but smoke and ashes at the royal court.

These late arrivals confirmed that the leader of the attacking force was undoubtedly Harold Godwinson. Some had seen and recognised him, others had heard riders talking to him and addressing him by his title.

Despite the gloomy news there was relief when it was confirmed by more than one, that the raiders led by Harold had left and returned eastwards. This would give Gruffudd time to regroup, contact his allies, raise an army to defend his kingdom and counterattack. Deganwy, the old royal capital, was only weakly garrisoned but was a good place to start the planning, with its access to the sea and the Conwy valley route to Powys and the south.

However, the following morning, Gruffudd was raging. He was furiously kicking the leg of the table, swearing and blaspheming continuously. It was some time before he was prevailed upon to settle and receive the full report on their position and to be grateful that he, his wife and daughter were alive and well.

He was told by some who had spoken to a few captured Saxons, that Harold and his raiding party had, acting on information received from a spy, left King Edward the

Confessor's court at Gloucester two days earlier and ridden directly to Rhuddlan. Their sole aim was to kill Gruffudd. Despite the fact that he had survived, Gruffudd was in an extremely angry mood and demanded to know how Harold had managed to ride through Mercia without being challenged or hindered in any way by his ally.

Their first day at Deganwy brought no relief. It wasn't a bad dream – it had happened. Rhuddlan was burnt to the ground, ships destroyed and soldiers killed. It was no wonder Gruffudd remained on the edge of a rage, bemoaning the loss of his court and the greater part of his fleet.

The talk of what to do next didn't start in earnest until midday. Everyone had a view, an opinion, and a suggestion. Some were for going back to Rhuddlan, some for going to Ireland for Viking help, but the majority were for moving to a safer place in the mountains. Gruffudd was unsure himself having been greatly shaken by the event. He wished above everything that Berddig was there to give his valuable advice. However, unfortunately, Berddig was in Gwent administering the lands given to him by Gruffudd years earlier.

Returning to Rhuddlan was deemed unsafe because Harold's cavalry, augmented by additional soldiers, could return to attack the area at any time. Ireland was also deemed unsafe, since it was rumoured that the Vikings of Dublin were now allied to King Edward of England. However, it was agreed that an envoy should be sent there as soon as possible to assess the possibility of a new alliance.

The role of Ælfgar, the earl of Mercia and Ealdgyth's father, was a puzzle. Why had he allowed Harold to use Mercia as a base for his attack on his ally at Rhuddlan? Ealdgyth herself was equally puzzled and volunteered to go on a mission to see her father. Gruffudd was very reluctant to see her leave and, at first, refused to consider the idea. He only mellowed towards it when it was said that she could be landed on Mercian soil in Chester and go from there to meet her father.

Ealdgyth meant too much to him to let her go but the fact was that there were few plausible alternatives. Ealdgyth and Nest would sail to Chester the following day and from there go on to meet her father. Gruffudd's trusted negotiator from the Maelor area would be sent a message to meet her at Chester.

Ealdgyth and Nest were prepared for the journey and the farewell on the beach was poignant. Gruffudd was deeply uneasy at the departure of his beloved wife. He was beside himself with concern for her safety and wellbeing, though many had pointed out to him that she was probably safer in Chester than she was in Deganwy. He embraced her and his child immediately before they boarded their ship. After they left shore, he did not leave the embarkation point nor stop waving his goodbye to her until the ship was out of his sight around the Gogarth.

The following day a messenger arrived by sea from Chester and told Gruffudd that his wife had landed safely, only to discover that her father Ælfgar had died shortly before Christmas. Since his elder son had died when returning from a crusade a year earlier, the new earl of Mercia was Edwin, Ealdgyth's brother, a young man far too inexperienced to challenge Harold and King Edward. So, Mercia hadn't been able even to warn Gruffudd of the impending attack, never mind prevent it.

CHAPTER 36

January 1063 to 5 August 1063

L ATE IN JANUARY 1063 the envoy sent to Ireland returned empty-handed. The Dublin Vikings were not interested in any alliance. The envoy felt sure he could see the hand of King Edward the Confessor and that of the family of the eight-year-old Gruffudd ap Cynan, of the old Welsh royal line, in this decision.

As for Mercia, the new earl was still grieving for his father and, in any case, hadn't the will to take part in a war. This left Gruffudd exposed on all fronts and without an ally.

Harold, however, was determined to blockade Gruffudd in the Welsh heartland of Gwynedd. So he and his brother, Tostig, started on their campaign in late May. Harold attacked the coast with a strong naval force moving from one port to the next, while Tostig crossed the border with a mounted force. Between them they laid waste large areas of the country and Welsh nobles were forced to pay tribute and give hostages to the brothers. The whole country was weakened by their devastating attacks and many deserted the cause of their own king.

Gruffudd was determined to resist, but his position was weakened daily, both from the attacks and the draining away of his support under such pressure. Even his half-brothers, Bleddyn and Rhiwallon, had remained in Powys, and under pressure from Harold they had deserted him weeks earlier.

In fear of an attack on Deganwy, the king led his supporters in their ships and boats across the Conwy estuary and along the coast to Aber Cegin opposite Anglesey, where they landed. There

Gruffudd had to abandon his royal ship, sinking it in the mouth of the river, but not before removing the gold-painted figurehead and taking it ashore with the rest of the royal treasure.

They retreated into the high mountains of Gwynedd away from the sea, where they were particularly vulnerable to onslaughts from Harold's naval force. They established a court at the northern end of Lake Padarn, on the banks of the River Caledffrwd where they had a plentiful supply of food and water. Situated about six miles from the sea, it provided them with a safe place against any landings on the coast, and it was also conveniently situated for a further retreat into the rocky mountains where it would be impossible for a mounted force to follow.

At this court they quickly settled to their routines and improved the structures of the buildings. They felt secure in this hideout but Gruffudd was in bad temper most of the time and missed his wife.

His sons, when not on recruiting or foraging expeditions, were constantly by his side, maturing rapidly and learning from their father. Elen and Rhys were also there at the court. She was tied to Gruffudd's cause by her sons and Rhys through his love for her.

People of importance in Gruffudd's administration called to see him for advice and to report to him. But his beautiful young wife remained in Mercia, now wooed by Harold Godwinson himself.

Then, in early July, reports arrived at the court that Harold's soldiers were camped at the mouth of the River Seiont and were scouting inland. Gruffudd and his group decided that they were vulnerable on the banks of the Caledffrwd and moved their base further into the mountains, establishing their new court on the small peninsula separating the two lakes, Padarn and Peris, at the foot of Snowdon.

They constructed rudimentary huts for themselves to see them through the coming autumn and winter. There was a plentiful supply of food between what they could get from the lake and through hunting in the high valleys of the rivers Hwch and Arddu.

On the fifth of August, a hot sweaty day, Elen and Rhys were descending from a walk they had taken into the high moorland of Cwm Deuthwch and its beautiful lake. They were following the banks of the River Hwch initially until it joined the Arddu, a river of cold, dark, almost black water which poured into the northernmost lake near their tiny cluster of huts.

They intended to stay in each other's company until the camp was almost in sight. Then she would walk down alone, with Rhys taking the circular route to arrive at the edge of the lake and then enter the camp.

They were still together when they arrived at the point where the ground became very steep, and was covered by short Welsh oaks, intermingled with birch along the edge of the river. The water flowed slowly through dark, deep pools and then rushed down through a narrow aperture in the rocks into the next pool until it came to an almighty fall. Here the river descended at an angle diagonally across the face of a high cliff for half of the fall. Then it tumbled outwards to produce a cold, white spray of water falling at speed and noisily, even in August, into a large, black, shallow pool. Then the water ran downwards rapidly through a narrow gorge and eventually past their camp and into the lake.

Elen and her partner were approaching the edge of the great fall from the west. She peered downwards at the massive waterfall and the pool it created about twenty yards below where they stood. Carefully avoiding the loose stones, the dry, dusty patches and making sure that their feet were well secured on bare rock, they started their descent.

After taking a few steps she thought she could hear the sound of a human voice competing with the roar of the falling torrent.

Rhys had also heard something and turned back to look at her.

She knew what was in his mind and said, "I think there's someone bathing in the pool."

He nodded and continued to stare between the tree trunks, branches and leaves. They both bent forward for a clearer view and moved their heads up and down and to the sides to find a better perspective, but it was difficult.

They could see that it was a man, a large powerful man and he was shouting against the noisy water. As they listened carefully and intently, his voice became more distinct and his words more decipherable.

It was Gruffudd. They could hear his powerful voice saying, "The greatest king Wales has ever known. I have expanded the boundaries of my country to the east, built a strong fleet and those areas that were lost I have regained and made them part of my kingdom. I have expanded beyond Offa's Dyke to our old boundaries. The South is firmly under my control…"

They could see that he was naked, the water of the pool came up to his middle. He was facing the waterfall and had his arms stretched outwards, resembling Christ's image on the cross.

Elen and Rhys, standing next to each other, exchanged a glance. The king slowly turned away from the wet cliff and started shouting again that he, the most powerful of kings, had been deserted by his cowardly brothers and others who had benefited under his reign.

At that instant, while still peering into the trees below, Elen's foot slipped on a small, rounded, loose stone. She lost her balance, fell backwards and immediately started to slide rapidly down the slope at an ever-increasing speed towards the pool and the king. Rhys lunged at her but she was on her journey past him before he could get a hold on her.

She screamed, but to no avail. The naked bather might have heard her or perhaps it was the sudden movement on the slope that drew his attention. He looked upwards.

A broad smile spread over Gruffudd's face as he saw and recognised the body careering towards him. It was like manna from heaven for him. It was recompense for all his recent sufferings.

She could see that developing smile. She knew it, she hated it as much as she feared it.

His large, heavy, muscular body started powering against the force of the dark water. His black beard looked larger than usual. His black eyes were happy. The trees shaded the narrow deep valley and very little light penetrated its depths. The black, peaty water contrasted sharply with the colour of the man's flesh straining his muscles to propel himself towards the shore to meet her. Behind him, the crystal white, oxygen-filled falling water appeared like countless arrows piercing the pool.

His strong, powerful legs were carrying him to the bank. She was sure she would arrive there before him but could she get to her feet quickly enough? She was in pain, her back was scratched and ripped by the rocks and stones.

At last, she came to a halt, flat on her back on the rocky bank with only her feet hanging over the water. But it was enough to prevent her having the foothold to raise herself quickly.

He grabbed her ankles and laughed out loudly. He had caught her, she was in his powerful hands.

He laughed a haughty laugh and pulled her closer, "Come into the water with me. Come on."

She shook her head desperately, and looked for Rhys but could not see him. She became frightened. Here she was again, threatened by this animal.

He stepped towards her, bringing his naked body further out of the water and made to grab her arm. But she avoided his grip by wriggling backwards. However he grabbed her knee and held it firmly, pulling her towards him again.

She knew what he was like. She'd experienced too much with him. He moved over her body. She was frantic, her arms flailing everywhere but her cries for help were drowned by the sound of the stream and Rhys heard nothing.

She knew under his full weight she would be powerless. She tried to push him off with her right hand while her left hand, desperately searching for a solid grasp, touched some soft material. He had left his clothes on the river bank. She struggled and felt the horn handle of the dagger she had seen so many times and dreamt almost as frequently of using to stab him at night. With great difficulty, unable to see what she was doing, she took a firm grip on it, brought it out of its scabbard and quickly thrust it at his side.

The expected response didn't come and she desperately struck him with it again. Then, to her horror, she realised that she was hitting him with the spherical pommel and not the blade. But it was enough of a distraction to stop his advance. There was silence as he picked himself up on his powerful arms, his face angry. She went to strike him again, with the sharp, pointed blade this time but he fell heavily on top of her. It was a second or two before she realised he was lifeless and was relieved that she had somehow killed him.

With considerable effort, she succeeded in pushing him sideways a little and there, protruding from his back, she saw the arrow. She had not killed him. It was the arrow that had saved her. It must have been Rhys but she remembered he only had his sword with him. She lifted her head to face the steep bank opposite and there she saw a man looking down at her while reloading his bow. Fearing the next arrow would strike her, she shouted, "He's dead. He's dead," as loudly as she could. The archer, however, continued deliberately with his preparation, took aim and fired. She closed her eyes and screamed. She felt and heard the thud as the second arrow hit Gruffudd's dead body.

She opened her eyes, looking directly at the archer who clearly had no wish to kill her, and thought the man was familiar. He looked at her briefly and coldly, and then turned to climb up the rocks behind him, scampering up on all four like a wolf, knowing that he had killed the king.

She sat up and screamed for Rhys. He arrived above her almost immediately. "Did you see who killed him?" she asked pointing at the man clambering up the cliff opposite.

"Not really, I was looking at you."

Holding her by her shoulders, he dragged her from under Gruffudd's body, releasing her to sit up gasping for breath before standing to gather her thoughts. "What shall we do?"

Weeping, she dropped the dagger and looked at her naked legs covered in his blood.

"Is he dead?"

Rhys bent down to look at the king. The lower part of his body remained covered by the peaty black water and two streams of blood flowed down his back into the river. He confirmed that Gruffudd was dead.

Elen shocked, shaken and confused, lifted her tunic with her blood covered hands, to find the front daubed in blood stains. She hardly heard Rhys, seeing her bare, blood covered legs, asking her, "Are you hurt?"

Dazed, she announced, "That is an end to years of misery for me." Then, in tears, she said quietly, "I'm glad he is dead but I don't want my children to know I killed their father."

"But it was the arrows that killed him. You didn't kill him."

Looking at Rhys through her tears she managed to say,

"I know, but who is going to believe me. I'm covered in his blood."

Sympathetic to her concerns as always, he led her a few yards to a shallow part of the river below the pool and helped her into the water saying to her, "Let's wash off his blood here."

He washed her hands, then cupping his hands he lifted water from the river and washed her legs clean of the king's blood. He then tackled her tunic and succeeded in diluting the stains but left the front soaked.

"Thank you." Recovering her composure she reassured him, "Don't worry about it being wet, I can dry it in the sun by the lake. You go back to the others and tell them you've found him killed."

They stepped out of the river and went back to the body lying on the bank face down, half-in and half-out of the water. She picked up the dagger that she had dropped, studied it intensely, or so it appeared to Rhys, before putting it back in its scabbard as if it had never been out.

"I have thought so many times, during the long nights I had to endure him, of killing him with that very dagger."

Rhys grabbed her arm and said, "Let's go."

They made their way together down the narrow gorge, carefully stepping from rock to rock and sometimes into the water until they reached the flatter, more open ground with larger, wider trees. Suddenly, they came face to face with Peter, sword in hand, and flanked by two others, similarly prepared.

Elen, shocked, stood petrified. There was no doubt that the man facing her, barely five yards away, was Peter. She could see his wolf-like features at close quarters, that horrible grin with the teeth showing and that 'I know it all' look in his eyes. Then she felt Rhys holding her arm and saying to her quietly, "It's alright, they won't harm us."

Peter, clearly a man of few words, nodded his head at her to confirm what Rhys had said, and he and the other two put their swords away.

Rhys was the first to speak, "Elen, I want you to meet Peter. His real name is Meurig. He is a nephew of Cynan ap Iago, of the ancient royal family of Gwynedd. But, more important still, Meurig had a brother called Madog who accompanied you on your journey from Pencader.

Peter then spoke, "I have dedicated my life to avenge my brother's death and I have killed the man who had him murdered."

Elen, in a cloud of confusion, tinged by annoyance, turned sharply to Rhys and asked him, "Do you two know each other?"

Rather sheepishly he replied, "If you remember, Peter first came to our notice years ago when we found him, inconveniently for us, hiding under the willow tree. I was, like you, concerned about what he had seen but decided to do nothing. A while later, you told me that this man was looking at you as if he knew something about us, which was unsettling you during your pregnancy. I decided then that I had to discreetly watch him and find out more about him."

"Why didn't you tell me?"

"You were pregnant and I had no wish to upset you. When that attempt was made to poison Gruffudd, you saw an extra spoonful of honey dropped into the jug. I also saw the extra spoonful dropped into the jug by a woman I had seen with Peter a number of times. She had scuttled off long before the man died. Later in the day I saw Peter and the woman aboard a ship leaving the port."

Peter nodded in agreement and added, "I'm proud to say she's my sister. It was really bad luck that the man drank from the wrong jug."

"After the poisoning attempt and, afraid that he suspected too much about you and I, I decided to challenge Peter directly when I saw him a few days later. I put it to him that he had tried to poison the king and that I had a witness who had seen his woman friend putting the poison in the jug and I threatened to tell the king."

"Of course, he countered and threatened that if I were to tell about him, he would tell about us. All three of us would be hung together then. I denied that there was anything between us of course, but he insisted we were lovers."

"Did you follow us to the oak tree to prove we were lovers?" Elen asked Peter.

Peter's nod showed her assumption was correct.

"I thought you had drowned in the river and I have felt guilty about it for years."

Peter grinned as he answered her, "Once you had left, Rhys came to the edge of the river and dragged me out. I was frozen but survived with his help."

Elen turned to Rhys and asked, "Is this true? Did you help him?"

"Yes. I wanted Gruffudd dead as much as he did, and Peter was my best hope. I knew what Peter was trying to achieve and since I rescued him from the river he must have known my wishes, though I never expressed them to him."

Elen, furious now, angrily asked Rhys, "Why didn't you tell me?"

"You have told me numerous times that you wished Gruffudd dead. But you didn't want to kill him yourself nor for me to be involved in his death, because of the risks to us. I thought it would be safer if you didn't know and so wouldn't be implicated in any way if Peter succeeded."

Elen was mollified somewhat, seeing the sense in what he was saying. But Rhys sensed there was some resentment for being kept in the dark and he added to clarify things further, "It was bad luck that we appeared at the waterfall at that moment.

If I had any knowledge of Peter's plan I would have kept you well clear of the place."

When she realised that he didn't know that Peter was going to attack Gruffudd at the falls that day, she softened further and became more content. She'd had her wish too; she was free of Gruffudd and Hywel's death was avenged. Peter had helped her and Rhys.

Peter intervened. Turning to his companions he said, "We had better leave before Gruffudd's soldiers will be crawling all over this place."

He nodded his goodbye to them and, as he turned to leave, he said, "I will be using my original name of Meurig from now on."

They separated with Meurig going back up the mountain while Rhys and Elen went towards the settlement. She turned left to head for the lakeside, while Rhys went directly to their base to report that the king had been killed in an ambush while bathing in the river. There was a rush of soldiers, women and servants to the pool and there was a lot of crying and wailing as the king's body was carried down to the settlement.

Elen had been some time rewashing the blood off her clothes at the edge of the lake and then trying to dry them in the August sun. When she returned, her legs clean and clothes dry, the initial excitement was over and the discussion over what to do next had started.

Some were deeply grieved by his death, others were relieved. There was a division of opinion as what should be done with the king's body. Some wanted it buried there by the lake. Others thought he should be buried on Wales's highest mountain, reflecting the man's greatness. Others still were convinced they would be well rewarded if they gave the body to his enemies and, sad to say, the latter opinion prevailed.

He was handed over to his enemies, his head cut off and

presented to Harold Godwinson, together with the golden figurehead of his royal ship. This brought the era of the Welsh kings to an end.

However, Tangwystl, the wife of Llywarch Olbwch, Gruffudd's chancellor, took the king's purple mantle and passed it on to her nephew, Gruffudd ap Cynan, who would wear it with distinction.

Elen hated Gruffudd ap Llywelyn but had no wish to see his head given to Harold. She was disgusted with her fellow countrymen. Gruffudd's death drew a curtain across Welsh independence but the boundaries of Wales established by him were to remain. On Elen and Rhys's lives the curtain opened. She was barely forty years old and they had a new life ahead of them.

Epilogue

Harold Godwinson married Gruffudd's wife Ealdgyth and became the king of England. He was killed at Hastings in 1066.

Gruffudd ap Cynan (aged about eight in 1063) came to rule Gwynedd, Powys and Deheubarth.

Gruffudd's half-brother, Rhiwallon ap Cynfyn, was killed at the battle of Mechain in 1069. His other half-brother, Bleddyn ap Cynfyn, survived the battle of Mechain to rule Gwynedd and Powys.

Gruffudd's sons who survived him, Maredudd and Idwal, died in 1069 after the battle of Mechain.

Also by the author:

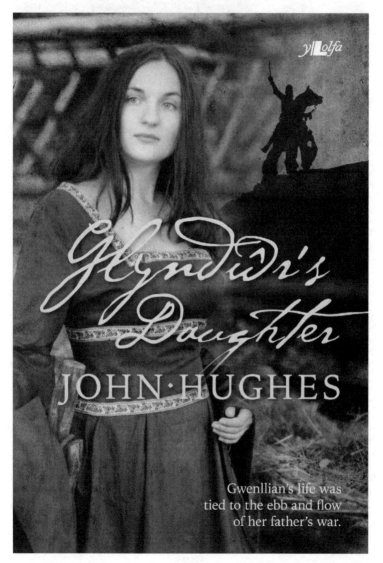

Gwenllian's life was
tied to the ebb and flow
of her father's war.

£7.95

Llywelyn

JOHN·HUGHES

A novel based on the story of the last Prince of Wales,
a young woman and a bishop

£8.95